Hound's Bite

Also by E.J. Stevens

Ivy Granger World

Ivy Granger
Urban Fantasy Series
Shadow Sight
Blood and Mistletoe
Ghost Light
Club Nexus
Burning Bright
Birthright
Hound's Bite
Blood Rite (coming soon)

Hunters' Guild
Urban Fantasy Series
Hunting in Bruges

Beyond the World of Ivy Granger

Spirit Guide
Young Adult Series
She Smells the Dead
Spirit Storm
Legend of Witchtrot Road
Brush with Death
The Pirate Curse

Poetry Collections
From the Shadows
Shadows of Myth and Legend

Super Simple Guides
Super Simple Quick Start Guide to Self-Publishing
Super Simple Quick Start Guide to Book Marketing

IVY GRANGER PSYCHIC DETECTIVE

Hound's Bite

E.J. STEVENS

Published by Sacred Oaks Press
Sacred Oaks, 221 Sacred Oaks Lane, Wells, Maine 04090

First Printing (trade paperback edition), July 2016

Stevens, E.J.
Hound's Bite/ E.J. Stevens

ISBN 978-0-9894887-3-0 (trade pbk.)

Printed in the United States of America

PUBLISHER'S NOTE
This is a work of fiction. Names, characters, places, and incidents either are the product of the author's imagination or are used fictitiously, and any resemblance to actual persons, living or dead, business establishments, events, or locales is entirely coincidental.

PRONUNCIATION GUIDE

Pronunciations are given phonetically for names and races found in the Ivy Granger series. Alternate names and nicknames have been provided in parentheses. In some cases, the original folklore has been changed to suit the city of Harborsmouth and its environs.

Ailinn: ah-lynn
Aleya: uh-LEE-yuh
Arachne: uh-RAK-nee
Athame: ah-thaw-may
Banshee: ban-shee (Bean Sidhe, Bean Sìth)
Barguest: BAR-guyst (Bargheist, Black Dog)
Bean Tighe: ban tig
Béchuille: beh-huh-IL (Bé Chuille)
Bema: BEE-muh
Bheur: ver (like air)
Blaosc: BLEE-usk
Bogey: BOH-gee
Boggart: BOG-ert
Boitata: boy-TAH-ta
Brollachan: broll-ach-HAWN
Brownie: BROW-nee (Bwca, Urisk, Hearth Faerie, Domestic Hobgoblin)
Bugbear: BUG-bayr (Bug-a-boo, Boggle-bo)
Bwca: BOO-kuh (see Brownie)
The Cailleach: kall-ahk (The Blue Hag, Cailleach Bheur, Queen of Winter, Crone, Veiled One, Winter Hag)
Cat Sidhe: KAT shee or kayth shee (Faerie Cat, Cait Shith, Cait Sith)
Ceffyl Dŵr: keff-EEL dore (Kelpie King, Ceff)
Chir batti: CHEER bhut-TEA
Clurichaun: kloor-ih-kon (clobhair)
Cu Sith: KOO shee
Daeva: DAY-va
Demon: DEE-mun

Djinn: JIN
Draugr: DROW-ger
Duergar: doER-gar
Each Uisge: erk OOSH-kuh (Water Horse)
Elphame: EL-faym
Emain Ablach: EH-van ah-BLAH
Faerie: FAIR-ee (Fairy, Sidhe, Fane, Wee Folk, The Gentry, People of Peace, Themselves, Sidhe, Fae, Fay, Good Folk)
Fear Dearg: far DAR-rig (The Red Man)
Fionn mac Cumhaill: FIN mac COO-will
Forneus: FOR-nee-us (Demon, Great Marquis of Hell)
Fragarach: FRAG ah roch
Fuath: FOO-ah
Gaius Aurelius: GUY-us aw-REE-lee-us
Galliel: GAL-ee-el (Unicorn)
Ghoul: GOOL (Revenant)
Glaistig: GLASS-tig (The Green Lady)
Gnome: NOHM
Goblin: GOB-lin
Griffin: GRIF-fin (Gryphon, Griffon)
Grindylow: GRIN-dee-loh
Gwarwyn-a-throt: GWAR-win-uh-THROT
Gwynn ap Nudd: gwin-AP-need
Hamadryad: ha-ma-DRY-ad (Tree Nymph)
Harborsmouth: HAR-bers-MOUTH
Henkie: HEN-kee
Hippocampus: hip-po-CAM-pus
Hob-o-Waggle HOB-oh-WAG-gul (Brownie, son of Wag-at-the-Wa)
Hy Brasil: HY bra-ZIL
Ignus fatuus: IG-nus FATCH-you-us
Inari: i-NAH-ree
Jenny Greenteeth: JEN-nee GREEN-teeth (Water Hag)
Kelpie: KEL-pee (Water Horse, Nyaggle)
Lamia: LAY-me-uh
Leanansídhe: lan-awn-shee (Lhiannan Sidhe, Leanhaun Shee, Leannan Sìth, Fairy Mistress)
Leprechaun: le-pre-khan (leipreachán)
Loup garou: LOOP guh-ROO
Mab: MAB (Unseelie Queen)

Manannán mac Lir: MAH-nah-nahn mac leer
Mauthe doog: MOW-thee DOO
Melusine: MEL-oo-seen
Mermaid: MER-mayd (male Merman)
Merry Dancer: MER-ree DAN-ser (Fir Chlis)
Murúch: mer-ook (Merrow, Moruadh, Murúghach)
Nixie: NIX-ee
Nuckelavees: NOOK-uh-LAY-veez
Oberon: OH-ber-on (Seelie King)
Peg Powler: PEG POW-ler (Peg Powler of the Trees, Water Hag)
Peri: PER-ee
Pixie: PIK-see (Pisgie)
Pooka: POO-kuh (Phooka, Pouka, Púca, Pwca)
Redcap: RED-kap (red cap)
Roca Barraidh: ROH-ka BAR-rah
Saytr: SAY-ter
Selkie: SEL-kee
Shellycoat: SHEL-lee-cote
Sidhe: SHEE (see Faerie)
Succubus: SUK-you-bus (male Incubus)
Tech Duinn: tek DOON
Tezcatlipocan: tehs-cah-tlee-poh-cahn
Tir na nOg: TEER na NOHG
Tir Tairngire: TEER TEARN-geer
Titania: ti-TAY-nee-uh (Seelie Queen)
Troll: TROHL
Tuatha Dé Danann: tootha DAY da-NAN
Tylwyth Teg: TILL-with TEEG (Seelie Court)
Unicorn: YOU-ni-korn
Unseelie: un-SEE-lee
Vampire: VAM-pyr (Undead)
Will-o'-the-Wisp: WIL-oh-tha-wisp (Gyl Burnt Tayle, Jack o' Lantern, Wisp, Ghost Light, Friar's Lantern, Corpse Candle, Hobbledy, Aleya, Hobby Lantern, Chir Batti, Faerie Fire, Spunkies, Min Min Light, Luz Mala, Pinket, Ellylldan, Spook Light, Ignus Gatuus, Orbs, Boitatá, and Hinkypunk)
Ynis Afallon: un-NIS AH-fuhl-on
Yue Fei: yweh-fay

I come from battle and conflict
With a shield in my hand;
Broken is the helmet by the pushing of spears.
I will address thee, exalted man,
With his shield in distress;
Brave man, what is thy descent?
Hound-hoofed is my horse, the torment of battle,
Whilst I am called Gwyn, the son of Nud,
—The Black Book of Carmarthen

CHAPTER 1

The night was broken by howls that sent icy claws skittering down my spine.

"What the Hell is that?" I asked, gloved hands reaching for my blades.

Ceff lifted his hands apologetically, mouth struggling to form words in a way that wouldn't upset me. I could read his discomfort in his stiff posture and the tightening of the skin around his eyes.

Torn had no such concern for my feelings.

"You didn't think you could enter Faerie without consequences, did you, Princess?" Torn asked with a mocking sneer.

So much for friendship. Apparently, returning to Harborsmouth had brought out Torn's snarky side.

The doors to Faerie had been sealed by Mab, Titania, and Oberon when they disappeared more than a century ago. The faerie paths no longer led to the Seelie and Unseelie lands. Lucky for me, I'd found a key to a hidden back door.

At least, that key had seemed like a stroke of luck at the time. I'd needed a way into Faerie, to the wisp court that promised clues to my father's whereabouts. Not that my journey had been easy. Nothing worth fighting for ever was.

The ability to come out of hiding? That was worth fighting for. I was tired of slinking around the shadows of my city.

The problem was that, even though I'd been raised human, the supernatural gifts I inherited from my father, Will-o'-the-Wisp, continued to grow like wildfire—burning me in the process. With no one to teach me how to control my growing powers, I'd broken the one rule that all fae live by. I used my powers in public, without glamour, and risked exposing the secret of our kind to humans—a crime punishable by death.

It didn't take the fae uppity ups long to send a faerie hit squad to take me out. The Moordenaar, a group of elite assassins, shot me full of poisoned arrows. I died. Thankfully,

I had a magic apple up my sleeve—an apple that resurrected the dead, and not in a creepy, zombielicious kind of way.

So, yeah, I died, but I got better. Take that faerie assassins. Ivy Granger: 1, Faerie assassins: 0.

With the fae believing I was dead, I used my father's key to enter the wisp court. As I said, it hadn't been easy. I did things there that were sure to give me nightmares—more than I already had—but I'd foolishly believed that the worst was behind me.

Surviving a trip through the land of the dead and into Faerie and back again—homicidal relatives and all—had left me hopeful. I'd learned how to control my powers. My friends and I had survived. Heck, I'd only been back a few minutes and already I'd managed to heal the wisps, who had been living in Jinx's father's junkyard, of their iron sickness. It was starting out to be a good day.

I should have known better.

But I had so many reasons for being hopeful. I was returning to Harborsmouth after demonstrating my newfound control to the Unseelie Court. The ruling fae had decided that I was no longer a threat to their existence. That meant no more hiding. For once, no one was trying to kill me. Even my relationship with Ceff was in a good place. My life was supposed to go back to normal.

Another hungry howl pierced the night, and I grimaced.

"This is no time for games, Torn," I said. Getting an answer from a cat sidhe was like following the metal ball in a game of Mouse Trap. I was pretty sure that Torn was allergic to straight answers, but I was sick of playing the mouse. Our journey to Faerie had been an exhausting one, and I was short on patience. The sooner we fought the big bad monster coming our way, the sooner I could go home and drop into my bed. "Did we wake the Hound of the Baskervilles, or what?"

Ceff and Torn exchanged a meaningful look, faces grim. I flashed Ceff a grin, hoping to lighten the mood, but he shook his head.

"Torn is right," Ceff said. "It would seem that our trip to Faerie was not without consequences."

"What consequences?" I asked, throwing my blade-laden hands in the air. "Will one of you just tell me what is out there? A heads-up might make killing the howling monster a little easier. Knowledge is power, yada yada."

"You will need more than mere blades to fight this enemy," Ceff said.

I ground my teeth while mentally stabbing a picture of my cryptic boyfriend with my "mere blades."

"Are you saying we should run?" I asked, eyebrows raised. "Because you should know me better than that."

"What he's saying, Princess, is that you woke up something too big for the three of us to defeat alone," Torn said.

That made me pause. We'd fought faerie queens, pyro demons, a lovesick necromancer, and a psychotic lamia, to name a few. I may not have come through those battles unscathed, or with all my guts still on the inside, but at the end of the day, we'd won. With my friends at my side, and a new arsenal of wisp powers at my fingertips, I felt nearly invincible.

I looked to Ceff, hoping he'd grab his trident and join me for some quick monster cleanup. I may not be on the clock for this one, but I didn't let hungry fae prowl the streets of Harborsmouth. And if Torn was right, I'd somehow let this one follow us out of Faerie. No way was I turning tail, no matter how tired I was.

But Ceff didn't reach for his weapon.

"We need allies," he said.

"And larger weapons," Torn said, with a wink.

The cat sidhe looked excited, which was a clue that I wasn't going to like the answer to my next question.

"And what monster do we need to gather our allies and weapons against?" I asked.

"Haven't you guessed yet, Princess?" Torn asked, eyes gleaming. "We're not just facing one howling beast."

Ceff turned to me, closing the space between us. In the moonlight, I could see my reflection in the dark pools of his kelpie eyes—eyes that were tight with worry.

"What are they?" I asked.

Ceff's voice was low and reverent, and tinged with the taint of fear.

"The Wild Hunt."

CHAPTER 2

I'd unleashed the Wild Hunt.

"Is it true what they say, that the Wild Hunt is led by Herne the Hunter?" I asked, trying to make sense of our predicament, and failing miserably.

Giggles lodged themselves uncomfortably in a throat gone bruised and dry.

You'd think after learning that my father was Will-o'-the-Wisp the king of the wisps and that my mother was Mab the Queen of Air and Darkness, I'd be more accepting of the fact that the Wild Hunt was real. I'd sat and had tea with the Celtic lord of the dead and his mistress the Morrigan, for Mab's sake. I guess there are some things that never stop making your mind spin and your heart race, no matter how jaded and world-weary you become.

That might not be a bad thing. I had a nagging suspicion that the day I got used to gods and faerie royalty popping into my life, was the day I'd end up dead.

"Yes, Princess," Torn said, licking his lips. "But the Huntsman is the least of our worries."

"We have something more to worry about than a pagan demigod?" I asked.

This was just getting better and better.

"It is true, though Herne is not a man to underestimate," Ceff said, staring into the darkness beyond the junkyard. "Gwynn ap Nudd, as Herne the Hunter was known before Mab set her hooks into him, has always been a formidable leader in battle."

"Whatever, Fish Breath," Torn said, waving his hand. "I'm not saying Herne is a pushover, what I'm saying is that we should be planning the best way to face off with his hunting party."

"I'm guessing we're not talking about some beer drinking guys in orange vests," I said.

"No, the Wild Hunt is much more interesting than that," Torn said.

"And by interesting, you mean dangerous," I said.

"Deliciously deadly, in fact," he said with a wink.

Great, that was just great.

"So what are we waiting for?" I asked.

I knew better than to run from a fae hunting party. I could feel it in my bones, but standing here like easy prey wasn't much better. Plus, Ceff and Torn had mentioned needing backup.

A horn sounded, joining the baying of hounds, and ripping the air from my lungs. After taking a moment to force my body to remember to breathe, I turned to see Torn smile.

"That, Princess," he said. "We were waiting for that."

"Which was?" I asked.

"The call to arms," Ceff said.

"One sound of the horn signals Herne's hunting party to come to him for orders," Torn said. "He'll round up his deadly host, and when he is ready, he'll sound the horn thrice."

"And what does three signal?" I asked, rubbing my arms against a sudden chill.

Ceff turned his face to mine, and I knew I'd regret asking that question.

"The beginning of the hunt."

With the horn still ringing out its death knell over my city, we turned and ran.

CHAPTER 3

"Where are we headed?" I asked.

I knew Ceff and Torn. Though their motivations varied, neither one of them would be interested in running from the Wild Hunt. Not without good reason. Ceff's sense of honor was much too strong, and Torn was way too curious to flee from an enemy as interesting as the Wild Hunt. I assumed we were about to gather those much-needed allies.

I just hoped we still had any.

When we'd left Harborsmouth, I hadn't been so sure of our survival. I also hadn't been at liberty to tell Jinx what we were doing. It didn't matter that she was my best friend. Jinx was human, and that meant that telling her about a secret back door into Faerie, and my father's key to open that door, would have put a target on both of our backs.

I'd already been killed by the Moordenaar. I didn't plan on being on the pointy end of their arrows ever again.

But right now, I was more worried about facing the wrath of Jinx. If she found out that I'd lied and taken off to Faerie without even telling her, the Moordenaar wouldn't be the only archers to be wary of. Jinx was a damn good shot with a crossbow.

Unfortunately, I had no idea how long I'd been gone. Time passes differently in the Otherworld, and we'd spent time in both Tech Duinn and Faerie. I wasn't sure what that meant for any potential homecoming.

From our perspective, we'd been gone over a year. But the wisps who I'd healed upon our arrival had still been alive. When Eben Braxton hired me, and I'd found the iron sick wisps in his junkyard, I'd assumed the wisps wouldn't have long to live. But I was no expert.

"I need to return to the harbor, and get word to my people and our allies the selkies and mer," Ceff said. "I will escort you as far as the Emporium. It is on the way."

"And I think I'll tag along and see what your witch friend has to say about a horde of barghests in her city," Torn said.

"Barghests?" I asked. "As in plural?"

"Yes, Princess," he said, stroking a tattered ear. "You do know how to make an entrance."

I groaned, and quickened my pace to catch up with the long-legged stride of the cat sidhe lord. Sweat trickled down my spine, and it had nothing to do with our hurried pace.

Years ago, one rogue barghest had threatened Harborsmouth, and numerous magic users and Hunters from the local guild had died in the ensuing battle to bring it down. One witch had survived, and I had a bad feeling about how she was going to react to the news that we'd led a bunch of the hellish hounds into her city.

If Jinx didn't kill me, Kaye sure as hell was going to. I frowned, but hurried toward the junkyard gates. Now wasn't the time for cold feet. Kaye was one of our most powerful allies, and I had a responsibility to do everything possible to save the innocent residents of Harborsmouth. I just hoped she wouldn't decide to turn me into a toad for my trouble.

CHAPTER 4

I was envisioning Kaye turning me into a toad when Jinx stepped out from behind a burned out car frame. My gasp of surprise was quickly replaced by a bark of nervous laughter when she raised her crossbow and trained it on my chest.

"Where have you been?" she asked.

"On vacation...with Ceff...and..." I stuttered.

"Don't give me that innocent crap, Ivy," she said. "You disappear for days, taking almost nothing with you except for your weapons, and you don't respond to any of my messages. Forneus is twitchy every time I mention you or Ceff, and when I tried to use all my powers of persuasion to find out what he knew, I got an earful of legalese."

"You're dating a demon attorney," I said. "Twitchy behavior and legalese should be the norm."

"He passed up sex, and tossed a fireball at Sparky when he snuck up on him," she said. The crossbow in her hand shook slightly.

"Is Sparky okay?" I asked.

"Sparky is fine, he thought the light show was a hoot," she said. She drew her shoulders back, and her hand stopped shaking. "So, I repeat. What the hell is going on?"

A howl split through the night, and Jinx's eyes widened.

"While I hate to break up this little reunion, especially when it involves an attractive woman holding a deadly weapon, we really should get moving," Torn said.

"Torn is right," I said. "You can shoot me later if you have to, but right now we need to move."

Jinx lowered her crossbow, but didn't put it back in her bag. Smart girl. With howling monsters on our tail, we needed to keep our weapons at the ready.

"Is your father here?" I asked as we ran for the junkyard gate.

Eben Braxton had hired me to investigate mysterious happenings in his junkyard. I'd feel responsible if I left him here to face another supernatural menace, especially one I'd somehow brought here from Faerie.

"No, he took your advice and gave his men the week off," she said. "Then I encouraged him to take a fishing trip upstate."

"Good," I said, mind racing. We'd been gone from Harborsmouth less than a week. That news might have made me giddy with relief if we didn't have a horde of fae beasts to deal with. "Ceff can you carry us to the Old Port?"

"I can try," he said.

His skin was ashen, but I nodded. It was likely that shifting into his kelpie horse form would be difficult here in a junkyard filled with iron and so far from the waters of the harbor, but it was a risk we'd have to take.

Ceff moaned, and fell to his knees, stripping his clothes from his body as spasms contorted his face in pain. Normally, Ceff made shifting shape look effortless, with his clothes coming and going at his will. The fact that he was clawing at his shirt and jeans was a sign of how difficult this shift was for him.

My jaw tightened, and I blinked away foolish tears as I put my back to Ceff with the excuse of guarding over him as he changed. Even Torn turned away, eyes searching the night for threats.

"I could drive us," Jinx said, dangling a set of keys in her fingers. "My dad took his truck, but he let me borrow his car so I could check on the place while he's gone."

I shook my head. The proximity of so much iron in the junkyard was already taking its toll on Ceff, and I was pretty sure the sweat soaking my shirt wasn't from our brief jog to the gate. My father, in his effort to protect me from Mab, had magically altered me as a baby, making me partially human to hide my highborn blood. But just as reaching maturity had begun to form cracks in the geis he used to cloud my memories, entering Faerie had changed me, exacting its own price.

I've never liked the close confines of a stranger's vehicle, too much risk of unwanted visions, but now I had a feeling that the option had been stripped from me entirely. If the oily sensation swirling through my gut was any indication, I wouldn't survive a ride to the Old Port Quarter packed inside a moving iron coffin. I was much more fae now than when I'd used my father's key to enter Faerie.

Another howl tore through the night, triggering a familiar ache between my shoulder blades. I wasn't sure of the limitations to my new powers now that I'd returned to the human world, and I wasn't quite ready to reveal all of my secrets to Jinx, but that didn't change the fact that wings like those of a damselfly longed to burst from the prison of my flesh.

Not for the first time, I had to wonder how much of my humanity—if any—I had left.

Movement at my back nudged me from my thoughts, and I spun on my heel as Ceff stood, snorted once, and pawed at the ground. I stepped forward, leaned close, and whispered in his ear.

"Are you able to carry us?" I asked. "Jinx can drive, and meet us at the Emporium, but I'd rather not split up."

Ceff nodded and lowered himself to the ground, his intention clear. I tugged at my gloves, and checked that my jacket was fully fastened before leaping onto his back. The awakening of my highborn blood did have some advantages. Even with the beginning of iron sickness, I was faster and more agile than before.

Of course, my uncle's brutal training, and my relentless pursuit of Ceff and Torn's captors had also honed my skills, but there was nothing from my time at the wisp court that wasn't tied to pain and suffering, so my mind balked at the memories and focused on my human friend as she struggled to gain Ceff's back without breaking her neck.

Jinx wasn't nearly as graceful as I'd been, but she managed to climb up behind me with Torn's help. I tensed as she grabbed my jacket to steady herself, but it wasn't skin to skin contact, so no visions came. Just a grouchy friend who looked ready to shoot Torn, whose hand lingered on her hip.

"Come on, Torn," I said with a scowl. "Cut it out. We don't have time for your games, and as much as I'd love to see Jinx shoot you, we can't afford the delay."

"You have a dirty mind, Princess," he said, raising his hands. "I was only trying to help."

"Help, my ass," Jinx muttered.

"Exactly," he said with an exaggerated wink.

I sighed, and Ceff pawed at the ground.

"Come on," I said. "Get on. We need to move."

"I thought you'd never ask," Torn said with a leer.

He leapt up behind Jinx, and from her squeal and his purr, I'd guess he was using the opportunity to cop a feel. As Ceff launched us forward at inhuman speed, I whispered a threat into the wind, knowing that Torn's fae ears could hear every word. He chuckled, but his laughter was cut short as once again howls ripped through the night.

Torn may have a cat's curiosity and a lust for battle, but even he had to respect the sheer might of the Wild Hunt. We fell silent, each of us weighing our chances to survive the night. Considering what Ceff and Torn had told me so far, I didn't like our odds.

CHAPTER 5

My current predicament, riding astride a kelpie at breakneck speeds to gather allies in hopes of saving my city from the Wild Hunt, was a reminder that there were many dangers that threatened not only my life, but the lives of those I cared about.

Jinx was human and vulnerable, which is why I hadn't left her unprotected when I'd gone to Faerie. As she clung to my leather jacket with white-knuckled fingers, I had time to realize that if she was just at the junkyard alone, then either something had happened to her boyfriend, or Forneus had broken his promise to watch over my friend. The demon better hope he was dead.

"Where is Forneus?" I asked, raising my voice so that Jinx could hear me over the rushing wind and the pounding of Ceff's hooves on pavement.

He wove us through thickening traffic as the sun crested to the east, bringing commuters into the city, but I was too angry to wonder at what his glamour forced humans to see as we passed. I was too intent on wanting to slay me a demon.

Jinx didn't answer, but her grip on my jacket tightened ever further, my silver reinforced collar nearly choking me as I leaned forward, trying to put a few inches of space between where we both sat astride Ceff's back. I was used to physical distance between us. It was the emotional distance that threatened to bring tears to my eyes, and light me up like a supernova.

I used the techniques I'd learned in Faerie to tamp down the urge to glow, but my magic did nothing to quell the anger rising to the surface. Ceff had barely stopped in front of the Emporium before I launched myself from his back and spun to face Jinx.

"Where is Forneus?" I asked, voice hard.

Jinx ignored me, and started to climb to the ground. I was ready to lunge forward if she fell—Jinx hadn't acquired her nickname for an ability to avoid injury—but there was no need. Torn was more than happy to lend his assistance...and a hand on her ass.

"Paws off, Torn," I said, one of my throwing knives hitting my gloved hand. It was sheer reflex, but he raised his hands and took a step back.

Ceff also moved away, giving me and Jinx space. With us all on the sidewalk and his horse form no longer necessary, Ceff began to shift. There was nothing I could do to ease his pain as his body contorted and contracted, so I focused once more on Jinx.

I raised an eyebrow, tapping my foot, and she sighed.

"I slipped some Ice into his wine, and snuck out before he woke up," she said, tossing her hair back. "Not that I have to explain myself to you, Ivy. It's not like you've been totally honest with me lately."

Jinx wasn't talking about frozen water. Ice was a powerful mix of narcotic and magic.

"Where the hell did you get your hands on Ice?" I asked, mouth dropping open.

Jinx folded her arms over her chest, but Torn was more than happy to tattle.

"They've been keeping it off the streets, ever since Puck was found dead in the Club Nexus storage rooms," he said. "According to my spies, our human and demon friend have become quite the Bonnie and Clyde of the supernatural underworld."

Oberon's eyes on a god damned stick! I'd been reluctant to support Jinx's decision to date a demon, but I'd backed down when I believed that Forneus would do anything to keep her safe. Becoming vigilantes; policing the city's supernatural criminals; and ripping off drug dealers wasn't safe, it was suicidal.

I should know.

I'd put my life on the line more than once to keep the monsters in check. Technically, protecting the city from rogue paranormals was the job of the local Hunters' Guild. Problem was the Guild was sworn to protect humans. They didn't often care much about fae or undead victims. That had been clear when I'd teamed up with my friends this past spring to rescue dozens of the city's faerie children who had been stolen from their beds while their parents slept.

Even with the help of my friends, and a well-thrown pixie nest, I'd barely escaped that mission with all my limbs still attached. I stalked toward Jinx, ready to give her a piece of my mind, but she held up a hand and shook her head.

"You know I have to do it," she said, eyes softening. "Ever since that night..."

Her voice trailed off, and I sighed.

"Yeah, I know," I said.

I did know. Not so long ago, Jinx had been slipped a supernatural roofie and was fed on by an incubus. The glowing marks were gone from her body, but that kind of violation left psychological scars. That kind of damage doesn't fade easily. If Forneus was tagging along while Jinx rid the city of a magic date rape drug, who was I to argue?

We all knew that Jinx had been struggling to regain her sense of control over her body, over her life. If this helped her retrieve that part of herself and become the confident woman I'd grown to love, then I needed to support that choice. Not try to talk her out of it.

If I gave Forneus any credit at all, I'd have to admit that he'd come to the same conclusion, and rather than bully her, he'd decided to go along with her crazy mission. Hell, he was even providing backup, and trying to keep her safe.

Tension eased from my neck and shoulders, and I sighed.

"Look, I get it," I said, rubbing a gloved hand over my face. "I get why you need to get Ice off the streets. But why drug your boyfriend? Why sneak out to your dad's junkyard in the middle of the night?"

I was missing something, and I was too tired and too busy worrying about the Wild Hunt to figure it out.

"Because I knew he was lying to me, about you," she said. "And don't try to tell me he wasn't. I know you and Ceff weren't off on some romantic vacation."

"No," I said. "We weren't."

She nodded, and started to pace.

"You've been acting weird for weeks, and it got worse when you took the junkyard job," she said. "So I figured it had something to do with wisps, and your dad. Then you made some cryptic comment about getting a possible new tip on his whereabouts and rather than clue me in on your plans, you go on *vacation*."

She growled out the last word, punctuating each syllable with violent air quotes. I was just glad her fingers were busy gesturing, and not on the trigger of her crossbow.

"And the second you left, Forneus started acting like I was some fragile freaking flower," she said.

I sighed, and shuffled my feet.

"That's my fault," I said.

"I figured," she said.

I'd asked Forneus to protect my friend, to keep her safe while I was gone. I hadn't known if I'd make it back from Faerie, and though she didn't know where I'd raced off to, Jinx probably suspected that I was up to something dangerous.

Taking off, lying about where we were going, and asking her boyfriend to double as a bodyguard had crossed a line. I got that.

I'd also do it again in a heartbeat.

"As much as I know you both need answers, we really should get inside," Ceff said as he strode to my side.

His feet were bare, but he'd taken the extra time to magically clothe himself in jeans and a dark green button-down shirt that showed off his eyes. The love and concern in those eyes reminded me that there were other secrets I'd kept from Jinx, news I hadn't been ready to share under the circumstances.

Before I left Harborsmouth, Ceff had proposed, and I'd said yes. I hadn't told Jinx, figuring it wasn't the kind of news to give before leaving town. Hell, she would have insisted on throwing a party, and setting a date, and a venue, and mailing invitations. I hadn't had time for any of that, nor was I ready for it.

Now with the Wild Hunt on our tail, the timing seemed even worse, but I had to tell Jinx soon. Torn knew, and though the cat sidhe liked his secrets, he liked tormenting me even more. I had to make some kind of announcement before Torn let the cat sidhe out of the bag.

I swallowed hard, and turned toward the entrance of the Emporium. I wasn't sure what was more unsettling, informing an irritable witch that I'd led the Wild Hunt to her door, or making a formal engagement announcement. I shook my head and snorted, striding forward.

It probably wasn't a good thing that I had less experience informing my friends of happy news than of telling them that death was once again at our door.

CHAPTER 6

As I suspected, Kaye wasn't happy that I'd led a pack of barghests to her city. Not one bit.

"You did what?" she asked, her power making my skin itch as it swarmed inside the confines of her spell kitchen.

We were in the back rooms of Madam Kaye's Magic Emporium, and I wasn't the only one eyeing the exits. Marvin, a young bridge troll, and Hob, the resident hearth brownie, had joined me, Ceff, Jinx, Torn, and Kaye. Arachne was out front in the part of the shop that was open to the public, helping human patrons who were oblivious to how close their fragile lives were to being swallowed whole by the supernatural creatures that secretly lived amongst them.

Normally, I pitied the young apprentice witch, but right now I envied her. Kaye had deemed her presence unnecessary. Sadly, I was stuck here in the hot seat, beneath the glare of one of the most powerful witches in America.

That too was my fault. I'd inadvertently helped Kaye regain the full strength of her powers, a surprising side effect of our recent temporary deaths and resurrection by magic apple. I was glad to have escaped the faerie bargains that had threatened my friend's lives and my own happiness, and it had been a relief when Kaye survived the poison she'd administered here in this very kitchen, but I couldn't help worry that I'd unleashed something dark and sinister when I'd restored Kaye's magical power.

Now I stood before the witch with news that threatened to tip the precarious balance of our friendship, and once again I needed her help. I swallowed hard, and tried to think of something positive to say.

"So, the good news is, I took care of the wisp problem out at Eben Braxton's junkyard," I said.

"And the bad news, lass?" Hob asked.

I should have been offended by the brownie's knowing look, but he had a point. Wherever I went, trouble was sure to follow.

"I may have unleashed the Wild Hunt on Harborsmouth," I said.

"No one can accuse you of doing anything by halves, Princess," Torn said, a grin tugging at his lips.

"I'm not the only one who went through that portal," I said.

I scowled at Torn, but my rebuttal was cut short by a flash of lightning that filled the kitchen with blue tinged light and made my teeth hum. I spun on my heel in time to see Kaye pocket one of her wands, and fold her arms across her chest. The fact that those arms no longer bore the tattoo marks of used power was a reminder of just how much magic the witch had at her disposal these days.

"So it was you," she said. "I should have suspected as much."

I fisted my hands at my side, ignored Torn's teasing remarks at my back, and winced as I met Kaye's steely gaze. Then her words sunk in.

"You already knew that the Wild Hunt was here?" I asked, eyes widening.

"Of course, dear," she said. "Give me some credit. I knew something powerful and fae had set off my alarms. I just wasn't sure what or why, although I suspected the Huntsman when I heard the sounding of the horn. I was waiting for confirmation from Janus, but I don't suppose we need to wait for the Guild to tell us what we already know."

"That Ivy in trouble?" Marvin asked.

Thanks a lot, big guy.

"The lass always be in trouble," Hob muttered.

"She *is* trouble," Torn said.

I shot Ceff a look, daring him to add his two cents, but he lifted his hands, palms facing outward.

"I am not saying a word," he said.

Smart man.

"What we know is that the Wild Hunt is here and that this Huntsman has blown his horn in some kind of call to battle," I said. Jinx snickered, but I pushed on. This wasn't the time for dirty jokes and double entendre. "But what does that mean exactly, and how do we stop him?"

Kaye stepped inside the magic circle that was marked by a ring of silver set into the kitchen's floor. She kept her eyes on me as she gathered spell components, set them on fire with a flick of her wrist, and then began moving her fingers in a sinuous dance through the noxious smoke.

"First," she said, voice filling the room and making my skin itch like spiders were dancing up and down my neck and crawling along my scalp. "We stop the Huntsman from sounding the horn again."

Judging by the way that Torn licked his lips and the muscles in Ceff's jaw twitched, stopping the Huntsman wasn't going to be easy. Stopping the evil supernatural forces that plagued our city never was.

"Fine," I said. "Let's go kick some Huntsman ass."

"You forget one thing, Princess," Torn said.

"And what's that?" I asked.

"His hounds," he said. "The Huntsman leads a pack of barghests, faerie beasts as fierce as hellhounds."

"Aye, and just as smelly," Hob said, wrinkling his nose.

"So we fight them," I said, fingering one of my blades.

I'd fought faerie beasts before. Heck, by some definitions, I was one now myself.

"I do not think a direct battle is what your friend has in mind, is it, witch?" Ceff asked.

Kaye nodded, and I tried to ignore the bile rising in my throat as black tattoos snaked across her chest and ringed her shoulders. Her hair danced around her head, and the circle set into the floor began to glow.

"The time to fight will come," she said, her voice a booming dirge that echoed off the walls. "But first you must bring me a piece of the Huntsman, so that I may bind his magic and keep the horn from sounding a second time."

"And what happens if this Huntsman dude blows his horn first?" Jinx asked.

Kaye whirled to face Jinx, arcs of blue energy trailing from her fingertips. My human friend blanched, but kept her head held high and I prayed that Kaye wouldn't turn her into a toad.

There were reasons why the power of magic users waned with use. It was one of the supernatural world's many checks and balances. Not least of all because of a disturbing trend for witches and sorcerers to descend into madness in the twilight of their lives.

I narrowed my eyes at Kaye and searched her face for warning signs, but she'd changed so much in the past few weeks. It was like looking into the face of a stranger, and I couldn't be sure if that was due to looming insanity or some other change.

I'd inadvertently helped Kaye recharge her magical power levels to that of a young witch, but she retained the knowledge and bitterness of someone who had lived for centuries. Someday there would be a reckoning for that imbalance of the natural order. I just hoped that day wasn't today.

She looked away from Jinx, and I let out the breath I'd been holding. Sadly, my relief was short-lived.

Kaye waved a hand through the smoke, and red liquid began to weep from the pile of charred herbs, spreading across the floor of the spell circle.

"Retrieve a piece of the Huntsman so that I may bind him and take hold of the power he has over his hounds, or with the next sounding of his horn the streets of Harborsmouth will run red with human blood."

CHAPTER 7

Blood pounded in my ears, so it took me a second to realize that someone had set off one of the Emporium's wards. The room trembled, and a hammering sound joined the rapid beating of my heart.

Kaye's head was tilted as if listening to a conversation the rest of us couldn't hear, and her eyes had glazed over.

"Kaye?" I asked, inching toward the door.

"What's going on?" Jinx asked.

Her hand went to her bag, but I shook my head. Jinx wasn't one of Kaye's favorite people. I couldn't guarantee the witch wouldn't attack my friend if weapons were drawn inside her domain, especially if that domain was already under siege.

"I don't know," I said, keeping my voice low. I moved slowly toward the door, careful not to make any quick movements. "But I'm going to find out."

"I will accompany you," Ceff said.

The set of his jaw brooked no argument, so I nodded.

"The rest of you stay here," I said. "And keep out of Kaye's way."

"Can't I come with you?" Jinx asked.

She bit her lip, but I shook my head. There was no way of telling what threat lay outside the Emporium. Kaye might be cranky and unstable, but she'd set powerful protection wards on her shop. The Emporium was one of the safest places in the city, so long as Kaye didn't snap and kill everyone.

"I won't be long," I said.

"Don't worry," Marvin said. "I protect you."

He grinned at Jinx, and a smile tugged at my lips.

"Thanks, kid," I said. "Keep her safe."

With that, I left the spell kitchen with Ceff at my side. Torn was trailing us, using his cat sidhe affinity for stealth to stick to the shadows. I tried to keep track of him, but once we were in the maze of the outer shop, I gave up. The Emporium's defenses were up, so it took all of my attention to make it through the magically shifting layout of the place.

The shop lights were flickering when Ceff and I reached the front of the shop. Arachne stood in front of the door, holding a broom like a weapon in shaking hands.

"You okay, Arachne?" I asked.

I'd tried to stomp my feet a bit, so as not to startle the kid, but she'd been too focused on the shop's entrance, and spending a year of Faerie time in the wisp court had made me unnaturally fleet of foot. Under other circumstances, Arachne might have thought my newfound ninja skills were cool. Not today.

She squeaked, and whirled toward my voice, lashing out with her broom. The kid nearly passed out when the wooden handle stopped dead in Torn's hand as he melted from the shadows. Apparently, I wasn't the only one showing off ninja skills.

"Sorry, sorry," I said, backing away from Arachne with my hands in the air. "We came to see what's going on."

"Something set off the alarm, and your witch boss is off her rocker," Torn said. "Figured it wouldn't be fair to leave you out here to have all the fun."

He winked at Arachne, and she blushed. I wanted to stab him for leading the kid on, but she'd stopped shaking. The cat sidhe lord was an insufferable flirt, but at least he'd managed to distract Arachne from her fear. She tucked a strand of purple and blond streaked hair behind her ear, and bit her lip.

"Um, thanks," she said.

"Miss Arachne, what has raised the Emporium's defenses?" Ceff asked. "And are all of your human customers safe?"

"Oh, yeah, they left as soon as the lights started flickering," she said. "Thought it was angry spirits...a Ouija board or tarot reading gone bad. They were gone before he even showed up."

"He?" Torn asked, releasing his hold on the broom handle. "Was it a cloaked rider on a black steed?"

"What?" she asked, brow furrowing. "No, it's that demon guy, Forneus. At least, I think it's him. It looked like Forneus at first, before Humphrey attacked him."

Mab's bloody bones. The Wild Hunt was in town, and my friends were busy being territorial pricks and seeing who had the biggest magical chops. Why was I not surprised?

"Humphrey would not attack without provocation, and Forneus has no reason to start a fight here," Ceff said. "This must be Kaye's doing."

"I know," I said, striding toward the door. "Let's go see if we can get Forneus and Humphrey to back down, and keep those two from killing each other."

We burst through the door and out onto the sidewalk just in time to catch a cloud of brick dust in the face. I coughed and blinked rapidly, trying to make sense of the scene before me.

Humphrey held a lamppost in his front claws like an oversized baseball bat as he jumped from a rain spout to the sidewalk to our left. Forneus faced us from across the street in all his unholy glory. I'd seen him in his fully demonic form once before when Jinx's life had been threatened, but the flaming hooves, glowing eyes, leathery wings, and horns spiraling from his head never ceased to make my stomach churn.

I frowned, taking in the scene. Forneus didn't like to reveal his true form, especially not while he was trying to woo my best friend. So why come here and do so now? He had to have been goaded into it. And as much as Humphrey didn't care for demons, he knew Forneus wasn't a threat.

If not civil, these two should have at least been able to tolerate each other, but from the missing bricks in the wall behind Forneus' head and the scorched crater at Humphrey's feet, they were out for blood. Ceff had been right. This had to be Kaye's doing.

She had the ability to see through the eyes of her sentinels and her familiars, and she was the one who gave Humphrey his orders. As the gargoyle guardian of this building, Humphrey would have to obey, even if his orders were to attack a powerful demon ally. Someone had to put a stop to this madness.

Fire danced along Forneus' fingers, and Humphrey growled and waved the lamppost menacingly as he leapt from perch to perch above our heads. A shower of stone dust and pebbles rained down to the sidewalk with each leap, and I stepped out into the empty street.

The humans who usually filled this part of town were gone, the busy intersection creepily silent except for Humphrey's gravelly snarling. Humans wouldn't be able to see through the glamour that hid Forneus' demonic form and the gargoyle from sight, but I suspected Kaye's magic had something to do with the empty streets. Most people were probably experiencing a desire to avoid the streets near the Emporium. Let's just hope it stayed that way.

"Forneus!" I yelled, turning my back on Humphrey.

The gargoyle may be under Kaye's orders to attack the demon, but I was pretty sure she didn't have any beefs with me. Well, mostly sure. Maybe. Let's just say, I wasn't about to go sprouting wings and reminding her just how much our relationship had changed recently.

"I suggest you return inside, Miss Granger," Forneus said. "The witch and I have unfinished business."

I winced as the smell of brimstone burned my nostrils, but I took another step closer to Forneus, and sighed.

"What the hell is going on, Forneus?" I asked, waving a hand from his horns to the cloven hooves that sparked as he turned to face me directly.

"I should ask you the same," he said, fire flickering ominously along his fingertips. "I was drugged, and when I awakened Jinx was gone. I have tracked her here to the Emporium, but the witch will not allow me to enter. Instead, she ordered her guard dog to attack me before I made it halfway up the street."

I looked over my shoulder, eyes tracking Humphrey.

"Is that true?" I asked. "Did you attack Forneus?"

"Yesss," Humphrey growled. "Kaye's orders. No demons."

"Fine, whatever," I said. "No demons in the Emporium. I get that we're on high alert." And that an all-powerful Kaye up to her old tricks was a royal pain in my butt. "Forneus will stay out here on the street, but no more fighting."

I held my breath as Humphrey tilted his head and communed telepathically with Kaye. After a tense moment, Humphrey nodded.

Forneus narrowed his eyes as Humphrey leapt to the sidewalk, but the gargoyle shrugged, straightened the kinks out of the twisted lamppost with a shriek of metal, and jammed it back into its concrete base.

"This solves nothing," Forneus said. "I will not leave until I have proof that Jinx is unharmed. By Lucifer, if anyone..."

I took a step forward and pressed a gloved hand against Forneus' chest, cutting off his tirade. Getting in a demon's face might not be smart, especially when he was already pissed off, but we were short on time, and Forneus had millennia to perfect his threats of what hellish torments he'd inflict upon his enemies.

The demon's eyes widened, and a sharp intake of breath came from Ceff and Torn's direction. I might also have gasped at my actions if I'd taken the time to think things through. Forneus was a Great Marquis of Hell, and I was standing with a few mere layers of leather between us. That leather was the only barrier between my sanity and an eternity of nightmare visions.

My time in Faerie had either made me extremely brave or terminally stupid.

"You have my undivided attention, Miss Granger," Forneus said. "I suggest you use it wisely while it lasts. I am quite short on patience."

"Yes, I can see that," I said, taking a step back. I started to wipe my gloved hand down my pants and frowned. I was dipping that glove in holy water as soon as I had the chance. "But it's not what you think. Jinx is fine. In fact..."

"Your girlfriend is the one who drugged you," Torn said, a grin tugging at his lips. "I've always said she was feisty for a human."

Forneus' eyes glowed red, and I sighed.

"Not helping, Torn," I muttered. "Ceff?"

"I will retrieve Jinx from the Emporium," he said. "What of Kaye and your troll and brownie friends?"

"Tell Kaye I'll bring her what she needs for that binding spell, so to be ready," I said.

"Hob and Marvin?" he asked.

"Tell them I have a special mission for them," I said. "But it means a trip to the suburbs."

"The suburbs?" Forneus asked, raising an eyebrow.

He didn't, I couldn't help but notice, ask why Jinx had drugged him. Perhaps he'd worked that out on his own.

"It's a long story, but first," I said, waving a hand in the air. "You might want to lose the horns and hooves."

Instead of smiting me with hellfire, he looked down at himself and sighed.

"Yes, perhaps for once you are right," he said.

With heavy, cloven steps, Forneus shuffled into a nearby alley. Ceff disappeared inside the Emporium, and Torn moved to my side.

"Demon's got it bad," Torn said.

"Yes," I said, turning to survey the charred craters on the sidewalk and scorch marks on the brick exterior of the Emporium. "I'm afraid he does."

After millennia of stealing souls, against all odds, a human had stolen his heart. Forneus was deeply, madly, unconditionally in love with Jinx, and he was prepared to use the entire fiery might of Hell to prove that love, and keep my accident-prone friend safe from harm.

Oberon save us all.

CHAPTER 8

Judging by Marvin's fist pumps, and the little jig that Hob was dancing, the two were pleased with the mission that I'd given them. It was a good thing that someone was happy. I studiously ignored the sour looks and barbed comments hurtling back and forth between Forneus and Jinx. I already regretted the make-up sex that Jinx would have to tell me about later, in excruciating detail.

I wrinkled my nose, and shook my head. I needed to focus. According to Kaye, we had until sunset to bind Herne's magic. In a rare stroke of luck, we'd returned to Harborsmouth just before sunrise, limiting the Wild Hunt's ability to ride. Not that the reprieve was a permanent one. If we failed in our mission, Herne would sound his horn, ordering an attack on the innocents of this city. I couldn't allow that to happen.

I focused on Hob who'd slowed his dancing.

"So you know what you each need to do?" I asked.

"Aye, lass," Hob said, looping his thumbs in the straps of his suspenders and puffing out his chest. "Ye can count on us."

"Secret mission," Marvin said, nodding and grinning from ear to ear.

"Okay," I said. "Be careful, and if you don't hear from me by sunrise tomorrow, send a message to Kaye or to Father Michael at Sacred Heart. They'll know what to do."

If I wasn't around to contact Hob and Marvin, then the worst will have happened and I'll be dead. I didn't want them out there on their own, but I knew that the suburbs were the safest place for them if the city was under siege. And even with Kaye's territorial display, I trusted that she would do what she could to keep the kid and the crotchety old brownie safe.

"I wish you well on your mission," Ceff said, bowing slightly at the waist. "Gentle tides."

"Safe travels," I said.

"Aye," Hob said. "Fresh breezes and safe travels to us all."

Hob and Marvin walked off, Marvin clapping his hands and Hob clicking his heels together.

"Keep them safe," I whispered.

I wasn't sure who I prayed to anymore. I'd never had a lot of faith in gods, but I'd seen too many things in recent months to deny the possibility that someone was listening.

I rubbed the back of my hand over my eyes, and Ceff came to stand beside me, a steady presence I'd come to take for granted before we'd left for Faerie. I'd lost him in the Otherworld. I'd mourned his loss for what had been months in that alternate time, and I'd only just got him back.

"I don't want to send you away," I said.

"Then let me stay by your side," he said.

I shook my head.

"You need to warn your people," I said.

"No, the kelpies and our mer and selkie allies are safe," he said. "The Wild Hunt will not enter our domain, and after the losses we suffered from the *each uisge*, they will not be eager to join this fight."

"Wait, you mean the Wild Hunt doesn't like salt water?" I asked, mind racing.

While defusing the Forneus situation and developing our secret backup weapon, I'd been struggling to come up with a plan for how to get a piece of the Huntsman without putting the lives of innocents at risk.

"They don't like any type of water, Princess," Torn said. "Hate the wet stuff nearly as much as cats."

"Good," I said, flashing my teeth in a grin.

Jinx and Forneus hesitated as they approached, and the demon cocked his head to the side.

"Did she hit her head?" he asked, eyes traveling over my face.

"Worse," Jinx said, shaking her head. "I think she has an idea."

"Not an idea, a plan," I said, licking my lips.

"Good thing I have nine lives," Torn muttered.

I ignored Torn, and hurried up the street.

"Come on, there isn't much time," I said.

"Time to do what, pray tell?" Forneus asked.

"Set a trap."

CHAPTER 9

"You do realize that it's never smart to corner a wild animal," Forneus said as we ran.

"No one ever accused me of being smart," I said, a fierce grin on my face.

"Nope," Jinx said from his arms.

We were running on foot across town, and as the only human, she had to be carried. Ceff had offered to change into his horse form, but part of my plan relied on him. I couldn't risk his being stuck in horse form once we got to where we were going.

Things had been tense there for a moment until Torn had rubbed a hand over his leather pants and offered Jinx a ride she wouldn't forget. After that vulgar display, Forneus hadn't hesitated to swoop Jinx off her feet, and she hadn't tried to stab him.

"Thanks for the vote of confidence," I said.

"Anytime," Jinx said.

Forneus' remark about cornering a wild animal brought a memory to the surface of a small demon dangling from the claws of a cat sidhe while cornered in a dark alley. I lost my footing and stumbled, slowing our run.

"Are you okay?" Ceff asked.

"No, I don't know," I said shaking my head, eyes wide. I whirled on Forneus and Jinx. "Where is Sparky?"

"I left him with..." Jinx said, hand going to her mouth and tipping her head back to read Forneus' face. "Forneus, where is Sparky?"

"Bugger," he said.

I took that to mean he'd been in such a tizzy that he hadn't thought about Sparky when he ran off in search of Jinx.

"We can't leave him on his own," I said. "He's just a kid."

"You would rather bring him into battle?" Ceff asked.

"Our choices are limited. The witch is not taking demon

visitors at the moment, and our allies at the Hunters' Guild would rather dip him in holy water than keep him safe."

"Marvin and Hob are already gone...I'm so sorry, Ivy," Jinx said.

"Wait, holy water, I might have an idea," I said.

I pulled out my phone, which I'd been able to charge at the Emporium, ignored the dozens of text messages from Jinx, and scrolled until I found what I was looking for. We needed someone who wouldn't mind babysitting a demon. That list was exceedingly small, but there was one man on my call list who would kill to get face time with hellspawn. Thankfully, he also had a protective streak and a soft spot for kids.

"Father Michael," I said when the priest picked up. "I've got a demon I'd like you to meet."

"You...you can't possibly bring Sparky onto holy ground!" Forneus sputtered.

I'd thought of that. I couldn't bring Sparky to Sacred Heart Church, but I sure as hell could send Father Michael to Sparky.

"Ah, an exorcism?" Father Michael asked, voice lifting eagerly. I could just imagine his bobbing head now. The birdlike little man was a friend, but one with an unhealthy interest in the supernatural denizens of Hell. "Let me get my things. A demon! I'll be right there. Wait, where is this demon exactly?"

"Not an exorcism, Father," I said. "And the demon is at my apartment."

"What the devil is a demon doing in your apartment?" he asked. "And not an exorcism you say? Then it is in its true form? I must see this for myself."

Father Michael had put me on speaker phone, and I could hear the priest rummaging through his office for supplies. I had to quell his excitement, or he'd be running off to my apartment armed with a demon hunting kit.

"Galliel, you there?" I yelled. I heard a whinny and the clop of hooves on floor tiles. "Good boy. Don't let Father Michael leave his office. Sit on him if you have to."

There was a thud and a clatter, followed by a muttered, "What the devil?"

"Did you just tell a unicorn to sit on a priest?" Torn asked.

I shrugged, and spoke into the phone.

"Father, the demon is a child and a friend," I said. "I need you to go to the loft and look after him for a day or two. Can you do that?"

"You want me to babysit a demon?" he asked.

"Yes," I said.

I crossed my fingers, and held my breath.

"Well, of course, my dear," he said. "I never thought you'd ask."

"Good, um, you remember where my office is?" I asked.

"Yes, yes, just off Wharf Street," he said.

I usually visited the priest at the church, since that was where Galliel resided, but Father Michael had come to my office once before to help with a demon problem. Thankfully, he seemed to remember how to get there.

"The apartment is above Private Eye, the next door on the left," I said.

I lowered my voice, and turned away from Torn who was watching me intently. He was probably too busy trying to come up with a new joke about a unicorn, a priest, and a wisp princess to listen in, but I didn't like taking chances. As it was, I was going to change my wards once I got home—if I got home.

"Speak the words 'Sparky likes ramen' to open the door at street level," I whispered.

"That's a terrible password," Torn said, sneaking up behind me and making me jump.

"I told her that God, pet names, and 666 were all overused, but she didn't listen," Forneus said.

"At least she added the bit about ramen," Jinx said with a nod. "That was my idea."

I sighed, giving up on keeping my ward info from Torn. I made a mental note to change it to "cat sidhe are nosy bastards" as soon as possible.

"There's a key to the apartment hidden inside a fake rock in the stairwell, Father," I said.

"And the demon child, does he speak?" he asked.

"Yes, he's a lot like a normal kid, but his fingers spark sometimes when he gets excited, hence the name, Sparky," I said. "Oh, and he likes to watch cartoons."

"Do not worry, I will take care of him," he said.

"Thank you," I said. "And, Father? There's something powerful in Harborsmouth. Can you see if you have anything in your library about the Wild Hunt, and text me if you find any info on its weaknesses?"

"Should I be worried for my flock?" he asked.

"Yes, Father," I said, shuffling my feet. "I'm afraid you should be. If I fail in my mission, we might all be in danger from the Hunt."

"Then I will pray that you are successful," he said.

A Cheshire cat grin crossed Torn's face as I hung up, and I shook my head.

"What?" I asked, running a hand through my hair.

"You keep your spare key in a fake rock inside a stairwell?" he asked.

"Why not?" I asked. "You have to know the ward to get inside, and it's not like it's the cleanest stairwell in the world."

I looked to Ceff for support, but his face was red from holding his breath.

"Oh fine, whatever," I said. "Go ahead and laugh. Next time I'll get the key holder that looks like dog poop."

"Now that might be a more believable object to find in your stairwell," Forneus said.

Everyone laughed, and I scowled, which only made them laugh harder.

"I'm not the worst housekeeper in the world," I said.

Forneus started wheezing, and Jinx had to dab at her mascara.

"Remember the time she came home after cleaning out that jincan nest?" Jinx asked, chest heaving as she broke into another round of giggles. "Covered in guts and slime, but she saunters to the kitchen and says she wants coffee. Not a shower, not clean clothes, coffee."

"Oberon's eyes, you guys," I said. I expected the teasing from Jinx. It was her way of motivating me to get off my ass and do my part around the apartment and the office. But I'd expected better from a bunch of immortals. "What are you all, two?"

"I will have you know that I have lived for at least three millennia, and I have never smelt anything quite as foul as the tray where you take off your boots," Forneus said, which set off a new round of snorts and chuckles.

I ground my teeth, and gripped my blades.

"Come on," I said. "Laugh time is over. We don't have all day."

They were still laughing, but nodded, and we headed out to follow the plan. My plan. Because no matter my other shortfalls, I'd become damn good at taking down the monsters that threatened this city.

CHAPTER 10

I planned on reminding Master Janus of my personal contributions to the protection of our city, but first I had to make it past the guard at the gate. Unfortunately, that guard was a huge Neanderthal of a man by the name of Hendricks.

Hendricks and I had met previously, and let's just say we weren't on each other's Christmas shopping list. No, I'm sure this guy had a spot for me on a list with a more unsavory name.

Last time, I'd had a little help from Jenna's friend Jonathan, a werewolf who had somehow become a member of the Hunters' Guild. Perhaps, he could help me again.

"Look if you're not going to call Master Janus, then go get Jonathan," I said. "He'll vouch for me."

"The whelp ain't here," he said, shooting a thumb over his shoulder. "Neither is that Lehane bitch, so get lost."

The local Hunters' Guild was located inside what used to be the old Herne School. The name of the place might be a coincidence, then again it might not. I imagine the Guild could have felt an affinity for a god of the hunt, even if he was in truth a faerie. What I was certain of was that the Hunters' Guild would never support an attack on humans by a supernatural force.

The Guild and I may have different methods, and frequently butt heads, but at the end of the day we both wanted the same thing—to protect the innocents of this city. My definition of innocents was more encompassing than that of the Guild, who only cared about human lives, but in this case, it didn't matter. The Wild Hunt was a major threat to those humans, the very same ones the Hunters' Guild had sworn to protect.

"I have news of a threat to this city," I said. "Master Janus will want to see me."

Hendricks spat, narrowly missing my boots.

"We'll see about that," he said.

His hand lingered over the handle of the battle axe strapped to his hip before picking up a phone that was bolted to the stone wall just inside the gate. The black receiver looked like a child's toy in his meaty grip. I had an image of Hendricks holding a teacup, pinky in the air, and had to stifle a giggle. Instead, I snorted and tossed my hair over my shoulder.

The conversation, once Hendricks got through to Janus' office, was blessedly brief.

"He'll speak with you, but you gotta leave your weapons, either here with me or with your associates," he said. "Looks like Janus don't trust you so much these days."

I shrugged, and started stripping off my blades. I hesitated, but he gave my boot a knowing look, and I sighed.

"Okay, okay," I said. "Just give me a minute to hand these over to my friends."

"While you're at it, give them a message," he said, his lips lifting in a one-sided grin. "You can come inside, but your friends stay where they are. They come one inch closer, and you'll be picking them out of the pavement for weeks."

I figured the Guild would have sentries on watch who could see my friends. Leaving them across the street had been a calculated risk. I knew that a cat sidhe, a kelpie, and a demon wouldn't be allowed inside, but I hadn't wanted to split up. The last time we had separated, Ceff and Torn had ended up in iron shackles inside my uncle's secret dungeon.

Of course, I was a lot more fae now than I'd been on previous visits to the Guild. I just hoped that they were willing to go by what they knew of me, rather than judge me by what I'd become. It gave me hope that Master Janus had knowingly allowed Jonathan, a werewolf, into his ranks. It meant that he, at least, wasn't a bigoted prick. I couldn't say the same for Hendricks, or the men targeting my friends with weapons.

"Relax, Hendricks," I said. "My friends are here to help us protect the city, nothing more."

"We'll see about that," he said.

I ignored the way Hendricks tracked my movements, the bulging veins on his neck pulsing in time to the compulsive flexing of his fists. Turning my back on a trained Hunter who probably had ogre blood somewhere in his family's past probably wasn't the smartest move, especially when he was obviously fantasizing about crushing my skull like a June bug, but there was no way I was letting Hendricks touch my weapons.

He was fully aware of my psychometry and touch phobia. Knowing his mean streak, and his ironic dislike of the fae, I wouldn't put it past Hendricks to take my blades into the nearest latrine or worse. I stifled a shudder, and hurried my pace.

"Hendricks, huh?" Jinx asked, wincing sympathetically at my approach. "No dice?"

"I told you the Guild would never help the likes of us," Forneus said.

"It's not that," I said, shaking my head. "I got permission to go inside. I just can't bring these with me." I turned away from Jinx and Forneus, and took a steadying breath. "Hang on to them for me?"

I handed my weapons over to Ceff, and he took them from me reverently. He knew how much the gesture cost me, and how far we'd come. I wouldn't have trusted my weapons with anyone not so long ago, especially not a kelpie king. Now, I couldn't imagine anyone I trusted more aside from Jinx, and she and I were still on the outs.

A cold hand gripped my gut, and I darted a look at my friend. I vowed to fix things with Jinx as soon as this was over. We suddenly had secrets between us, too many secrets. I had to resist the urge to confess everything now, but I was afraid that if I started unburdening myself of all the things I was keeping locked inside, I wouldn't be able to stop. Now wasn't the time for honesty and tears.

It was time for action.

"Torn, while I'm in there, you think you can contact your spies without setting off the Guild's trigger-happy sentries?" I asked. "Hendricks warned that there are Hunters just itching for a reason to take out the potential enemies on their doorstep. I don't want to give them an excuse to attack, but I'd rather not rely solely on their intel...or on Kaye." I hesitated. "I'm not sure how much I trust Kaye and Janus right now."

It was the first time I'd voiced my concerns about Kaye outside the privacy of my own skull. My mouth went dry, and I had a sudden wish for extra strength antiperspirant.

"One step ahead of you, Princess," Torn said. His lips lifted in a lopsided grin. "I wondered how long it would take you to realize the witch has gone batshit crazy."

"Amen to that," Jinx muttered.

Forneus winced, but nodded.

"I would think it obvious after the unprovoked attack on me," he said. He lifted a brow and spread his hands innocently. "Why on earth would the witch wish me harm? She is drunk on power."

I snorted. I could think of plenty of reasons why someone might wish Forneus harm. Sadly, for all his grandstanding, he still had a point.

"Drunk on power and a few tarot cards short of a full deck," Torn said.

I wanted to rage at Torn and Forneus. I wanted to defend Kaye, who had been a longtime acquaintance and one whose wisdom I'd come to rely on. But they were right. Kaye had changed since regaining the full force of her powers. Her little stunt on the Old Port streets had proven just how much that power was clouding her judgment and influencing her actions.

Kaye had always had a temper, and a mischievous streak, but the woman I knew would never stage a demon/gargoyle death match in the streets. Not only had she done so, but she'd brought trouble to her own doorstep. A niggling voice inside my skull had been warning me that the witch was itching for the kind of fight where she could test the renewed strength of her magic.

I hate it when I'm right.

Ceff, who had been standing as silent sentinel, cleared his throat.

"I find it troubling that she is so easily distracted from the task at hand," Ceff said. "The Wild Hunt is a very real threat to this city and its human inhabitants. Not even the fae are safe from Herne's insatiable bloodlust."

"Like I said, I don't fully trust Kaye right now, but that doesn't change the fact that we need her help," I said. "We can't stop the Wild Hunt without that binding spell. Not unless we learn of some new weakness we can exploit."

"Then we better hope either the Guild or my spies turn up something useful," Torn said.

I nodded, casting one last longing glance at my weapons, and marched across the street. I was about to go unarmed into the lion's den. With a little luck, a lot of bluster, and a bluff or two, I just might make it out alive.

CHAPTER 11

Hendricks scowled down at me longer than necessary before letting me through the gate. I kept my breathing slow and steady, and let my hands hang loose at my sides.

The walk across the old school grounds to the main building took about five minutes, but it felt like a century. It's amazing how time crawls when you're doing the walk of shame.

I may not be slipping out of some man's bed after a night of overindulgence, but my face flared hot all the same. I'd come here in the past claiming to be half human, but that was a lie. I hadn't known the truth, but that didn't change the fact of the matter. I was a fraud.

I had to hold on to my glamour just to make it across the grassy parade grounds and up the stone steps of the building where Master Janus waited. I was the wolf in sheep's clothing. I was the monster hiding amongst humans.

Hunters stopped and stared as Hendricks led me to my meeting, and my glamour was all that kept my glowing eyes and skin from their notice. In fact, if they were wearing faerie ointment, they'd be able to see the glowing evidence of my discomfort. That would explain the way they all gripped their weapons as their narrowed eyes tracked my movements.

I tried to remember my uncle's training, the control I'd gained through months of practice. But I was no longer in Faerie, the source of all fae magic, and the thought of my uncle and his betrayal only made things worse. A tingling began along each shoulder blade, and I nearly gasped with relief when I made it inside the building and escaped the staring Hunters. I didn't want to think about what would have happened if wings had sprouted from my back.

I remembered a long-ago visit to Harborsmouth's small natural history museum and a display of winged insects beneath glass, a sharp pin thrust through each of their bodies, holding them in place to be ogled by dusty scholars and bored schoolchildren. The anxiety that had plagued my march through the Guild's grounds was slowly replaced by a growing

anger. I hadn't asked to be born fae, and I'd had no knowledge
of my father's magical sleight of hand when it came to my true
origins. What I had done was prove over and over again
through my actions that I valued the lives of the humans of
this city, and that I was willing to risk my life to protect them.

If these Hunters couldn't see past the ends of their
blades and their own prejudices, that was their loss. I'd held
some of those same ignorant beliefs at one time, when I'd been
the only one to see monsters walk our streets and had no one
whom I could trust to share that knowledge with. But once I
began to learn more about the fae, and even the undead, I came
to realize that, like humans, there will always be those who are
good and those who are bad. Even when I questioned my own
humanity, I never truly doubted that deep down I was a good
person. I was flawed—hell, I was so broken that some days I
didn't have the energy to get out of bed and try to reassemble
the pieces—but I wasn't evil just because I wasn't human.

But if the Hunters decided to make me and my friends
their enemy, I had no doubt that I could become their worst
nightmare.

Surprisingly, that thought gave me the strength needed
to stroll through the halls of the Hunters' Guild without so
much as a flicker. The glowing was gone, and I held my chin
high as I strode into Master Janus' office.

Hendricks, of course, was pissed.

"You bitch, you can't just go in there without my say so,"
he growled.

He hurried to head me off, but I rolled my eyes and
crossed my arms.

"Hey, Janus," I said. "Sorry if I broke protocol or
something, but time is of the essence, and the door was open."

"That's 'Master Janus' and..." Hendricks sputtered, face
flushing red.

Apparently, I should have waited to be properly
announced. The thing is, I'd spent the equivalent of a year
watching supplicants come and bow and scrape in a faerie
court. My first action when I'd been given the power to rule
that court had been to hand it over into the care of my hearth
brownie friend Skillywidden who was now in the process of
creating a democratic council for the future rule of the wisp

court. I'd had it up to my glowing eyeballs with pretentious introductions and red tape.

I sauntered over and sank into the chair opposite Janus' desk. The message was clear. I was here, and I wasn't going to budge any time soon.

"It's fine, Hendricks," Janus said. The guild master came to his feet, and though he stood a foot shorter than the guard, he managed to look menacing. "Return to your post."

"Yes, sir," Hendricks said.

He bowed, and backed out of the room. Janus came out from behind his desk, and followed Hendricks to the door. He watched, making sure that Hendricks didn't linger in the hall, and then shut the door. Silence fell on the room, filling the office with palpable tension, as we studied each other.

"So," he said, eyes lingering over my shoulder. "You wanted to see me."

I had to fight the desire to reach behind my back and check to see if I'd unleashed my wings.

"Yes, I think Kaye already alerted you that a powerful faerie has set off her wards," I said. He nodded, and I swallowed. "The Wild Hunt is in Harborsmouth."

He swore, his hand going to the sword at his hip.

"Give me a status report," he said. "Where were they last seen?"

I leaned forward, gloved hands resting on my knees. Where to begin? I had a nagging suspicion that withholding facts from Janus might be as bad as lying in his eyes, and he was a man I'd like to someday count as an ally. I took a deep breath, nodding as I made up my mind.

"They're on the edge of the city, in an industrial area near my friend's junkyard," I said.

"How'd you happen to come upon the Hunt?" he asked. "Was it dumb luck, or is there something more to the story?"

My heart raced, and the room started to spin. This was it, the moment where I had to decide whether to hold my cards close to my chest or go all in.

"They followed me and my friends back from Faerie," I said. "You could say I was there to get my wings."

I smiled, showing too many teeth. But Master Janus was a tough man and didn't so much as flinch.

"I thought there was something different about you," he said. "You're not even a little bit human, are you?"

"I didn't lie before, if that's what you're asking," I said. "What I told you about being half human was true at the time, and you know how I was raised, but you're right. Human blood no longer runs through my veins."

We stared at each other, my fingers itching for weapons I didn't have. It was probably a good thing I'd been ordered to leave my blades behind. If I had them on me, the desire to draw them might have gotten me killed. As it was, Janus took his time before nodding and moving his hand from his sword.

I let out the breath I'd been holding. The Guild might have archaic rules, rituals, and red tape, but their guild masters weren't fat old men who sat around ordering others to do their dirty work. Their leaders earned their positions through blood, sweat, and sacrifice. That made Janus a formidable opponent, even if he hadn't stood there armed with a blade.

"I'm guessing you're not going to share how you got into Faerie when all the pathways are said to be sealed," he said.

"Nope," I said.

"Didn't think so," he said. "Then what else can you tell me about the Wild Hunt."

"Herne has some kind of magic horn that he uses to control his hounds, a pack of barghests," I said. "He's already sounded his horn once. Kaye said that was a rallying call to bring his hounds to him. We have to stop him before he sounds the horn again at sundown."

"And what did she say will happen then?" he asked.

"The hunt begins," I said. "We can't allow that to happen."

"No, that we can't," he said with a sigh. "I've also had word from Kaye, but it doesn't hurt to have it confirmed. Are you the one she's enlisted to aid with the binding?"

"Yes," I said, head snapping back to look him in the eye. "You know about that?"

"There's this thing called a telephone," he said, a grin on his lips as he glanced at the phone on his desk.

"Could have fooled me," I muttered.

I'd never been able to get Master Janus on the line.

"Anything else?" he asked.

I shrugged.

"I'm supposed to get a piece of Herne for Kaye," I said. "My friends and I have a rudimentary plan for making that happen, but I could use more intel. Maybe even backup. I know I'm a faerie, and probably not your favorite person, but I was hoping we could set aside our differences to protect the people of Harborsmouth."

He nodded, and clasped his hands behind his back.

"Since you have been honest with me, it is time that I am honest with you, Miss Granger," he said.

"Um, okay," I said.

I had an idea of what might be coming. Jenna had gone to extreme lengths to get me a message about a war on the horizon—a war that would pit supernaturals against humans. It wasn't as black and white as that. Things involving the fae rarely are.

There was a faction of supernaturals, the most bloodthirsty of the fae and the undead, who believed that humans were little more than a food source to be dominated and fed upon at their leisure. There were some who missed the thrill of the hunt, the intoxication of chasing down their prey and leaving chaos and terror in their wake.

These supernaturals balked at the rules that demanded hiding and suppressing what they believed to be their true nature. I'd seen the horrors of that nature in the basement of Club Nexus. The chained corpses of ravaged victims and the reek of blood and terror still filled my nightmares. I didn't want to imagine that kind of wanton violence and disregard for human life on a larger scale.

"What I'm about to share with you is not common knowledge, even amongst my men," he said. His face darkened, and he fixed me with a stare that had been known to bring trained Hunters to their knees. "Do ye ken my meaning?"

The last he said with such intensity, and in a brogue so thick, it took me a moment to parse out the implications of what he was saying.

"Yes," said, nodding and swallowing hard.

One of the most respected leaders of an ancient organization whose sole purpose was to police rogue supernaturals, an organization that guarded their secrets like a dragon hoarded gold, was about to share something with a faerie. By Mab, the guild master had my full attention.

"Good," he said. "First, what do you know of Fae and Vampire Law?"

I fidgeted in my seat. I didn't envy the students who had Master Janus as an instructor. I wasn't even in a classroom, and I had the unsettling feeling that this was a pop quiz and I'd spent the night before goofing off instead of studying. I had to force myself to concentrate and remember that I was a trusted peer, not one of his novitiates.

"Vampire law states that feeding on humans must be done discreetly," I said. "The vampire council encourages vampires to take blood slaves from the fringes of society, the homeless, addicts, and runaways whose disappearances are less likely to be noticed. But whether taking blood slaves or feeding on the fly, they use their glamour and a mind altering drug released in their saliva during feedings to keep their existence secret from humans. The fae have a similar law. All fae must hide their existence from the human media, or face execution."

"Exactly," he said. "We protect innocent humans by taking down rogue supernaturals who would do them harm. Members of the Guild put their lives on the line every day in cities around the world. But how much more difficult would our job be if the fae and vampires weren't already policing their own?"

My mouth went dry. We already had our hands full with rogue vamps, ghouls, and fae. It was hard to fathom what the world would be like if they were allowed to come out of the supernatural closet and feed on humans with impunity.

"You're talking about anarchy, total chaos," I said.

Not all supernaturals were blood-crazed psychopaths, but I had to admit that even some of the more peace-loving fae liked nothing better than to mess with humans. The implications of Janus' words kicked me in the gut, knocking the air from my lungs.

"Aye, and more bloodshed and terror than we've seen in centuries," he said. "And it will come on the heels of a war that will take more lives than any plague or cancer."

"So there are vampires and fae who want to go against the vampire council and the faerie courts to break the old laws, and they're willing to wage war with us as well," I said. I shook my head. "Immortality won't protect them from a stake through the heart or a sword in the gut. It seems like a big risk."

"But one with huge rewards for those who desire to hunt humans without repercussion from their own kind," he said. "And they've begun amassing magic weapons that could give them an edge in the coming battle."

"So, are you saying that the Wild Hunt being in Harborsmouth is part of this war?" I asked. "You think someone in the Unseelie court managed to slip the Hunt through before the portal closed behind us?"

He rubbed a calloused hand over his face, and for a moment the guild master aged before my eyes.

"That I can't say for certain, but it's a good theory given what facts we know," he said. "What I do know is that Kaye means to bind the Wild Hunt and use them as a weapon."

"Wait, what?" I asked. "That's not what she told me."

But I had to admit it made a sick kind of sense. Kaye was drunk on power and she faced an opponent that gave her a chance to exact revenge on a pack of barghests for the friends she lost at the hands of a rogue barghest long ago, all the while knowing that a larger threat loomed on the horizon. It wasn't all that farfetched.

What hurt was that she'd lied and manipulated me into being a part of her plan.

"I suspected as much," he said.

"So do you agree with this plan of hers, to enslave a group of fae to fight for you?" I asked.

I held my breath, waiting for his answer.

"It leaves a bad taste in my mouth, if that's what you mean," he said. "But there's some who'd say that all is fair in love and war."

"Well, I'm not one of them," I said.

I thought of the tormented looks that crossed Ceff's face when he thought no one was looking. I recalled living through the worst moments of his captivity through the visions I'd had dozens if not hundreds of times. The torture by iron had been painful, but the most heinous acts had been his own.

Ceff was highly skilled with water magic, but there are some things that water can't cleanse. The *each uisge* had stolen his bridle, and with its magic forced Ceff to fight against his own people. He would never wash that blood from his hands.

"We cannot win this war if we are being assailed on all fronts," Janus said.

He was staring at a map hanging on the wall above his desk. It depicted the city, and was covered in a complicated maze made up of thumbtacks and colored string.

"Then we need to defeat the Wild Hunt before this battle makes it to our doorstep," I said.

"Any idea how to do that, aside from Kaye's binding spell?" he asked.

"I have a few ideas," I said. "But we'll need your help if there's even a chance in hell of pulling this off. Can I count on the Guild?"

A slow smile spread across Janus' face, tugging at the old scars that crisscrossed his cheek.

"Aye, by Athena, you have my word," he said. "Now let's invite your friends in so we can have us a chat."

CHAPTER 12

"That was the strangest hour of my life...lives," Torn said. "And I've got nine of them, as you recall."

A ridiculous smile split my face in two. For all of my friends' bewilderment, anxiety, and at times flat out ire, I'd spent the meeting with the Hunters' Guild like a pooka hopped up on Jimson weed.

Skillywidden had warned me that I was showing extreme signs of depression, but I hadn't listened. I'd had Ceff and Torn to worry about. Now my friends were all here, and they were safe and we had a plan that not only made sense, it included the local Hunters' Guild.

My smile wavered when I thought of Kaye's duplicity and mental instability, but I quickly shrugged it off. I'd lived under the tutelage of my uncle. Not only was he the poster child for lies and manipulation, but the man was as unstable as a losing move in a game of Jenga.

He'd also let me down so hard, I'd barely been able to pull myself up out of bed that first day. But I'd done it. I'd grit my teeth, and made myself stand. Now I was ready to do more than stand, more than walk, more than run into battle.

I was ready to fly.

There's something completely freeing about being decisive. I wasn't sure if this was the right decision, but I'd finally broken free of the mental stasis that fear, and loss, and pain had chained me into.

Not so long ago, Jinx had been my only friend. Hell, she'd become my entire family. Now I counted so many amongst my friends and allies. I was even working to repair ties with my mom, there was hope of reuniting with my father, and Ceff wanted to spend immortality together.

None of those relationships were perfect, but they were mine. I hoarded and protected them greedily. I'd experienced so much loss and loneliness that the fear of reliving that pain had come to drive my every thought, my every move.

But I finally had to make a choice. One that I'd known was coming ever since the changes that Faerie had wrought on me. I chose to embrace the truth of my fae lineage while remaining true to the morals that my life amongst humans had instilled. I'd been racing toward this moment all my life, and everything seemed clearer now that I'd made up my mind of how I was going to handle things.

I chose to be me.

This city was my home, and I valued the life of every person in it, no matter the blood, dust, or ichor that flowed through their veins. My time in Faerie hadn't changed the fact that I was a hero of this city, one who had vowed to use her gifts to protect its inhabitants—all of her gifts.

If using those gifts would save the city, then it was worth the fallout. And if some of my friends or allies couldn't face the extent of my faeness, then perhaps they weren't really worth having in my life after all. I think, for the first time, I was learning when it was okay to let go.

Look at me adulting.

I wore a deranged grin that made most of the men and women nearest me grab at their weapons. I'd made the decision to do everything possible to save Harborsmouth from any threat. Right now, that threat was the Wild Hunt. I was about to become Herne's worst nightmare.

Well, with the help of my friends, the Hunters' Guild, and a gaggle of pookas. There was strength in numbers, and right now, we were legion.

And we weren't done assembling our ramshackle troops. There were a few more pieces to the puzzle, and the next move was Ceff's. Until now, we'd both insisted on sticking together. But if our plan was to succeed, I needed to face down one more fear, and let Ceff go.

"It's going to get weirder," I said to Torn. "You up for it?"

"Does a bugbear shit in the woods?" he asked.

"And you wonder why I chose the demon," Jinx muttered, shaking her head.

"Oh, I can think of numerous reasons, least of all the cat's use of foul colloquialisms," Forneus said, stroking a hand down her side to rest at her hip.

Jinx shivered, and I sighed. If we weren't on a tight timetable, I'd tell those two to get a room. There was nothing like a demon overdue for make-up sex to make a person crazy.

"Are you certain you wish for me to leave your side," Ceff said. "I can see the value in harnessing the strength of the water fae, but..."

I held up a hand, and shook my head.

"I wouldn't ask you to go if I didn't believe it could change the outcome in our favor," I said.

"Then I will feel your loss like a bottomless trench in my heart until we are reunited on the waves of battle," he said.

"I love you too," I said.

My smile became less manic as we said our goodbyes, but we didn't touch. There was no time for kisses or an embrace. The moment our skin touched, I would be thrust into a sea of visions, and though I'd grown accustomed to much of Ceff's past, the mental wounds of his recent captivity were still too raw. I needed to keep my head in the game, not lose my way inside someone else's.

"What now, Princess?" Torn asked as Ceff turned a corner and was lost from sight.

I cast a look over my shoulder at the assembled Hunters, and that ridiculous grin once again tugged at my lips.

"Now, we get into position for the fight of the century," I said. "You coming?"

The cat sidhe were fickle allies, so it was a valid question. Thankfully, I'd spent enough time with Torn to get the hang of cat sidhe psychology. For all his secrets, the man was an open book. Dangle a new experience in front of him, especially one rife with danger, mayhem, and possible death, and Torn went for it like catnip.

"Well, when you put it like that, how can I resist?"

CHAPTER 13

Movement in the sky had me jerking my head back and shielding my eyes with one gloved hand, the other already reaching for one of my silver and iron blades.

I'd probably need to have new iron-free weapons crafted soon, but I'd keep using my old, faithful blades for as long as I could take the side effects of a growing iron allergy. Wearing leather gloves helped—for once my touch phobia was a blessing, giving me the advantage of having always trained with gloves on—but having iron strapped to my forearms, belted to my lower back, and stuck inside my boot made my skin itch, and left a sickly sheen of sweat on my brow. For now, the edge those iron weapons gave me against fae assailants was worth the mild discomfort.

It was better than being dead.

Speaking of which, a shadow fell over us like a shroud, and a chill ran up my spine. There were six gigantic owls circling high above our heads, and I doubted their arrival was a good thing.

"Holy crap," Jinx said, her eyes following mine. "Am I the only one who feels like we just stepped into the fire swamp?"

"The what?" Forneus asked, eyebrow raised.

"Princess Bride reference," I said, keeping my eyes on the circling predators. "Rodents of Unusual Size, except in this case they have wings."

"Owls of unusual size," Torn said with a grin. "That would be Herne's minions. Interesting."

"Shit," I said. "I didn't know he had airborne forces. That complicates things."

I was hoping that our plan to stop the Wild Hunt would work, but if we failed, we'd have to rely on my original plan to get a piece of Herne for Kaye's binding spell. Problem was, that plan relied heavily on pookas, pookas that would be bite-sized morsels those giant owls could pluck from the sky like moths.

A pooka clan had helped me before in exchange for a home in my old, childhood treehouse. I'd sent Marvin and Hob there with a message for the pooka leader, a diminutive fellow who liked partying and screwing, not necessarily in that order. The pooka clan treated life like a perpetual rave, right down to the glow-in-the-dark condoms they wore on their heads and the psychedelic herbs they liked to smoke.

So long as I let them live in the treehouse, which has become party central for the small fae who live out in the burbs, and brought them the occasional munchies, the pooka clan was usually willing to do the odd recon job. But they have sticky fingers and love a dare, especially a double-barghest dare, which is why I thought they'd be good for this mission.

Until now.

"It might be sensible to warn our new Guild allies of the arrival of Herne's spies," Forneus said.

"Let me guess, Herne sees what they see?" I asked. "Like a witch's familiar?"

"Precisely," he said. "At least they are at a disadvantage, for now."

"Right, 'cause those sharp beaks, talons, and wings the length of baseball bats are total disadvantages," Jinx said, rolling her eyes.

"Aside from those notable attributes, Herne's great horned owls, just like the rest of the Wild Hunt, are nocturnal," Forneus said.

"And this helps us how?" I asked.

"For one thing, Princess," Torn said, stepping from the shadows where he'd been once again meeting with one of his cat informants. "If we'd encountered those owls at night, you never would have seen them. The first you'd know of their existence would be the pain of their talons crushing your rib cage and piercing your heart."

Now that was a pleasant thought. Leave it to Torn to dredge up the most gruesome image possible.

"You sound as if you speak from experience," Forneus said, narrowing his eyes at Torn.

"I'm on my ninth life, and I spent one of those entirely in cat form," Torn said, showing his teeth. "So, yes, I know what it's like to be attacked by a great horned owl. They're not called winged tigers for nothing."

"Is that where you got your scars?" Jinx asked, eyes tracing the puckered flesh that lined his face, arms, and tattered ears.

"A few of them," he said, unlacing his leather pants. "Want to see where the bastard's rear talon pierced my femoral artery?"

He winked, and licked his lips as Jinx leaned forward, and I had to bite the inside of my cheek before I stepped between them and Forneus. The last thing I wanted was to stand any closer to a half-naked cat sidhe, but now wasn't the time to make the demon jealous.

"Lace 'em up, Torn," I said, holding a blade an inch from the bulge in his trousers.

Our proximity made my hand shake, but it could have been worse. If I'd hesitated any longer, he would have been stark naked. Take it from someone who knows, stripping off leather is never easy, even if it's cold out and you've coated the inside of your leathers with talc. I had a nagging suspicion that getting naked was some kind of cat sidhe super power. Or maybe it was just Torn. He was the kind of guy who would spend immortality practicing that trick.

Jinx pouted until Forneus cleared his throat from over my shoulder.

"If you are interested in scars, love, all you had to do was say so," he said.

I ratcheted my free arm behind me, aiming a blade at Forneus' chest.

"Don't even think about it," I said. "Whatever you have in mind, just don't. You're all making me want to puke."

We stood there in our awkward standoff long enough for my shoulder to begin to ache. Jinx looked amorously at Forneus until Torn broke the silence.

"Did you know that owls regurgitate to feed their young, and that when they shit their turds are all hair and bone?" he asked.

Jinx blanched, and I snorted. I'd actually heard that before. Unlike Jinx who was a city girl through and through, I'd grown up in the suburbs. There had been a small farm not far from my old elementary school, and the kids used to call the owl feces "squirrel loafs" for their furry appearance. I suspected that some of those squirrel loafs were made up of bunny parts, but I didn't have any friends to share that with at the time, which was probably a good thing. The kids already thought I was a weirdo.

"Charming, cat," Forneus said.

"That's what the ladies tell me," Torn said.

"What can you tell me about Herne's owls, aside from their excrement?" I asked.

One of the owls swooped down to perch on the roof of a nearby warehouse. At this distance, the bird's unusual size was impossible to ignore. While they'd been circling overhead, I'd imagined the owls to be about the size of a Labrador, but this thing was on par with a Tibetan Mastiff. If a regular great horned owl could crush a rabbit, what the hell was this creature capable of?

I shivered, and Jinx shuffled her feet.

"Can we stop talking about owl poop?" she asked.

"Of course, but perhaps we should walk as we converse," Forneus said.

His meaning was made clear by Torn's next statement.

"There's more than one reason Herne uses his owls as spies," he said. "Most important is their keen hearing."

"Oh, right," I said, a snippet of a nature documentary coming back to me. "They hunt by sound."

"Which means if we stand still beneath that one sitting on the warehouse, we might as well be talking to Herne on speakerphone, right?" Jinx asked.

Torn made a strange series of hand gestures toward a nearby alley, and cats began to yowl and cry.

"Good thinking," I said, flashing Torn a rare smile. I was careful not to thank him for the cover sound he was orchestrating for our benefit. The consequences of thanking the fae were very real for me these days. I needed to watch my tongue, or I'd be in Torn's debt. "But are your cats going to be safe out here with those owls flying around?"

"Oh yes," Forneus said, stepping forward. "Herne's owls won't bother with lowly street cats. Not when they have much more important targets."

Not for the first time, I had the unpleasant sensation of a having a bull's eye painted on my back. I figured being pierced by those talons would be about as much fun as being pierced by the Moordenaar's arrows had been.

"I really hope you mean the Hunters in their shiny armor," I said.

"Not a chance, Princess," he said, licking his lips and rubbing his hands together. "They're following us."

Of course, Torn would think being the primary target of some mutant, super-sized "tigers of the sky" was fun. Not to mention the fact that we were already up against Herne and his pack of blood-crazed barghests. Could this day get any worse?

I should know better by now than to ask that question.

"More specifically," he said, tilting his head in my direction. "I think they're following you."

CHAPTER 14

"Haven't you ever wondered why the Wild Hunt is here, in Harborsmouth?" Torn asked.

"Sure," I said, shaking my head. "But at first, I figured it was just our bad luck that they somehow followed us through the portal before it closed."

I'd become used to seeing monsters and villains wherever I went. It was an occupational hazard. When the Wild Hunt had followed us into the human world, I hadn't given why much thought. I needed to protect innocent people. It must be a day that ended in the letter Y.

"Yes, but what if this wasn't simply a case of Herne being an opportunist?" he asked. "What if he had help?"

I nodded.

"The thought crossed my mind," I said with a frown.

It wasn't a pleasant thought. I hated to think that Herne had help since that meant we had more enemies out there somewhere, but it was damn likely. Master Janus had made a similar assumption.

"You're implying that the Wild Hunt's arrival was orchestrated by someone on the other side of the portal," Forneus said. "Someone in Faerie."

"About that," Jinx said, pulling me back to the present. "I'd still like to hear that story. You've managed to dance around the topic like a spider on a hot skillet, but I will get the truth about your 'vacation' and what the hell you were secretly up to the past few days."

I winced.

"I couldn't tell you about our plans because it would have put your life in danger," said. "I still can't share with you how we got there, but I promise to tell you the rest as soon as this is all over. Okay?"

There was a lot about meeting my uncle and discovering that I was Mab's biological daughter that I needed to work through. Talking it out with Jinx would help us both heal, if we lived that long.

"Okay," she said.

I nodded, and focused on Torn who was watching us in amusement. My fingers drummed along my thigh as I thought about the possibility that someone had helped Herne escape Faerie.

"Who would benefit from the Wild Hunt coming to the human world?" I asked.

"In my experience, most things are motivated by greed, lust, or revenge," Forneus said. "But I fail to see how lust could be a factor in this scenario, and aside from your witch friend's desire for revenge against any barghest that enters this city, I've seen no evidence of revenge being a factor."

I reached into my leather jacket and pulled out and flipped open the notepad that had somehow made it through my journey to the Otherworld and back again. It was beat up, and curling on the edges, but it would do. When working a case, taking notes often helps me sort through the details, and determine what is relevant and what is the extraneous flotsam of a person's life.

I forced myself to think back to the events just before our departure from Faerie. My uncle's betrayal, our visit to the Unseelie Court, their verdict against him, and their ruling to absolve me of being a traitor to the fae had been so all-consuming that I hadn't spent time focusing on much else beyond getting the assembled fae to allow our use of their secret portal to the human world.

I'd wanted so badly to go home. I hadn't even asked questions when our guide to the portal had been reluctant to follow the path into the woods, just assuming he was afraid of the Forest of Torment's bloodthirsty trees. He'd remained behind at the castle while I'd rushed headlong toward the portal, thinking of nothing but my friends and longing for my own bed. I cursed my own stupidity. It was exactly the kind of situation an unscrupulous member of the Unseelie Court might take advantage of. Had I walked blindly into a trap?

I hadn't been paying much attention during our short stay in the winter castle, but that didn't mean that I'd been oblivious to my surroundings. I was a detective, and that meant collecting even the smallest of details was second nature. I closed my eyes, hoping that my skills hadn't grown too rusty while I'd been away.

"The clipboard..." I said, closing my eyes and pinching the bridge of my nose.

"What, Princess?" Torn asked.

"Give me a minute," I said.

When the giant yetis guarding the entrance to the winter palace had opened the frost gates, we'd stepped into the frozen palace courtyard and been quickly surrounded by curious fae. A goblin female with a clipboard had been the first to approach us directly, but when I'd announced that I was the daughter of Mab the Queen of Air and Darkness, the faeries had fled inside the castle.

I remembered the goblin woman's bulbous nose bouncing as she turned and ran, but more importantly, I recalled her clipboard and stylus falling from shaking hands. It was the clipboard that interested me. As I'd stepped over it with blood and snow-covered boots, I'd read a list of agenda items. Knowing what was on the Unseelie Court's docket seemed like a good idea at the time, but I'd soon been consumed with my own troubles, and cast the mental list aside.

Eyes closed, I took a deep breath, and cleared my mind of everything but the goblin's clipboard. The scrawled list swam before me in a blur, slipping and sliding from my grasp, remaining just out of reach. Not so long ago, I would have given up. But I'd honed my mental skills while learning to control my wisp magic. Now, I applied those principles to years of detective work, and the list came into focus.

I quickly discarded the prominent items on the list. Minor cases of theft and land squabbles in Faerie had little relevance to our current predicament. But there were cases that had already been brought before the court, and been subsequently crossed off by the goblin administrator. It was those cases that now drew my interest, and set my detective skills tingling.

"The day we arrived at the winter palace, the Unseelie Court had already adjourned three cases," I said.

My heart raced as random words and glances began to fit together like pieces of a puzzle.

"How do you know that, Princess?" Torn asked. "I don't recall anyone telling us that at the time. In fact, I recall those faeries shitting their fancy pantaloons when you told them who your mother was."

"The clipboard the goblin woman dropped in the courtyard," I said. "There was a list, and the first three cases were crossed out."

"And you remember what those cases were?" Forneus asked, eyebrow raised. "You've never seemed interested in any legal discussion in the past."

"She just isn't interested in your legal cases," Jinx said, elbowing him playfully in the ribs. "You do go on a bit."

"I do remember, and I don't think what's happening is a coincidence," I said. "That morning the Unseelie Court was petitioned by a man named Gerald as a representative for a Y.F., and from the notation, it looked like they were requesting some kind of magical diversion."

"You think Y.F. stands for Yue Fei, the vampire?" Torn asked.

"Yes, Yue Fei and some of his men were here in Harborsmouth the last time I visited Gaius," I said. "And we all know Gerald is a weasel. It wouldn't surprise me if those two are working together to take the city from Gaius."

"You think they got their request approved, and the magical diversion the Unseelie Court sent is the Wild Hunt," Torn said.

"Holy crap," Jinx said.

"Yes, we got used," I said. "I thought they accepted my request to use Mab's portal a bit too readily."

"It's the perfect plan," Torn said, nodding. "So devious, I wish I'd thought of it. They accept your request, make sure the Wild Hunt slips through the portal behind us, and leave you to take the blame."

"Meanwhile, we are all distracted while Yue Fei takes out one of our allies, and becomes the new vampire Master of the City," Forneus said.

"Gaius Aurelius is a pompous prick with a flair for the dramatic, but he's been an ally, and more importantly, he's kept his vampires in line," I said. "From what I've heard, Yue Fei was a samurai warrior who left legions of corpses on the battlefields of ancient China while serving his master. Perhaps, he wants to return to a time when vampires can hunt humans freely."

"I've heard Yue Fei is a man of honor and loyalty, but Sir Gaius would be foolish to blindly believe his loyalty to the

Master of the City of Harborsmouth would usurp loyalties from his homeland," Forneus said.

"So the Unseelie Court sent the Wild Hunt here as a distraction so that a samurai vampire can overthrow Gaius and take over as Master of the City for some badass, ancient vamp back in China?" Jinx said. "Why?"

"To give them a leg up in the coming war," I said. "Jenna warned me that the war would begin in Harborsmouth. If she's right, this could be the first battle in a much bigger fight."

"The Unseelie Court acts in Mab's interest," Torn said, tugging at a scarred ear. "You think Mab's finally made contact with her court?"

"It does seem her style, doesn't it?" I asked.

"Yes, but what can we do about it?" Torn asked. "I'm all for beating Mab at her own game, but how can we help Sir Gaius while the Wild Hunt poses a more urgent threat?"

I smiled, showing my teeth.

"We change the rules."

CHAPTER 15

"You want to try talking to Herne?" Torn asked. "You do realize he's here to hunt us and steal our souls for his ragtag group of slavering barghests, all while Yue Fei takes over the vampires and sets them to feed on the city's humans."

"Yep," I said.

"You think that's going to work?" Jinx asked.

"Not really," I said. "But I want a closer look, and if I can reason with Herne while I'm at it, all the better."

"Just don't smile at him," she said.

"Or offer to cook for him," Forneus said. "I seem to remember burnt macaroni as the apex of your culinary skills."

I scowled, and shook my head.

"Am I really such a failure?" I asked.

"Not at causing trouble, or at killing things," Torn said. "It's what I like about you."

"Glad I still have some redeeming qualities," I muttered.

Torn winked, and Jinx hefted her crossbow onto her shoulder.

"What about those owls?" she asked.

"Let's keep things friendly," I said. "Keep an eye on them, but don't shoot unless they attack first."

She sighed, and I stifled a grin. I wasn't the only one who'd acquired a taste for violence. Our Hunter friend Jenna Lehane had trained us before being shipped off to Europe. If only she could see us now, with a squad of Hunters at our back.

"Well, you better hope those guys got the memo," she said, shrugging a shoulder toward the Hunters.

"They did," I said. "Master Janus is in agreement, and he's issued orders. One squad will cover our backs, but will not engage unless we're attacked."

"And the other Hunters?" Torn asked.

"They'll stay here and hold the line until we return," I said.

"And if we don't make it back alive?" he asked.

"Then they'll rendezvous with Ceff and the water fae, and follow the plan without us," I said.

"Are we ready then?" Forneus asked, tugging at his gloves.

"Almost," I said. "Torn, were your spies able to get word to Benmore?"

"Yes, Princess," he said. He tilted his head, and smiled. "In fact, here he comes now."

I ran a hand over my hair and tugged at my jacket and pants, smoothing hair and straightening my clothes. I couldn't do anything about the blood stains, I hadn't bothered to return home for a change of clothing, but I drew myself to my full height, and tapped into my magic enough to improve my glamour. I wasn't sure if dwarves could see through faerie glamour, but I wanted to at least make an effort.

Benmore was the leader of the local dwarf clan. Centuries ago, drawn to the ley line power that attracted so many supernaturals to Harborsmouth, the vampires had come and ousted the dwarves from their halls. Since then, Benmore's clan had struck an agreement with the vampires. I was unsure of the details, but the dwarves claimed to rule the city below from above while the vampires ruled the city above from below. I suspected their alliance had to do with things like mining rights, daytime protection, and shared access to sewer tunnels, but the exact terms weren't important.

The dwarves and the vampires had an alliance that was now being threatened. Gaius Aurelius had honored the mysterious treaty with Benmore and his clan, but I doubted Yue Fei would be so generous. The samurai had his own loyal men-at-arms. He'd have little use for miners and even less use for anyone who'd allied with Gaius. That gave me a potential friend in this fight.

"You sent for me, m'lady?" Benmore asked.

He pulled off his bowler hat, and bowed, beard wagging. The last time we'd met, the dwarf had been delivering a message for Gaius. I'd been grouchy, and far from civil. I forced a smile, and waved a hand at Benmore.

"No need to bow," I said. "I've asked you here as a friend."

Benmore took one look at my face, blanched, and stumbled back a step. He held his hat against his chest, and turned it in a circle, his beard twitching. I guess I really did need to work on that smile.

"If I've done somethin' to offend..." he stuttered.

"No, this is no trick, and I wish you no harm," I said. "But I do have a warning for your clan. Yue Fei, with the help of his men and a vampire named Gerald, are making a move against Gaius Aurelius."

"A move against the Master of the City?" he asked. "That's preposterous. No offense, m'lady."

"Have you heard that the Wild Hunt is here in Harborsmouth?" I asked.

"Aye, the Master called a meeting," he said. "He was worried Herne and his hounds might pose a threat to the...the food supply, as it were. Yue Fei said Herne could not act until sunset, which pleased Gaius just fine. The vampires are to gather in the council chambers at dusk. If the problem remains, then the vampires will march, fully rested, on the city."

"Yue Fei doesn't intend to protect this city, or the vampires' food supply, from the Wild Hunt," I said. "He's the one who orchestrated the Hunt's arrival. He will likely execute Gaius in his chambers then let loose his vampires on this city."

"But...what are we to do, m'lady?" he asked.

"We have our hands full with the arrival of the Wild Hunt, but if you can get a warning to Gaius, and perhaps help him escape, it would save us all a great deal of bloodshed," Forneus said.

"What makes ye think we can do that?" Benmore asked, eyeing the demon with open suspicion.

"Because dwarves are smart, and those halls were yours long before the vampires came to Harborsmouth," I said. "You must have built escape routes to the surface, and I'm guessing you know every tunnel in the Hill. Perhaps, every tunnel in all of Harborsmouth."

He put a pudgy, calloused finger to his nose, and winked.

"That be true," he said. "But what's in it for my clan? The humans have never done us no favors. Why should we protect them from Yue Fei? Maybe we let the vampires kill each other, and decrease the number of leeches in our halls."

"If I thought we could rid this city of vampires, and restore you to your home, I would," I said. "But Yue Fei is a master of military strategy. He wouldn't make his move unless he was sure he had every piece in place to succeed."

"By the Mother Mountain," he said, stumbling backward. He clutched at his chest, spittle on his bearded lips. "The suits of armor."

"What?" Torn asked. "Is he having some kind of fit?"

"Are you saying that Yue Fei has been smuggling in his men in suits of armor?" I asked.

I'd seen his men use a similar ruse to stand silent guard inside vamp headquarters.

"He said they were valuable antiques, precious to him," Benmore said, nodding slowly. "We were to help sneak the crates into the city, and the undercity below, as a surprise for the Master from Yue Fei's Master in China. Priceless relics that could not be exposed to sunlight."

"Where are these crates now?" I asked.

"In the council chamber," he said, voice barely a whisper.

"The same chamber where Gaius is to meet Yue Fei at dusk," I said.

"It's a trap," Torn said.

"What can I do?" Benmore asked.

"Do you know Gaius' daytime resting place?" I asked.

Vampires guarded the secret of their resting place, often having multiple coffins to confuse their enemies. But Benmore was an ally, and one who wasn't nocturnal. It was possible that he and his clan knew of the place in order to stand guard when needed. I crossed my fingers, and held my breath.

"That I might," he said, eyes twinkling.

"Then go to Gaius," I said. "Wake him, and warn him of Yue Fei's treacherous plans. Help him get his most trusted men to safety."

"And what of the traitors?" he asked.

"Might I make a suggestion?" Forneus asked.

Benmore nodded, and Forneus smiled.

"I propose we sneak into the council chambers and burn them all."

CHAPTER 16

With our help, and under the cover of cats yowling, Benmore slipped into an ally and down a sewer grate. I'd convinced him to leave behind his bowler hat, which was currently being worn by an excessively shaggy coon cat. It wouldn't fool an observer on the ground, but I hoped to confuse Herne's owl spies for as long as possible.

Forneus had wanted to go with Benmore, but I convinced him to stay with us awhile longer. He'd meet Benmore on the Hill an hour before dusk, when they would make their move on the vampire council chambers. Ever since his spat with Kaye, the demon had been itching to burn something to the ground. He'd get his wish soon enough, but in the meantime, he would focus on keeping Jinx safe.

"Are you certain you will not return to the loft?" he asked, stroking her face. "There is time to return you there before my mission."

"No, I'm fighting this Herne guy," Jinx said, shaking her head and moving away from his touch.

"But you could protect, Sparky..." he said, eyes pleading.

"Father Michael can do that," she said. "And if we kick ass, the Hunt will never even make it to the Old Port."

"And if we lose?" he asked.

"Then I know we did everything we could," she said, thrusting out her chin. "All of us. Even the weak little human."

"I know you are not weak, my love," he said.

"Then stop acting like I'm made of glass," she said.

"You want me to grab your ass?" Torn asked with a wink. "Don't mind if I do."

"Do it and lose your hand, cat," Forneus said.

"Cut it out, all of you," I said. "We're almost there."

We rounded the corner, and I stopped dead in my tracks. In the distance, on the opposite end of a deserted, concrete lot between rundown warehouses, was the Wild Hunt.

Hounds the size of grizzly bears slept in a protective
ring, and in their center sat a man astride a black horse. The
rider wore a hooded cloak, but above his head, the ghostly glow
of antlers flickered in and out of existence.

"Am I the only one who can see that?" I asked.

There was something off about those antlers, something
both familiar and stomach churning. It was like the red eyes
and black cloak were part of a powerful glamour, and the
antlers were a glimpse at the Huntsman's true form, whatever
that may be. I squinted and turned my head, hoping my
second sight would cut through the illusion—it's easier to fight
what you can see rather than wave my blades at smoke and
mirrors—but the cloaked figure remained seated atop his black
horse.

An eldritch glow like witch light lit the antlers from
within, and for a just a moment, I had the impression of a
stag's head on a man's body. Then the forlorn face of the stag
and the glowing antlers were gone.

"See what?" Jinx asked. "The scary ass Ringwraith
wannabe guy on a horse? Or maybe you mean their creepy,
twinsy, glowing red eyes?"

Now that she mentioned it, the eyes were creepy.
Herne, the horse, and the few hounds roving the grounds as
sentinels all had the same glowing, red eyes.

"No, I meant the antlers," I said, shaking my head. "But
never mind. They're gone."

"Antlers?" she asked. "Like a deer? Not horns?"

"Got a thing for horns?" Torn asked with a leer.

"Actually, cat, she does," Forneus said.

Horns emerged slowly from his head. Instead of scream
or shy away, Jinx leaned forward and stroked one of the horns.
Forneus' eyes became heavy-lidded, and Torn hissed. Jinx
ignored Torn, and kissed Forneus before stepping away and
grabbing her crossbow.

"Baby, you know I love your horns, but
they're...distracting," she said.

I shook my head. Mab's bones, she was practically
panting. I will never understand those two.

Forneus retracted his horns and smirked at Torn.

"Are you certain that what you see are antlers?" Ceff asked, stepping out of the shadows, and lowering a pair of binoculars.

Ceff had returned from the harbor just in time to join us in our reconnaissance mission. After an hour with Torn, Jinx, and Forneus' bickering, he was a refreshingly sane and calming presence at my side.

"Yes, like a deer," I said. "In his true form, the Huntsman might have a stag's head. But there's something weird about his glamour."

"That's because it's not glamour, not entirely," Ceff said.

"So what am I looking at?" I asked. "Is it some other kind of spell?"

"I believe you are seeing both the man and the spirit that has taken up residence within him," he said.

"You mean he's possessed?" I asked.

"In a way, yes," he said. "Some say that the entire Wild Hunt is possessed, though that's a misnomer. The Huntsman is possessed by the Spirit of the Forest, but his horse and hounds are the souls of men enslaved to join the Hunt."

He shuddered, and my stomach clenched. Ceff had been enslaved by the *each uisge*, tortured and forced to fight with them in the bloody harbor battle. He'd slipped away from his royal guards for a brief moment of privacy, and had paid dearly. The *each uisge* had ambushed him, stolen his bridle, and made him their bitch. He still had nightmares, and I relived the darkest moments of his captivity each time we touched.

That kind of violation of a man's will leaves scars, not only on him, but on us all.

"It's okay," I said. "Your bridle is safe. It won't happen again. Not ever."

We'd had his bridle reinforced and shielded magically. It had taken favors, some of which he wouldn't speak of, but it had been done. No one would ever again steal the control of this kelpie king.

"Oh how I wish for your ignorance in this one thing," he said.

"What do you mean?" I asked. "Did something happen?"

"What he means, Princess, is that all it takes is one bite from a hound of the Hunt for Herne to gain control and become their master," Torn said. "Man or fae, no one can resist the call."

"The hounds...they're not real barghests?" Jinx asked, brow wrinkling. "That's good, right? If they're just men, we can kill them."

I looked at the hounds, focusing all of my power and will to cut through their glamour to see the men within. Instead, all I got was a pounding in my skull. My eye twitched, and a slick oily sensation filled my gut.

"That's not glamour," I said. "The barghests are real. But how?"

"Magic," Torn said.

I thought about Ceff and how broken he'd been after suffering such a short time at the hands of the *each uisge*.

"Is there anything left of the men they once were?" I asked, watching the hounds pace at the feet of their master.

"No," Ceff said. "Once they kill for the Huntsman, their transformation is complete."

"Ceff is right," Forneus said. "Their souls have been in torment for so long that they have come to lust for blood and for the praise of their master. Their souls are black with it."

"Is there nothing we can do to save them?" I asked.

"Yes," Ceff said. "We can end their suffering, and break them free of this foul, unnatural bondage."

"Sometimes death is a mercy," Torn said.

"Then let's go be merciful."

CHAPTER 17

I wanted to swoop in like an angel of mercy, providing quick deaths to all of the enslaved members of the Wild Hunt. I only managed to take two pig-headed steps before Ceff grabbed the back of my leather jacket, stopping me in my tracks. I bared my teeth, and my blades, but he shook his head.

"Our allies are not yet assembled," he said. "To fight Herne and his hounds now would mean our deaths."

My hands tightened on my blades, and I shook him off, but I didn't continue marching blindly into combat. As much as I despised what was being done to the members of the Hunt, Ceff was right. He'd gone to the harbor and asked for the help of the water fae, but our plan was not yet fully in place. Ceff was still waiting to finish negotiations with his allies, and might need to return to the harbor at any moment. We also had left most of our trigger-happy Hunters' Guild backup more than two blocks away. It would be foolish to make any move yet, beyond peaceful negotiations.

I can be stubborn, and impulsive, but I'm no fool.

"Fine," I said. "No killing, yet."

"Then perhaps you should put your weapons away, Princess," Torn said.

"And let me do all of the talking," Forneus said, stepping forward. I gaped at him, but he raised an eyebrow. "What? I am obviously the most qualified to act as negotiator."

I grit my teeth, but he was right. The demon attorney was the most skilled at negotiating contracts. He had even more experience than my kelpie king boyfriend. Whether I liked it or not, Forneus could talk the Pope out of his soul and still come out smelling like roses. I, on the other hand, tended to become ensnared in unfavorable bargains.

The demon was our best chance of talking our way out of this mess. Oberon save us all.

"Fine," I said. "Let's go tell Herne that hunting season is over. If we're lucky, he'll pack up and go home."

*****

"HAVE YOU COME TO SURRENDER?" Herne asked,
his booming voice reverberating against nearby buildings.
"YOU WOULD MAKE A FINE ADDITION TO MY HUNTING
PARTY."

I winced, gritting my teeth. Herne sat astride a massive
black horse, his horn strapped to the saddle. The day had
grown overcast, and his owls circled overhead, like seagulls
before a hurricane.

Father Michael had texted me that in some stories, the
Wild Hunt presaged war or plague. With the growling of
barghests, the thunder of his mount's hooves as he rode to meet
us, and the whip crack power of his voice, I could well believe
that Herne and his Hunt was a mighty storm with the power to
destroy and bring death in its wake.

And though we'd let Forneus take the lead, Herne
settled the full force of his glowing red gaze on me. I bit the
inside of my cheek, and tried not to fidget.

"What are the rules of engagement?" Forneus asked,
waving a hand to gain Herne's attention.

"YOU HAVE UNTIL THE SUN SETS IN THE
WESTERN SKY," Herne said.

"And then?" Forneus asked.

"AND THEN WE HUNT," he said.

I couldn't be sure, there was a chance it was a
coincidental flickering of his glowing red eyes, but I could have
sworn that the bastard winked at me. I'd had enough. Herne
wasn't interested in negotiating with Forneus, but he did have
an interest in me. It was time I used that to get some answers.

"Why are you here?" I asked.

Torn muttered something unflattering, but I ignored
him and Forneus' sulfurous sigh. Herne and Kaye had both
said we had until sunset before the Wild Hunt would make its
move. I didn't plan on provoking the Hunt into battle, but I
wanted answers. Perhaps we could learn something with the
right person asking the questions.

"THE SPIRIT OF THE WOOD REQUIRES
SACRIFICE," he said. "AND SO DOES MY QUEEN."

I knew something of hungry wood spirits. I'd fed my blood to The Forest of Torment, the sentient woods that protected my mother's winter palace. Those skeletal trees had supped on my blood and found me worthy of safe passage, but I didn't fool myself. My ties to Mab were as much a curse as a blessing.

My mother had enslaved the Spirit of the Wood inside the mighty general Gwyn ap Nudd, creating Herne and his monstrous Wild Hunt. I didn't think he'd thank me for my mother's devious handiwork, so I made sure not to mention my relationship to Mab when I raised my next question.

"Did Mab send you here?" I asked. "Is she part of the coming war amongst supernaturals and humans?"

"BEWARE WHEN MY HORN SOUNDS THRICE," he said.

I shivered. It was hard to see inside the shadows of his hood, but I got the impression Herne was grinning. This conversation was taking a decidedly sinister turn, but I tried to keep him talking. Maybe he'd accidentally give us some detail we could use against him. That's what the evil villains do in movies, right?

I should have known an ancient spirit twisted to my mother's will wouldn't have anything to say worth hearing.

"Why?" I asked. "What happens then?"

"I WILL BREAK YOU, AND BEND YOU TO MY WILL," he said, his booming laughter echoing through my skull.

"Yeah, like I haven't heard that before," I said. "You'll find I'm not so easily broken, old man."

"I WILL BREAK YOU," he said. "YOU WILL BECOME ONE OF MY FAITHFUL HOUNDS, AND, ONE DAY, I WILL GIFT MY QUEEN YOUR SOUL."

Before I could think of a witty comeback, Forneus stepped forward.

"I happen to be something of an expert on souls, Herne," he said. "So, I am curious. Why do you think Mab would want this one's soul?"

I held my breath. Had Herne or the twisted spirit living inside of him been able to sniff out the truth of my blood? Was he already aware of my parentage when he followed us through the portal from Faerie? Or was his interest in me, and my soul, mere coincidence?

"THE ONE THING STRONGER THAN A MOTHER'S LOVE IS MAB'S THIRST FOR VENGEANCE," he said.

"Then Mab, or her minions, sent you here?" Forneus asked. "To what purpose? To capture Ivy, or to presage war?

"HAVE YOU NOT FIGURED IT OUT, DEMON?" he said. "WE ARE ALL PAWNS IN MAB'S GAME. THE WAR. THE GIRL. ULTIMATE POWER AND CHAOS. MY QUEEN WILL GAIN EVERYTHING SHE DESIRES."

CHAPTER 18

"Well, that was fun," Jinx said, wiping a shaking hand across her forehead.

When it became obvious that Herne wasn't willing to negotiate, we walked from the empty lot, with his booming laughter taunting our every step. Once out of sight of Herne and his hounds, we made a hasty retreat to the warehouse where our Guild allies had assembled.

"Yes, let's do it again," Torn said, a grin tugging at the scar that crossed his face.

"That was sarcasm, cat," Forneus said. "Though I fear you'll get your chance to fight Herne and his hounds soon enough."

"What I still don't get is what this Queen Mab wants with Ivy," Jinx said. "Does this have something to do with what you were doing on your supposed vacation?"

I sighed, and rubbed a gloved hand over my face.

"I went to Faerie, and to the wisp court in Nithsdale," I said, suddenly bone weary. "I had an uncle there."

"Oh my God, that's awesome, right?" she asked. "Did he know where to find your father?"

"If he did, he never told me," I said. "My uncle, Kade, had once loved Mab, and over time became obsessed with her, but she chose his brother, my father, over Kade. Kade was jealous and never forgave my father."

"Kade was a bastard," Torn said. "You should have let me kill him slowly."

Jinx's eyes widened, but I shook my head.

"Perhaps, but he is my uncle," I said.

"When you say that Mab chose your father, does that mean what I think it means?" she asked, pulling a face. "Like, bow chicka bow bow? Your dad and Mab?"

"Yes," I said.

"Holy shit," she said. "But I still don't get why she'd be pissed at you."

"Because..." I said, taking a deep breath. "I am Mab's daughter."

"Oh hell no," she said, blinking rapidly. "But...what about your mom?"

"My dad stole me away from Faerie, and from Mab, as a baby," I said. "He brought me here to the human world, and used his magic to put me in a kind of stasis until he could be sure that we hadn't been followed."

"Mab has eyes and ears everywhere," Torn said with grudging respect. "Her network of spies rivals even my own. It wouldn't have been easy to hide from her agents. Willem would have had to go underground for a long time, and kept you hidden all the while, even from his friends."

"Yes, but Mab left Faerie, and disappeared for over a hundred years," I said. "My father met my human mother, brought me out of stasis, and began a new life."

"Until Lucifer meddled," Forneus muttered. "Interfering with the Unseelie queen's former favorite, and knowing the knife's edge your family was on would have been a temptation too great. He always did most enjoy gambling when the stakes were high."

"The devil tricked my father into carrying the cursed lantern, and to keep us safe from the lantern's curse, he left us," I said.

"To keep you safe, he also put a geis on your human mother that forbade her from speaking of the fae, or him, and he used magic to block your childhood memories of him," Ceff said. "But he was no longer around to maintain the magic that kept you human. With time, your powers grew, your gifts manifested, and your memories began to filter back."

"Yes, but that geis is still strong," I said, hands fisting.

"He did it to keep you both safe," he said. "And a geis over a human is not likely to fade. I'm sorry."

"It's just...never mind," I said, shaking my head. "I wish I could speak freely about all this with my mom, especially now, but what's done is done."

"Maybe when you find your dad, he can lift the spell on your mom," Jinx said.

I loved that she still said "when" you find your dad, not "if" I found him, but I no longer shared her confidence in my success. I'd traveled to Faerie and back, and I was still no closer to finding my father.

"Maybe," I said, forcing a smile.

"So, Mab's daughter," she said. "That's heavy."

"You don't know the half of it," I said with a sigh. "I'm not the person you thought I was. I'm not...I'm not even human. Not even a little."

"Is that what all the secrecy is about?" she asked. She put a hand on her hip, and wagged a finger at me. "You better not be wigging that I'd care that you're pure fae, or that you're some evil faerie queen's spawn."

"Spawn?" I asked with a snort. "Thanks."

She winked.

"Anytime," she said. "You'll always be my best friend, Ivy. But no more secrets. No more lies."

"Deal," I said.

A heavy weight settled on my shoulders, and I struggled to suck air into my lungs. I blinked past the dizziness, knowing it would pass. I'd made a bargain with Jinx. I just hoped it was one I could keep. If not, it would kill me.

But if I couldn't agree to be honest with my best friend, I might as well be dead.

"Are you alright?" Ceff asked, leaning in.

"Never better," I said.

"That will be a difficult bargain to keep," he said, keeping his voice low.

"I'm willing to take that risk," I said. "I refuse to become like my mother."

I may be Mab's daughter, but I vowed never to be anything like my evil, manipulative mother with her deadly web of secret plots.

"Then let us go put a stop to her schemes," he said.

CHAPTER 19

We were on our way to meet with Master Janus when my ringing phone made me jump. According to the caller ID, it was Father Michael.

"What's up, Padre?" I asked. "Any new info on Herne or the Wild Hunt? We're looking down the field at a Hail Mary pass and the end zone has sharp teeth and glowing red eyes. Any weaknesses we can exploit would come in handy to help tip the odds in our favor."

"I...no...I mean..." he stuttered.

Father Michael seemed at a loss for words. Had I offended the priest? Was naming a pass a Hail Mary some form of blasphemy? Heck, I wasn't even sure where the football metaphor had come from. I was no sports fan. Must be too much television, I thought, shaking my head. Ever since Sparky moved in, the TV was on twenty-four-seven. If it wasn't cartoons, then the kid was watching something with lots of clapping and cheering, and that usually meant some kind of sports show.

"Sorry," I said, wincing. "I didn't mean to dump on you. Pre-battle nerves making me speak before I think, I guess. Everything alright at Casa Granger and Braxton?"

I was babbling, not giving the priest much chance to answer. I had to bite my lip and hold my breath to keep from rushing on. Something had set my nerves jangling, and I knew from experience that in times like this it was better to sit back and listen, but that didn't make it any easier.

Something bad was coming. I could feel it.

"No...everything is not alright!" he said, voice becoming shrill.

"Okay, okay, tell me what happened," I said.

I waved a hand at Ceff, then at Jinx, Forneus, and Torn, to get their attention. They raised a few eyebrows, but came to a stop when I gave the signal to halt. Ceff and Torn tilted their heads, and I knew they'd be listening in to the rest of the conversation. Fae hearing had its advantages.

With Herne's spies around, I'd rather not put the priest on speakerphone.

"I do not know how it is possible," Father Michael said, voice shaking. "He was right there, watching his cartoons. I went to make more of that noodle concoction..."

"Ramen," I said reflexively.

"Yes, yes, ramen," he said, taking a shuddering breath. "I turned away to set the water to boil, and when I looked back, he was gone."

"Gone?" I asked.

"Sparky," he said. "Someone has taken him."

I put a gloved hand out to steady myself, gripping a rusting railing that ran alongside a warehouse loading dock.

"That's impossible," I said, voice barely a whisper. "The wards..."

"The wards are still active," he said. "I have checked, and double-checked. I know of these things, but I do not know how an enemy found a way inside. You were quite thorough in your security."

Of course, Father Michael knew of supernatural security measures. He'd had to circumvent more than a few in his move to steal ancient treasures from the Vatican archives. If he said the magical wards guarding our apartment were still active, then I believed him.

I took a deep breath, forcing air in through my nose, and held the breath to the count of three before exhaling. I needed to think. If the wards were still up, then how did Sparky disappear? A kidnapping, or demon-napping in this case, didn't seem all that plausible.

Then again, I'd teamed up with fae, demon, and Hunter allies to take down Herne and the Wild Hunt. In Harborsmouth, anything was possible.

"Are you sure Sparky didn't just run off?" I asked. "Maybe he was scared by something, or was lured outside?"

Jinx blanched, catching on to what the conversation was about. I looked away, focusing on the case. I'd handled child abduction cases. In recent months, I'd become something of an expert.

A few months ago, when someone was stealing dozens of fae children from their beds, I discovered that the kidnapper used a lure to tempt the children outside their homes. Could something similar have happened to Sparky? The kid was a sucker for food, cartoons, and shiny things.

But that's what didn't make sense. Why go with some stranger if he already had his cartoons and Father Michael in the kitchen whipping him up his favorite food?

"There was nothing to scare the little tyke," he said. "God forgive me, I don't know what else I could have done to keep him safe."

If there was nothing to scare Sparky away, then he had to have been lured from the apartment. But that left the question of how. Not everyone had their apartment warded against every possible threat, no matter how mundane, but I did. I was paranoid that way. Growing up being the only one to see monsters roam the streets had that effect on a girl.

"You heard nothing?" I asked, running a hand through my hair and starting to pace.

I couldn't face my friends' worried looks right now. I needed to focus on getting Sparky back. That meant treating this like any other missing persons case.

"No, the cartoons were playing, but not very loudly," he said.

"There were no broken windows, no sign of a break-in or a struggle?" I asked, ticking off possibilities.

Not that a break-in was likely. Not with the apartment warded with the best Kaye had to offer. Considering her newly juiced magic, that was a lot.

"No, certainly not," he said.

"Okay, let me think," I said, biting my lip.

Someone had managed to slip through my front door, past Kaye's magical protective wards, and into our apartment where they quickly and silently convinced Sparky to leave a perfectly good dinner and playtime with someone who was great with kids. That narrowed the suspects to my closest friends.

An oily sensation churned through my gut, and I gripped the phone so tight it made a creaking sound of protest. I raised my eyes to meet the worried looks of my friends, and Torn sighed.

"We must all be thinking it," he said.

"Thinking what?" Jinx asked, turning on Torn, then me. "What the Hell is going on?"

"Sparky's been kidnapped," I said.

"From the loft?" she asked. "But that...that's impossible. You said...we paid..."

"Yeah, that's what Torn is hinting at," I said with a heavy sigh.

"You mean?" she asked.

"Yes," I said, an icy chill running up my spine. "Those wards were keyed so that only specific friends of ours can pass through. That's not a lot of people. Most of us are here, which eliminates us as suspects, and there's no way that Marvin or Hob would harm one floppy ear on Sparky's head. They already love the kid like family."

"He has that effect," Forneus said, rubbing the back of his neck.

Was that a tear on his cheek? If so, I wasn't about to mention it. I didn't feel like taking a fireball to the chest.

"So, it really is her?" Jinx asked.

"Yes," I said. I hesitated. Saying it would make it real. "Kaye took Sparky. It had to be her. No one else could have waltzed through those wards, and into our apartment."

"And Sparky knows her," she said, nodding. "She doesn't like demons, but she was never outwardly mean to him. Not in any way he'd notice."

"Yes, he is...was...he IS naïve in that way," Forneus said. "Always seeing the best in people."

"A peculiar trait in a demon," Torn said.

I thought Forneus might lash out, but he nodded.

"Yes, I always thought so," he said. "It's probably why he left Hell, the first chance he got."

I sometimes wondered about what Sparky's life must have been like before he came here, and how exactly he'd managed to get trapped in a vessel with a bunch of fire imps. He was a tezcatlipocan demon, which meant he should have grown up to dominate other demons. In the demon plane where tezcatlipocan demons ruled, torture and violence would have been a daily occurrence—business as usual.

I shuddered. At least there was no way his own kind could have entered my apartment, or Harborsmouth. If demons were behind this, then they were acting through Kaye. That was unlikely considering her abhorrence of demons.

Unlikely didn't mean impossible.

At the moment, I didn't have a lot to go on. Kaye seemed our prime suspect, but there was no clear motive for her actions. My best guess was that she intended to use Sparky as a pawn, a bargaining chip if I chose not to bring her what she wanted. But her motives could be darker, much darker.

Tezcatlipocan demons are a rarity here in the human world. There were spells that called for rare ingredients. Kaye may have walked the line in the past, sticking to using her magic for good, but she'd changed since her death. She'd been reborn a darker and more powerful woman, one who might be capable of harming a demon child if doing so helped to quench her thirst for strong magic.

"What does she want with Sparky?" Jinx asked, her question echoing the one raging inside my head. "Do you think...will she hurt him?"

"If she harms that child, no pet gargoyle will stand in my way," said Forneus, eyes flickering. "I will hunt the witch, and I will drag her to the deepest depths of Hell and acquaint her with my brother. He would enjoy torturing a witch of her power. It's been decades since he had such a challenge. Even Hell grows dull over the centuries."

He said the last with a shrug, and I stifled a shudder. Thank Mab, the demon counted me an ally. We'd got off to a rocky start, but we weren't enemies. Right now, I was extremely glad of that fact.

Forneus was focusing all of his anger on Kaye, and he wasn't the only one.

Nobody threatened a child without facing Ceff's wrath, not even Kaye. She may have done us favors in the past, but if it turned out she'd harmed Sparky in any way, Ceff would drive a trident through her heart without a second's hesitation.

I wouldn't be far behind him.

Kaye had been a mentor to me, and a friend. At one time, when I'd felt abandoned by my own family, she'd been like a surrogate mother. She'd helped me navigate a world that I could see, but didn't understand. When I learned that I was indeed a part of that world, she didn't judge me or turn me away.

She helped me to adapt to being the daughter of Will-o'-the-Wisp, and she gave me the tools to survive in a city filled with threats. I was alive because of Kaye. I would never forget what she'd done for me, but I would do whatever it took to keep Sparky safe. If Kaye threatened that kid, I would take her down.

We all would.

Looking around at every face, I could see that truth. It was written in the lines between Jinx's eyes, the widening of Torn's pupils, and the set of Ceff's jaw.

We were all ready to rush off, blades and arrows out, running like the hounds of Hell were hot on our tail. Every one of us cared about Sparky, and wanted to bring him home safe. But our lives weren't that simple, and we were short on time.

With sunset fast approaching, and Herne unwilling to negotiate, things were about to turn bloody. Forneus would soon be needed to aid Benmore and the dwarves in their assault against Yue Fei and the rogue vampires. The Wild Hunt would soon attack, likely tearing their way to the heart of the city.

We were already threatened on multiple fronts, and we were the last line of defense this city had against supernatural threats. If the human police got involved, they wouldn't stand a chance. And with the penalty against revealing our existence to humans being death, we would all face execution if we warned the media.

The most we could do was call in bogus reports of an incoming storm, and hope innocent civilians stayed indoors. The thunder of Herne's horse riding through the portal, the howl of his hounds, and the sounding of his horn helped substantiate those rumors. Humans have an uncanny ability to overlook the supernatural and find a rational, mundane explanation for what they don't understand.

That combined with glamour would hide the truth of the Wild Hunt from humans right up until Herne's hounds tore out their throats. Then the One Law would be moot. You can't tell the world that monsters truly exist when you're dead.

"We can't all go," I said. "With both the Wild Hunt and the rogue vamps preparing for a fight, we can't just leave this in the hands of the Hunters' Guild."

"Are you saying you want us to stay here, and let you face Kaye on your own?" Jinx asked.

"Not on my own," I said.

I took a deep breath, and nodded. They wouldn't all like my decision, but that was too damn bad. I wasn't about to leave this city vulnerable, no more than I'd let Kaye harm Sparky. But I knew just how bad this could go. If Kaye went homicidal, it would be better if some of us survived. Otherwise, there'd be no home for Sparky to come back to.

"Torn, you're with me," I said. "I'll call back Father Michael and have him meet us outside the Emporium. He's still at the loft which is an easy hike over, even for the priest."

Torn raised an eyebrow at my choice, but nodded.

"Can't let you have all the fun," he said, lip lifting in a lopsided grin.

"And the rest of us, Miss Granger?" Forneus asked, flames flickering in his eyes. "You can't possibly expect us to sit idly by while there is a threat to the little one."

"We all have jobs to do," I said, shaking my head. "Yours is to kick vampire ass. Until then, keep Jinx safe."

"He doesn't need to stay here to keep me safe," Jinx said, hands on her hips. "I'm not staying. I'm coming with you."

"No, you're not," I said. "I need you to stay here with the Hunters."

"No way," Jinx said.

"Look, I know this sucks, but..." I said, running a hand through my hair.

"But I'll just slow you down," she said.

"Yes," I said with a heavy sigh. "Torn and I can run faster unencumbered. Plus, she may not despise you as much as she does Forneus, but you and Kaye have never really gotten along."

"Yeah, I know," she said. "She's not my biggest fan."

"This is our best shot," I said. "And you're all needed here. If we don't make it back before sunset, kick some barghest ass for me."

"You will come back in time for battle," Ceff said, dark eyes locking on mine. "If I have to grab the moon to change the tides, you will be here."

His threat was clear. He'd stay here and work with the water fae and the Hunters' Guild to coordinate our attack plan. But if I was running late, he'd drop everything to come find me. For a second, I almost felt bad for Kaye.

"Don't worry, Fish Breath," Torn said, eyes roving over my body, lingering on my chest before turning to Ceff with a wink. "I'll take good care of her."

I turned tail, and started running toward the Old Port with Torn on my heels. Coward, me? If it walks like a duck, and talks like a duck.

I'd rather face an angry witch than listen to one more second of Ceff and Torn's arguing. Too bad the witch was likely to turn me into a frog. I swallowed hard, and eyed the sky as I ran. Only good thing? I'd be too small for the giant, killer owls to bother with.

CHAPTER 20

I would have recognized Father Michael by his nervous head bobbing, even if he hadn't been the only soul pacing up and down the sidewalk. In this case, I spotted the lanky priest from over a block away. The area was unnaturally silent, without a car or person in sight. The entire street was deserted.

"Creepy," I muttered, halting to scan the area before rushing headlong into a potential trap.

"Even my cats are wary," Torn said, narrowing his eyes at the intersecting streets. "I suspect our witch friend has cast some kind of look-away spell to keep prying eyes away."

"Great," I said, waving a hand at the normally busy section of the Old Port Quarter. "She could have staged this all—Sparky's abduction, even Father Michael's call to us—just to get me here."

"Do you really think she'd go to all that trouble for a clandestine meeting?" he asked. "Seems a lot of trouble, even for you, Princess."

"Yeah, well, I know Mab is gunning for me, but nobody seems to know where she is," I said. "The abduction of Sparky moments before a battle we know she orchestrated seems both evil and convoluted enough to be one of Mab's schemes."

"Let's hope you're wrong, Princess," he said. "As much as I enjoy a fight with poor odds, I'd rather not face the Queen of Air and Darkness and the strongest witch on the damn planet. Not at the same time and without backup."

"What am I, chopped liver?" I asked.

"What you are is stalling," he said.

Torn was right. I was stalling.

"Everything about this stinks," I said. "But you're right. Putting it off won't help. Whatever is in there, we need to face it and get this over with before sunset."

Father Michael looked up and started toward me, recognizing us. Not that we were hard to identify. Torn looked like a rocker who enjoyed the underground fight scene with his leather pants and scarred body.

"Miss Granger, I am so sorry that this happened," Father Michael said.

"Not your fault, Padre," I said. I was pretty sure that blame lay squarely on me. "Any news?"

"No, I checked all through the apartment one final time, then ran here as you requested," he said.

"Any sign of Kaye or her pet gargoyle?" Torn asked.

I frowned. I liked Humphrey, but Torn had a point. Kaye had Humphrey on a magical leash. She could take control of the gargoyle, making him a fierce enemy. It was something to keep in mind.

"Gargoyle?" he asked, head bobbing. "Yes, yes, he has been scrabbling along that wall, up to the stone rainspout and back to the door lintel. I think he was surprised that I could track his movements. Must not be accustomed to a priest who wears faerie ointment, I should think."

It made sense that Father Michael would be wearing the magic ointment around his eyes. It was the only way to see through glamour, and he'd been in a faerie's home babysitting a demon child. The ointment was a wise precaution, and would come in especially handy now.

Although it did make for some awkward, furtive glances at Torn's slit-pupil eyes.

"Cat sidhe," Torn said. "In case you were wondering."

"Oh, no, I mean, I wouldn't dream of..." Father Michael stuttered.

I held up a gloved hand.

"He's just messing with you," I said. "It's what he does. But right now we need to focus on Kaye."

Torn rolled his eyes, and Father Michael fidgeted.

"Do you have a plan?" Torn asked.

"Yes," I said. "Father Michael, you stay behind me, and if I say run, hightail it as fast as you can out of there. If we get split up, meet us back at the loft. Torn, you cover our backs."

"So the plan is to go in fighting?" he asked. "If so, I like this plan."

"No," I said. "But be ready for a fight."

Torn lifted one hand, and razor-sharp claws slid from his fingertips.

"Always."

CHAPTER 21

"Hey, Humphrey!" I yelled, getting the gargoyle's attention.

He tilted his head to the side with a grinding sound that set my teeth on edge. I liked Humphrey, but he was a behemoth of solid stone that could crush our bones like matchsticks. A behemoth who might not currently be in control of that bone crushing body.

I waved a hand at the street, and smiled.

"Quiet out here today," I said. "We should liven things up. Break out the *rock* n' roll."

Torn groaned at my pun, and muttered something unflattering. Father Michael paled, and inched away from Torn's grouchy remarks. I tried to ignore them both, keeping an eye on Humphrey. My bad puns were part of our usual banter, and the easiest way I knew of how to tell who was in the driver's seat.

"Can't brrreak rrrocks," he said with a rumbling chuckle. "Even you know that, Ivy."

"Yeah, buddy, I do," I said, letting my shoulders relax. "Glad to see you're feeling more yourself."

That was an understatement. The gargoyle's ears drooped, and he looked away.

"Sorrry about earlierrr," he said.

"You can make it up to me by answering a few questions," I said. "Has Kaye left the Emporium at all today, and did she bring a demon back with her?"

Humphrey looked up and down the street, although I knew Kaye had eyes and ears everywhere, including the ability to see and hear through the gargoyle if she turned her attention that way. He held up his arms to his head, indicating longer ears than his Doberman style ones, and my heart sunk.

"Small, with long, floppy earrrs," he said.

"That sounds like Sparky," Father Michael said.

Humphrey shifted, looking over my shoulder at the priest.

"You herrre to send it back to Hell?" Humphrey asked.

"N-n-no, Sparky is but a child," he said. "We only wish to bring him safely home."

"Nobody's sending anybody to Hell," I said.

At least, I hoped that was true. With Kaye's newfound power, she might be able to open a portal straight to Hell, and bring through or send back whatever, or whomever, she chose. I slid a gloved hand to my wrist, feeling the reassuring shape of my knives beneath the leather jacket.

Humphrey met my eyes, and nodded.

"I suggest we take that as an invitation," Torn said, eyeing the street at our backs.

The sun was already sitting lower in the sky, casting ominous shadows across the empty pavement.

"Later, Humphrey," I said. "As for earlier, we're square...or round. Cool as glacier rock."

"Laterrr, Ivy," he said.

I ducked my head, and reached for the front door of the Emporium, knowing that next time we came through that door, I intended to have Sparky with me. I just hoped that didn't mean we'd have to fight our way through Humphrey.

He was the only guy I knew who enjoyed my bad puns.

CHAPTER 22

"Ivy, what are you doing here?" Arachne asked, eyes going wide.

Arachne was Kaye's assistant. That meant the good-natured teen spent most of her time running the touristy part of the shop, schlepped boxes on delivery days, and once in awhile learned a bit of magic. Trouble was, with Kaye the spell was just as likely to backfire on her apprentice, the older witch's idea of a practical joke.

But the fear in Arachne's eyes had nothing to do with hazing. The kid looked genuinely afraid. Her hands were fidgeting atop a pile of books she'd been pricing at the counter beside the register, and within seconds of our entrance, she started chewing on a strand of purple-tipped blond hair. Arachne was shaking in her Chuck Taylors.

I looked over my shoulder at Torn, but he shrugged. Guess it was up to me how to handle this. We knew that Kaye had this place magically bugged to the brim of every oversized witch hat, and the tip of every broom. That complicated things.

It was obvious that Arachne knew something, but was terrified of being questioned. Not that I blamed her. If she pissed off Kaye, which was likely if she started to spill the beans on the witch's nefarious dabbling with kidnapping, the kid could lose more than her apprenticeship. Arachne pulled the hair from her mouth, and tucked it behind her ear, lifting her chin. She'd made a decision, and I just hoped it was one we didn't all come to regret.

"I need..." I said, but Arachne cut me off.

Her hand hit a packet of herbs that had been resting beside the books on the counter, and her face momentarily lit up. Breathing heavy, she lifted the packet with forced cheer.

"Oh yeah, you totally texted to say you needed these herbs for Ceff," she said. "How is he? That gash to his leg must be pretty serious to bring you all the way here. By the Goddess, Ivy, you've even got a priest."

She started wrapping the bag of herbs in tissue paper, and stuffing them into a Madam Kaye's Magic Emporium gift bag. Her hands were shaking, but she kept smiling as her eyes pleaded with me to follow her lead.

She'd come up with a logical reason why we might come around, one that had nothing to do with snooping for a backstabbing kidnapper. I wasn't sure if she was just trying to buy us some time, but I decided to roll with it.

The kid wasn't stupid. Working for over a year as Kaye's apprentice had made her a quick thinker. You learned to think creatively and act rapidly when your boss was a nutty, old witch with a penchant for nasty tricks.

And that was before Kaye's transformation. I can't imagine what it must have been like working here over the past few weeks. I reminded myself to make some time for the kid if we survived this mess.

"Yes, the…gash…on his leg is pretty bad," I said.

"She still finds it difficult to talk about," Torn said, stepping forward. "I told her not to worry. If he loses the leg, it's not the appendage that really matters."

He slid a hand to his belt, and Arachne blushed. I would have smacked Torn upside the head if it wasn't for the fact that his lurid flirtations had distracted the kid from her fear, at least for now. Arachne's hands were steady as she wrote out a sales slip, and put it inside the bag.

That last was unusual, since I typically ran a tab at the Emporium. Paydays were often few and far between, especially with the recent necessity of playing dead. It's hard to collect payment on a job when you're supposedly six feet under.

At a guess, I'd say that either my line of credit had finally been cut off, or Arachne had found a way to slip me a note right under Kaye's nose. Clever girl.

"That is why I am accompanying Miss Granger," Father Michael said. "For emotional support."

Crafty devil. I'd be more surprised if I wasn't already aware of Father Michael's past. Most priests wouldn't have been so comfortable with lying, or so convincing. I guess a youth of grand larceny came with a few beneficial skills.

"Um, cool," Arachne said. "Well, I guess you need to get this to Ceff right away. Gotta save that leg, and all."

"Here is the payment we owe," Father Michael said. "We appreciate your help. And if you are ever near Joysen Hill, please stop by Sacred Heart. You are always welcome to join my flock."

Arachne came from a long line of Wiccans, but that didn't matter. The priest's meaning was clear. If she ever needed help, she'd just earned sanctuary within the walls of Sacred Heart. Since that church came with its very own unicorn defender, it was a significant offer.

She smiled more easily, and nodded.

"Thanks," she said. "Good luck, you guys."

Our eyes met, and so much more than a simple goodbye passed between us, but that was all I let past my lips.

"Goodbye, Arachne," I said. "Safe travels."

"May the Goddess be with you, Ivy," she said.

We walked out the door, and I would have missed Arachne's final words if it weren't for my enhanced fae hearing.

"May the Goddess save us all."

CHAPTER 23

"What..." Father Michael asked, but I cut him off.

"Come on, Padre," I said. "I won't be able to live with myself if we're not in time to save Ceff's leg."

I figured sticking to Arachne's story was the smartest move, for now. Thankfully, Father Michael was a quick thinker.

"Oh, y-y-yes, of course," he said, catching on.

"Yes, don't they shoot horses with bad legs?" Torn asked.

I rolled my eyes at Torn, and hurried my pace. We needed to get out of Humphrey's hearing range before discussing Sparky or Arachne's mysterious bag of herbs. Leave it to Torn to find a way to make every second even more agonizing.

"I'll shoot you if you don't keep your mouth shut," I said, showing all my teeth in a smile.

"Lord, they do not mean these things they say," Father Michael whispered.

"True, I'd never shoot him," I said. The priest started to smile, but it froze awkwardly on his face as I finished. "I'm not much of gun person. I'd use one of my blades, or a fireball."

Father Michael was only momentarily fazed, his mind latching onto my mention of magic. The man was a sucker for the supernatural. He peppered me with questions, head bobbing and hands fluttering in excitement, until we turned the corner a good two blocks from the Emporium.

Torn scanned the sky and the rooftops, while my eyes darted into darkened doorways and alleyways.

"All clear?" I asked, raising my eyebrows at the cat sidhe.

"Yes, Princess," he said with a nod.

I forced my fingers to relax their death grip on the Emporium shopping bag, and dug out Arachne's note, careful not to let the bag or its contents touch any exposed skin. Normally, that wouldn't be much of a problem, but my trip to

Faerie had done a number on my gear. My leather jacket, and the shirts and wrist sheaths I wore beneath it, had seen better days.

"What does it say?" Torn asked, leaning in and licking his lips.

Father Michael wasn't much more patient, shifting his weight from one foot to the other.

"Oberon's eyes, give me a second," I muttered.

I lifted out the slip of paper between a gloved finger and thumb as if it may bite. Since it had come from the Emporium, it wasn't a bad guess. I just had to hope that Arachne was truly on our side, and trying to help. I flipped over the paper, and frowned.

"It's...it's just a sales receipt," I said.

"Witches," Torn said with a hiss. "Nothing is ever what it seems when witches are involved."

Father Michael nodded sympathetically, though the same could be said of dealing with the fae. Rather than remind Torn of that fact, I considered his words again. Nothing is ever what it seems when witches are involved.

"Torn, you're a genius," I said, rocking back on my heels.

"Yes, I know, Princess, but what does that have to do with the deviousness of witches?" he asked.

"I'm willing to bet that there's more to this receipt than it seems," I said, a grin tugging at my lips.

"Ah, like a code?" Father Michael asked, hands fluttering. "I am quite good at ciphers. Perhaps, I can help to crack this code...or were you thinking something less mundane? A secret message hidden by magical means? That would be quite brilliant really. If I only had access to my library, I could begin researching encoding spells..."

I shook my head, and cut him off. If not, the priest would have rattled on all day with his theories, and we were nearly out of time as it was.

"Let me try something first," I said. "It might not be that complicated."

At least, I was hoping that Arachne wasn't requiring the magic equivalent of an Enigma machine to decode her message—if there was a message at all. I thought back to the kid's worried face, and meaningful glances. I had to believe that she had information about Sparky, and was willing to help us, even if that meant going against her uber-powerful witch boss.

That was a lot of faith to put in one person, but this was Arachne. She might be young, but that didn't mean she wasn't just as passionate, and stubborn, about what she thought was right. And, let's face it, she'd screwed up recently. Big time. This was her chance at redemption. I just hoped that she knew me as well as I thought she did, and had decided to play to my strengths.

I lowered myself to the sidewalk, and sat cross-legged with the receipt on my lap, ignoring the heat of the pavement seeping through my jeans. I took a deep breath, and began stripping off my glove.

"You sure about this, Princess?" Torn asked, eyeing the receipt in my lap like it was a viper ready to strike out at my bare hand at the littlest provocation.

I swallowed hard. The exposed skin made me vulnerable, and there was no saying what vision Hell I'd be sucked into once I touched the Emporium receipt. There were too many variables that could make this go inexorably wrong.

Even if Arachne was motivated by the best of intentions, the receipt book could have been handled by various persons, or kept in storage with a number of arcane items of dubious provenance—any one of which could fry my mind, permanently. I shook off the creeping chill of fear, and focused on calming my breathing before responding to Torn.

If Arachne was willing to risk Kaye's ire by leaving us a message, then I could damn well suck it up. And if this really was a trap, intentional or accidental, then at least Ceff wouldn't be here to see Torn slit my throat and put me out of my misery. The cat sidhe could be a fickle, impulsive pain in my ass, but I knew I could count on him to be ruthlessly efficient in doing what needed to be done. Leaving me to an eternity of madness, a situation that Mab was likely to exploit, wasn't an option.

"I'm sure it's the right thing to do," I said, meeting Torn's furrowed gaze.

He hesitated, then nodded and turned his attention to the darkening street. Shadows were lengthening as the sun slid behind the brick buildings of the Old Port Quarter, and I was glad to have Torn on lookout. Most fae have enhanced night vision, but nothing rivaled the cat sidhe's affinity for shadows and darkness.

"A-a-are you...I mean..." Father Michael stuttered.

"Yes, Padre," I said, recognizing the eager gleam in his beady eyes. "I'm going to touch the receipt and see if I can learn something from the vision."

I sent up a silent thanks to Jenna for doing something similar not so long ago, otherwise, I might not have thought to give this a try. Then again, I might be barking up the wrong tree—an unpleasant irony considering our current situation with Herne's hounds—maybe even walking into a trap.

"Fascinating," he said, head bobbing in excitement.

I sighed. At least someone would be enjoying this.

Father Michael started to prattle on, but I tuned out his discussion of everyday uses for supernatural abilities. I closed my eyes and reached out with my bare hand, fingers brushing the thin paper. I frowned, and cracked open an eyelid. Maybe I needed to touch the spot where Arachne had written in the price, or where she'd signed her initials at the bottom corner of the page?

I slid my fingers along the paper, and gasped. As my fingers touched Arachne's signature, I threw back my head, body going rigid. I caught a glimpse of towering brick walls before my vision narrowed, and darkness swallowed me whole.

CHAPTER 24

I blinked, heart racing. Whatever I'd been prepared to see, it wasn't this.

I was inside a storage room where the boxes had been rearranged to resemble a table and chairs, and the box table was set with an altar cloth and topped with mugs and a platter of cookies. Sparky was running around his chair, long ears trailing behind him as he giggled, stopping only long enough to shove fistfuls of cookies in his mouth.

I'd been sucked into an impromptu demon-witch tea party. If it wasn't for the perspiration soaking my shirt, or the ominous location of the windowless storage room, I might have thought the two kids had run off for a bit of harmless fun.

Too bad that wasn't the case. I tried to make a mental note of every detail, hoping it would help me find Sparky and figure out how to bring him home safe.

I tasted shampoo as Arachne chewed on the ends of her hair, but my time training with my uncle was paying off. Successfully using faerie magic required unwavering concentration. I'd had my concentration tested repeatedly with beatings from uncle Kade, and eventually, I'd mastered the basics of controlling my wisp magic. Taking the reins while riding out a vision worked on similar principals.

I forced my real body to inhale deeply, and I focused my mind, managing to experience what Arachne had felt earlier today, yet holding on to my own sense of self.

It wasn't easy. Everything that I was seeing, smelling, tasting, and feeling was from Arachne's memories. It would be so simple to just relax and let the vision take over.

The door to the storage room opened with a blast of magic, and Arachne tensed, nearly breaking the pen that continued its looping signature on the piece of paper beside her on the table. She only flicked her gaze to it once, but it was long enough to realize that the pen wasn't filled with normal ink. Suddenly, the vision's clarity made perfect sense.

Arachne was doodling the loops of her signature over and over again, in her own blood.

"M-m-madam Kaye?" she asked in a weak, stuttering voice.

How much courage had it taken the kid to hold that connection with the paper, knowing that she was documenting all of this in hopes of sneaking a message to me? Double-crossing Kaye meant facing the wrath of one of the most powerful, and possibly unstable, witches on the entire east coast. Arachne must have been terrified.

My heart, no *Arachne*'s heart, pounded as Kaye strolled into view. The bells on the old witch's skirts were jingling, a sure sign that she wanted to attract attention. If she wished to, Kaye could move as silent as death.

Sparky paused in his cookie chewing, tilting his head.

"Jingle bellllls!" he sang. "Jingle belllllls! Jingle all the waaay!"

He started dancing a circle around the box that was his chair, singing and clapping his hands. Cookie crumbs crunched beneath his tiny feet, and Kaye frowned.

"I told you to keep the demon busy, not fill him full of sugar," she said.

"You said to keep him safe...u-u-until the ritual," Arachne said.

"Yes, I suppose," Kaye said with a toss of her hand. "The spell won't work if he's dead. More's the pity. That's what makes this spell so difficult, and powerful. Tezcatlipocan demons are rare enough, but the blood of a living one is rarer still."

"So, you want me to, um, keep him safe?" she asked. "Here in the Emporium?"

Smart girl.

I could have kissed Arachne. She was letting me know that, for now, Sparky was safe with her. At the time of the vision, they were at the Emporium, and in one of the storage rooms by the look of it.

The public areas of the shop, and Kaye's office and spell kitchen, were most heavily guarded by spells that kept out intruders. Sparky could get up to no end of trouble if allowed to wander the building. I figured that even if Arachne had to step out into the shop now and then, she'd keep Sparky in the storage room for as long as possible.

Kaye may not want Sparky dead, yet, but I couldn't say the same for The Emporium. A tangled network of spells had been laid on that place for so long, magic had seeped into the very wood grain and brick mortar. More than once I'd been convinced the place had a disturbing sentience that reflected Kaye's moods.

With the witch's rapid descent into madness—the only explanation for her actions my brain could possibly begin to believe—I had no illusions about what The Emporium would do if it trapped a demon within its walls of power.

I was so busy planning a way to get inside The Emporium, and battling images of Sparky being crushed by bookcases and suffocated by packets of herbs, that I nearly missed Kaye's reply. But I needed to focus, for all our sakes.

I pushed through my anger, and Arachne's fear, and listened.

"Of course, you foolish girl," Kaye said, tone sharp. "I need the creature close by for when I do the binding ritual. Until then, I will tolerate no interruptions. Keep that in mind, and keep that thing in here."

Arachne flicked her eyes upward. I looked for potential clues, but the movement may have been nothing. All I saw on the ceiling was a skylight with an unhelpful view of a fluffy cloud above the Emporium. Without a frame of reference, it was difficult to even pinpoint time of day from my vantage. Other than the fact that there was still daylight, the glance skyward had provided nothing new to work with. I focused instead on Arachne's words.

"The *CIRCLE* will stop you if they find out what you're doing," she said. "I won't interrupt you, but if they come, I'm not strong enough to keep them from taking Sparky."

What the hell was the Circle? It sounded like a coven, or maybe a governing force for witches, but Kaye had never mentioned them before.

"And how will they find out, child?" Kaye asked, dark thunderclouds swirling in her eyes. She lifted a hand above Arachne, and the kid tensed. "Will you tell them?"

"N-n-no, no w-w-way," she said, shaking her head, eyes wide. Her gaze flicked to Sparky, and she flinched. "If the

CIRCLE found out, they'd come and stop you. If they knew about your power, and your, um, plans, they'd take you away. I'd never learn anything then."

"Ah, your concern for your own rise to power is endearing, child," Kaye said. "I knew I chose my apprentice well."

"Yeah, well, um, it wouldn't do me much good with you in one of the Circle's prisons," she said.

"No, child, it wouldn't," Kaye said. "You'd be wise to remember that."

Arachne nodded.

"I will," she said.

"Good," Kaye said, an eager gleam in her eye. She pulled a length of rope from one of her skirt's many pockets, and tossed it onto the table, making Sparky jump. He tilted his head, and Arache froze, her only movement the slow scrawl of her pen on the piece of paper. "Now tie the fiend up. I need you back in the store. I have more preparations to make, and you need to be out there in case Granger or one of her allies arrives with the piece of Herne that I requested."

"And, um, if Ivy stops by with the ingredient…this piece of Herne, should I bring it to you in the kitchen?" Arachne asked. "Or will you be leaving the Emporium for your spell prep?"

"Of course, I will be in my kitchen, foolish girl," she said with a quick snort. "Where do you think I would be preparing the binding spell, out in the city streets? I have enough meddlesome interruptions without making a spectacle for the rest of the idiot humans and fae. No, I'll have my revenge soon enough. Those barghests will wish they never entered my city when I'm through with them."

"A-a-and Sparky?" Arachne asked. "He'll be fine after the spell, right?"

"Don't be daft," Kaye said. Shadows seemed to gather around Kaye as she drew herself upright, spine rigid, and she fixed Arachne with a piercing, black-eyed stare. "We'll bleed them all dry, starting with the demons and the hounds. Then I'll do what should have been done years ago."

Kaye spun on her heel, and whirled toward the stockroom door. Arachne's hand shook as she continued to trace her name with the blood-soaked pen, but her voice barely quivered as she asked her final question.

"What should have been done?" she asked. "What work will you have me assist you with next?"

"Isn't it obvious, girl?" Kaye asked, spittle forming at the corner of her mouth as a frenzied smile curled her lips. "I will bind all of the vampires, faeries, and other unnatural creatures who've dared to enter my city and I'll march them all to the painful death they so justly deserve."

"E-e-even Marvin and H-h-hob?" Arachne asked, flinching as Kaye leaned toward her.

"Of course," she said, eyes gleaming and a sickly line of tattoos pulsing along her brow. "We'll finally rid our city of those vermin once and for all."

CHAPTER 25

I gasped, gulping air into my lungs. I'd maintained my sense of self throughout the vision, but that didn't mean it was a fun or easy experience. My head was pounding, and my throat felt raw as I struggled to drag a ragged breath deep into my lungs.

Visions are often like drowning. Thankfully, this particular vision had been well worth the discomfort.

I'd learned the full extent of Kaye's madness. As difficult as it was to believe, the witch blamed supernaturals for all of this city's problems and intended to rid Harborsmouth of every demon, vampire, and faerie—including those she'd until recently considered her friends and family. Thank Mab I'd sent Marvin and Hob away to the suburbs.

As far as I knew, Kaye hadn't killed anyone yet. I just hoped I could rescue Sparky in time to keep him from becoming her first victim. I also needed to get Arachne out of Kaye's clutches before the kid was forced to do and see things she might not recover from. Even Humphrey was at risk.

My head spun, and a cold sweat trickled down my spine.

"Going to live, Princess?" Torn asked, a bemused grin tugging at his lips.

His face loomed above me, and I let out an annoyed growl. It was meant to be intimidating, but the effect was ruined when something caught in my throat. I rolled to my knees and hacked, trying to dislodge the object.

My eyes bulged, tears streaming down my cheeks, as the object scraped the inside of my throat. What the hell had I swallowed? If I hadn't known better, I'd say there was something crawling inside me—something with multiple spiny legs, and hooked claws.

That thought finally pushed my gag reflex over the edge, and with a shuddering gasp and an involuntary spasm, I retched painfully, bringing up my breakfast. The motion also dislodged the spiny thing from my throat.

A hard object about the circumference of a half dollar hit the wet pavement, and scuttled toward the shadows. I barely had time to shudder before Torn used his catlike reflexes to trap the creature beneath the half moon of a crystal bowl. I ignored the fact that the bowl looked suspiciously like the ones we'd had in the wisp court, and turned my attention to the thing trying to climb the sides of the curved surface of its prison.

"Neat trick, Princess," Torn said, eyes locked on the creature as it flipped onto its back in an unsuccessful attempt to escape.

"Is that a beetle?" I asked.

"Scarabaeus sacer," Father Michael said, rubbing dry hands together. "Commonly known as the scarab beetle. They were revered by the ancient Egyptians, who worshiped the sun and sky gods. It was most often used as a symbolic representation of Khepri, the morning manifestation of the sun god Ra. The scarab beetle would roll its dung across the sand just as Khepri rolled the sun across the sky."

"You mean the princess swallowed a dung beetle?" Torn asked, eyes going wide. "That thing rolls around balls of poop?"

Mab's bones, I'd never live this down. Too bad I could do nothing to come to my own defense. I was too busy gagging, and spitting up bile.

If there was dung in my throat, I wanted it out, now.

"I h-h-hate you," I said, scowling at Torn as I pulled out a tissue and wiped my mouth.

"Why, Princess?" he asked. "It's not like I put that thing in your throat."

"You know I'm vulnerable during a vision," I said, coming to my feet with a shaky breath. "The least you could have done was to make sure that random beetles didn't go flying into my mouth."

"Perhaps it crawled there..." Father Michael said. I'm sure he was just trying to help, but I held up a hand, and shuddered.

"Sorry, Padre," I said. "But I'd rather not know how it got there."

"Um, Princess," Torn said, frowning at the shop receipt he now held in his hand. "Does that mean you don't want to see this?"

"What?" I asked, tugging on my gloves. The sooner I got my hands covered, the better. I'd had enough of psychic visions for one day. "Did you find something?"

"Those loops there," he said, extending one sharp claw to trace the loops and whorls of Arachne's signature. "Anything about these lines look familiar?"

I wiped away the tears still clinging to my eyelashes, and squinted at the receipt.

"Now that you mention it," I said, flashing him a frown.

"Scarabaeus sacer," Father Michael said, awed voice barely a whisper.

"Well I'll be a bugbear's uncle," Torn said. "I'm right, aren't I?"

As much I hated to admit it, he *was* right, but I had no idea what to make of it. I tried to think of everything we knew about that receipt. Arachne had hidden a doodle of a scarab beetle in the swirling loops of her signature, a signature written in blood.

Arachne was Kaye's apprentice, and now the senior witch was exhibiting uncharacteristically unstable, and dare I say flat out evil, behavior. There had been hints of instability, signs that Kaye was having difficulty adjusting to her newfound power, but I'd brushed it off.

Aside from an instinctual wariness, I'd tried to pretend that what my friend was going through was the normal growing pains associated with a physical and magical transition. I hadn't wanted to admit that she'd gone completely off the rails. The why of that reasoning was like a punch in the gut.

If a physical and magical transition could make someone with Kaye's many years of experience become a danger to her friends and allies, then what had my own transformation done to me?

"Princess?" Torn asked.

I shook off memories of my uncle, and the blood, sweat, and burned flesh that characterized our training sessions. I'd have plenty of time to brood over those memories later, so long as we survived the night. And if not, well you can't worry about the past when you're dead.

I grimaced, and turned my thoughts back to Arachne and the curious sales receipt.

"Yeah, it looks like a scarab," I said.

I refused to call the thing a dung beetle. The very thought made bile rise to burn the many tiny lacerations inside my throat.

I may not be a big fan of the method used, but I had to give Arachne kudos for creativity. She'd risked Kaye's wrath sneaking me that message. Even now, Kaye would be in her kitchen preparing her binding spell, readying for the moment when I delivered the final ingredient, a piece of Herne. At any moment, she would call for Arachne to bring her Sparky so that she could add his blood to the spell.

I swallowed hard, a searing pain making my eyes water as bile rose in my throat.

I think in Kaye's broken mind, she was doing the right thing by finally seeking revenge for the death of her friends so many years ago. I'd bet she even thought she was still protecting this city. Arachne was Kaye's apprentice, which meant Arachne wasn't much more than a servant to do her bidding, one more tool to be used to rebuild a Harborsmouth free of us pesky supernaturals.

The kid was between a rock and a hard place.

Rock and a hard place. Normally, that line of thought would have me chuckling and making a mental note to share the story with Humphrey. He always tolerates my poor attempts at gargoyle humor. But Humphrey's situation was no less desirable than Arachne's. They were both ensnared by Kaye, a powerful witch whose powers had recently been unnaturally amplified by yours truly.

Both kids were trapped, and Sparky had been kidnapped, and it was my fault. I'd gotten us all into this mess, and no matter what it took, I was going make things right.

"So what do we do now?" Torn asked.

"We go rescue my kids," I said.

"Even if that means battling an all-powerful witch?" he asked.

I palmed my blades, and locked eyes with Torn.

"Whatever it takes."

CHAPTER 26

"What do you think the scarab means, Padre?" I asked, glancing at the priest from the corner of my eye as we walked.

As much as I'd like to forget about that damn beetle, I was sure its appearance was significant. I didn't believe in coincidence.

When you're a P.I., you realize early on that coincidence is a handy word for laziness. There's always a connection. If something seems like a coincidence, you just haven't figured out how all the clues are related yet.

But figuring out the meaning of the beetle wasn't my biggest reason for keeping the priest talking. He'd refused to return to the loft apartment, or the safety of Sacred Heart Church, and I'd had to admit we might need his help in freeing Sparky, Arachne, and Humphrey from Kaye's clutches. But the man was a priest, a scholar. He was a human civilian about to enter a powerful, mentally unstable, vengeful witch's domain.

Keeping his mind busy would keep him from thinking too much about the dangers we were about to face. Or, maybe, I was just trying to comfort myself. There was only so much a girl can take, and I still had a demigod and his pack of bloodthirsty hounds to battle before this night was over.

I just hoped that our knowledge of Herne was correct, and he wouldn't launch that fight before sunset. I knew that magic operated by its own rules, and that those rules were often governed by things like the ebb and flow of the sun, moon, and tides. That didn't keep me from scanning the sky for oversized owls, looking over my shoulder for a mounted rider, or listening for the howling cry of Herne's hounds.

"I believe that you may have been hexed," Father Michael said.

"Wait, what?" I asked, stopping dead in my tracks.

I blinked trying to make sense of what he'd said. Maybe I'd heard him wrong.

"The sudden manifestation of the scarab beetle so soon after your vision, and the drawing that was left for you in the young witch's blood, all point to a hex," he said. "It is the logical conclusion."

You know your life is weird when a hex that causes a freaking beetle to claw its way out of your throat is the logical conclusion, and that the person who laid that hex is a friend who you're on the way to rescue.

"Arachne is just a kid, and she was trying to help us," I said. "Why would she put a hex on me?" It makes no sense."

"Actually, Princess," Torn said, with an apologetic shrug. "It does make sense if Arachne was trying to send you a message."

"You mean the beetle is a clue?" I asked.

"I agree with Sir Torn," Father Michael said, head bobbing. "I believe that the young witch used what tools she had at her disposal. She reached out to you with a vision, but added the hex spell in the event you missed a clue that was integral to her plan."

"You're assuming Arachne has a plan," I said, rubbing the back of my neck with a gloved hand. "She managed to get us a message about Sparky's capture, but she's just a kid."

"A kid who has been apprenticing under a powerful witch," Father Michael said.

"But why a hex?" I asked. "Why curse me, and make me puke up a beetle? I can't believe Arachne would do that to me, or to anyone."

I folded my arms across my chest, and dug in my heels. Arachne had made mistakes, but she was a good kid. I couldn't believe that she'd be involved in dark magic spells against me.

"Look at it this way, Princess," Torn said. "What other choice did she have?"

I thought over the events of the past few months, and the impact of those events on the inhabitants of the Emporium. Kaye had regained the magic of an all-powerful witch, but at an age when such power could corrupt, decay, and destroy. Humphrey had been at her beck and call, and Arachne was her loyal assistant. Even if they'd begun to suspect Kaye of wrongdoing, what could they possibly do to stand against her?

If, like me, they'd waited for concrete proof, then we'd all postponed the inevitable, and given Kaye the opportunity she needed to gain a stranglehold on us all.

"Kaye never taught Arachne any truly powerful magic," I said, thinking aloud. "Not before, when she was in her right mind."

"But after?" Torn asked. "I'm with the priest on this. We've all seen what Kaye is capable of, and I've no doubt that Arachne's been exposed to dark magic these past few weeks."

"That is precisely my thinking," Father Michael said, hand fluttering to his chest. "That poor child."

The priest was greedy for all knowledge of magic, dark or light, but he drew the line at the use and abuse of children. It was why he'd insisted on joining us in our impromptu rescue mission. There were some things worth dying for. Rescuing those kids was one of those things.

"So you think Arachne learned hexes, and used one on me to send me a message?" I asked.

Father Michael nodded.

I chewed on my lip, mulling over what we knew. There were still too many questions.

"But what does the beetle mean?" I asked.

"Well, Princess," Torn said. "Beetles roll feces."

"Not helping, Torn," I grumbled.

"Scarab beetles are associated with the sun and the sky," Father Michael said, eyes flitting nervously to the lengthening shadows that surrounded us.

We were running out of time before Herne launched his attack. We needed to rescue Sparky and Arachne before that happened.

I shook off the sickly squirming in my gut, and focused on the details of my vision. Arachne had shown me a storeroom inside the Emporium where she was keeping Sparky safe until Kaye began her binding spell. There was the paper receipt, the blood filled pen, the cookies on the cardboard box table, and...a ceiling broken only by a large skylight.

"The skylight," I said, voice barely a whisper.

"What, Princess?" Torn asked.

"Scarab beetles are symbolic of the sun and the sky," I said, looking up to meet his questioning gaze. "There was a skylight in the storage room where Arachne was keeping

Sparky. It must be why she hexed me. It has to be the message she was trying to send."

"A skylight?" Father Michael asked.

The priest frowned, but Torn licked his lips and grinned from ear to ear. Cat sidhe were spies and thieves. He recognized what I was saying, and nodded, claws flexing.

"It's more than a skylight, Padre," I said. "Right, Torn?"

Torn's cat eyes gleamed as he waved his arm dramatically, gaining the priest's full attention. Not that I could blame him. Arachne had given us exactly what we were looking for.

"Thanks to the witch, we have exactly what we need," he said.

"A way in."

CHAPTER 27

My revelation of the skylight located in the ceiling of the Emporium's storeroom led to a frenzied line of questioning from the priest and Torn. Apparently, amidst my beetle retching and vision induced nausea, I'd forgotten to mention a few details from my vision.

While I could understand their need for information, I was growing weary of their questions. I was also painfully aware of the lowering sun. If we were going to attempt this rescue mission, we needed to act now.

"Enough talking," I said, hitting send on a final text to Ceff.

I'd sent messages to Jinx, Forneus, and Ceff providing updates on our current situation, and the potential consequences of angering our powerful witch ally. So far, I'd only heard back from Jinx. Ceff was busy rallying the water fae, and Forneus was likely out of cell phone range, deep beneath the city on his mission to destroy Yue Fei and the rogue vampires who threatened the city's human population.

I'd clued everyone in on our current situation—everyone except for Kaye's old friend Master Janus. The two had been allies for a long time, and I had no idea just how far the witch's madness would truly take things, but I couldn't risk Janus trying to stop me from doing what needed to be done.

I also couldn't risk distracting our Guild allies from the looming battle with the Wild Hunt. Herne was a powerful adversary, a pawn of the Queen of Air and Darkness. Mab had sent the Wild Hunt to take us down and make Harborsmouth the first in a long line of cities to fall to the most bloodthirsty of the fae and undead. That was a fight we had to win. Hence my impatience.

"But, Miss Granger..." Father Michael said, Torn cut him off with the shake of his head.

"No, the princess is right," he said. "If we're to rescue the demon and witch children, and free the gargoyle, we have to do it now. We've no time to lose."

"What he said," I said. "Come on."

"But...what is my role?" Father Michael asked.

"You're our backup, Padre," I said over my shoulder. I stopped, took a deep breath, and met his worried gaze. "And it's your job to get the kids to safety. If we don't make it out, you're their last hope."

"I won't let them down," he said.

A steely glint entered the priest's eyes, and I nodded. If he said that he'd get the kids to safety, he meant it. When it came to protecting children from the evils of this world, the priest was a man of his word.

I could trust Father Michael, even though one of those children was a demon and the man was a priest. At the end of the day, it didn't matter. Whether he admitted it or not, Father Michael was a hero.

Just like me.

Not that I let it go to my head. In fact, at the moment, I was starting to wonder if I'd fallen on that head a few too many times during my training in Faerie. I palmed one of my knives reflexively, and lifted my hand to point over the priest's shoulder with my blade.

"Anyone else see what I'm seeing?" I asked.

Father Michael lost his look of steely determination, and took a fumbling step away from the building at his back. But after mere seconds, he crept forward, leaning in to peer more closely at the writhing mass of beetles that had assembled on the wall's brick surface.

"What on earth...?" he asked.

"Oberon's great silver balls, Princess," Torn said, eyes widening. "You do keep things interesting."

Torn watched the beetles in amusement, always pleased for the rarity of a new experience to break the tedium of a long, immortal life, but Father Michael was already hastily making notes in a small notepad he'd pulled from his shirt pocket. Judging from his scribbling, the priest was most intrigued by the size and number of scarab beetles, and the fact that they'd manifested magically so far from their native habitat.

But aside from an involuntary shudder triggered by the scuttling sound of so many chitin-covered exoskeletons scrabbling along the brick face of the building, I ignored the fact that they were beetles at all. What interested me most was what they were doing.

The creatures weren't just swarming. The bodies moved in a rhythmic dance that was dizzying to watch, but I didn't allow myself to look away. A pattern was slowly emerging, but years of detective work had taught me to pay close attention to orderly patterns that appear amongst natural chaos.

I hardly dared to blink as the beetles scurried, climbed, and scrabbled. But my P.I. instincts had been right. Within seconds, a circular form emerged from the writhing mass of dark bodies. The beetles formed an ever-spinning circle.

It was a message. Of that, I was certain.

"A circle?" Father Michael muttered, hands twitching. His entire body seemed to quiver with unleashed energy as he watched the beetles raptly. "Interesting...possibly indicative of, but no...hmmm..."

"Is there some reason why they're moving like that?" Torn asked.

I sighed, and rubbed a gloved hand over my face. How could I be so stupid? I'd become so focused on the post-vision beetle incident, and chasing after Sparky, that I'd forgotten all about Arachne's mention of the Circle.

"It's from my vision," I said, letting my hands drop to my sides. I looked away from the dancing beetles, and met Torn's curious gaze. "Arachne mentioned something called the Circle. From what she said, it sounded like a coven. Maybe even a governing body for witches."

"The Circle?" Father Michael asked, moving toward me so quickly, I took a hasty step back and almost tripped over a fire hydrant. Thankfully, I had faerie reflexes rather than Jinx's propensity for painful accidents. "What did she say? What else do you remember?"

I held up a hand, halting his forward assault.

"Give me a minute," I said.

I pinched the bridge of my nose, and closed my eyes. Slowing my breathing, I used the focusing techniques my uncle had taught me. I mentally placed myself back in that storage room, and inside the mind and body of a teenage girl who I was beginning to realize had a hell of a lot of moxie.

"Arachne told Kaye that if the Circle found out about the dark magic she was doing, that they'd stop her," I said.

"She also mentioned something about the Circle having its own prisons."

I opened my eyes. That was all I got. I just hoped it was enough. I was done with visions and hexes, especially a hex involving bizarre beetle behavior. I swallowed hard, and ran a gloved hand through my hair.

"So the beetles were sending you a message, again," Torn said.

"Yeah, and I'd bet that these Circle people could help us take down Kaye, and maybe even give us an option for safely containing her if it comes to that, but I don't know of any group calling themselves the Circle," I said.

"Neither do I, Princess," he said. "And I know all there is to know about this city's secrets."

"That's because the Circle has had no need to step foot in Harborsmouth for quite some time," Father Michael said, tugging at an unkempt eyebrow.

"Wait, you know about this Circle?" I asked.

"Of course," he said. "There are numerous references to the Circle in the Vatican archives. As you hypothesized, they are a governing body of witches policing rogues within the magical community. They are most prevalent in North America, though the Circle and I have never crossed paths."

I was surprised that the priest hadn't sought this group out, but I kept my questions to myself. He'd stolen arcane items from the Vatican archives, and had likely been trying to remain under the radar when he came to this country. Seeking out a group of high profile witches probably would have attracted too much unwanted attention from Rome.

But the priest's hunger for supernatural knowledge was insatiable. I found it hard to believe that he wouldn't have kept tabs on a group with so much potential information on witchcraft.

"Do you know where we can find the nearest Circle members?" I asked.

"Or one of their prisons," Torn said, eyes flicking in the direction of the Emporium.

There had been no sign of Humphrey since we'd left Arachne earlier, but we'd be smart to be cautious. Kaye could have eyes and ears anywhere. I hoped she was just too obsessed with revenge to make the effort.

"As much as I hate to think about it," I said, keeping my voice low. "That might be our only option."

It sure beat the alternative. I'd much rather subdue Kaye, and help her overcome her madness, than have to take her out. I'd killed when necessary, but that was blood I'd never wash off my hands. I still had nightmares, and those I'd killed had been enemies. I'd do what I had to to rescue those kids, but I couldn't imagine coming back from killing a friend. Some things you can't recover from.

"Yes," Father Michael said, nodding. "But the nearest Circle facility is a day's ride away, assuming you can knock the witch out that long."

I slumped.

"Damn," I said. "I was hoping for help."

"Oh, but that is just the nearest prison," he said. "Help should not be difficult."

"Stop speaking riddles, and spit it out, priest," Torn said. "We're running out of daylight."

"I didn't already say?" he asked. "Sorry, it's the kind of thing I forget isn't common knowledge. Hardly seems worth mentioning." Torn growled, and the priest hurried on. "B-b-but of course, it is w-w-worth mentioning. Their location, that is. I mean to say, there's a meeting house in nearby Branford Falls."

"That's not far," I said, licking my lip. "Ten minutes by car, twenty at the most."

"There is one more thing," he said, eyeing Torn. "It may not be pertinent, but I've long suspected certain local covens of harboring inactive Circle members."

"Like sleeper cells?" I asked.

"Yes," he said. "It is not an inapt analogy."

Torn cocked his head to the side, raising a scarred brow.

"Who would these secret Circle members be?" Torn asked.

His eyes were cold, and I felt a momentary pang of sympathy for whoever had hidden themselves so well as to draw the ire of the cat sidhe lord. His question was also a good one. I couldn't shake the idea of a sleeper cell of Circle members snaring us all in a web of deceit. I was used to seeing what no one else can, so I was just as irritated as Torn, perhaps more. There is something innately terrifying about powerful magic users who can hide in plain sight.

"And how do we know we can trust them?" I asked.

"Oh, yes, well...I don't think that will be a problem under the circumstances," Father Michael said. "You see, I have the strongest suspicion that they are led by Fern Greatoak."

"Fern Greatoak?" Torn asked. "Sounds familiar. Who is she?"

My jaw dropped open, and I shook my head. I too was familiar with the name.

"Arachne's mother," I said.

CHAPTER 28

It all made sense. Arachne's family pawning her off on a grumpy, old witch. How many times had I heard Arachne proudly say how her family had been trying for generations to enlist one of their sons or daughters as an apprentice to Kaye O'Shea.

Arachne had been the first, and she might be the last.

"It was all about checks and balances, wasn't it?" I asked.

"I do believe you are right," Father Michael said. "Kaye has long been the most powerful witch in Harborsmouth. If the Circle wished to keep an eye on her, having a person on the inside would be the most effective method."

"They sent a child into that lion's den?" Torn asked.

I thought it over, and nodded.

"And if I had to bet, I'd say Arachne did so knowingly," I said. "Maybe not at the start, but she's certainly become more vigilant lately."

"I did think she'd started acting strangely, even for a human teenager, but I assumed it was a response to my unearthly charm," he said, running a hand down his leather-clad chest.

"Are you referring to the use of faerie glamour?" Father Michael asked, brow furrowing.

"No, Padre," I said with a snort. "I'm pretty sure Torn here thinks all women want him."

"Well, don't they?" Torn asked, giving me a smoldering, heavy-lidded look.

I shook my head in the negative as the priest muttered, "I should think not."

"As much as I hate to admit it, Arachne did have a crush on you, but I agree she's been different lately," I said. "And not just when you're around. I thought it was the result of her starting to grow up, especially after the fiasco with those fire imps she accidentally set loose on the city, but now I'm not so sure."

"If Arachne has infiltrated the Emporium for the Circle, do you think she will have managed to get a message to her mother and the other Circle members?" Father Michael asked.

"I sure as Hell hope so, Padre," I said. "For all our sakes."

CHAPTER 29

Our attempts to reach Fern Greatoak were a bust, but Father Michael agreed to continue his efforts to contact the Circle so long as he remained our backup for getting the kids to safety. Getting the priest's help was the easy part. In our haste to rescue the kids, and to enlist the help of the Circle, we hadn't discussed the remaining details of this mission.

Now we were less than a block away from the Emporium, which meant there was no time left for procrastinating. Apparently, Torn had come to the same conclusion.

"I take it my job is scaling the building and climbing in through the skylight?" Torn asked, rolling his shoulders.

"Not exactly," I said. "I have a different plan."

"Why do I have the feeling I'm not going to like this plan?" he asked.

I explained what I had in mind, and Torn scowled.

"Stop complaining," I said around a mouthful of granola bar. I wasn't hungry, and the food tasted like ash on my tongue, but chewing kept me from grinding my teeth. Plus, it helped wash the vile taste of beetle puke from my mouth. I also suspected that talking with my mouth full grossed Torn out, and these days I get my kicks where I can. "If you keep frowning like that, you'll have permanent lines on your face."

It was something Jinx had threatened me with a million times. Unlike me, Torn was vain. He stopped frowning. Too bad that didn't keep him from speaking.

"I am the stealthiest of us all, and you know it, Princess," he said.

"Yes, and that's exactly why they'll suspect you'd be our first choice for infiltration," I said. "So they won't suspect a thing if you approach from the front, and keep Humphrey busy."

"Everything we know about Arachne, even her connection to the Circle, is mere speculation," Father Michael said. "How can you be sure this isn't a trap?"

Food lodged in my already raw throat, but I swallowed hard, and forced a smile.

"We can't," I said. "But I don't think Arachne hexed me with something as nasty as a bug in my throat without a good reason. She wanted me to see that skylight."

"Even if you are right and this is not a trap, how can you be certain there are no protection wards set to keep out intruders?" he asked. "If I were a witch as powerful as Kaye, I'd have every means of entry booby-trapped. She probably even has cameras set to watch their heads explode."

He made a fist, then expanded his fingers dramatically to illustrate his point. Great, exploding heads. Just what I needed.

"No," I said, shaking my head with feigned confidence. "The kid may be running scared, but Arachne is resourceful. I have to trust that she'll find a way to disarm any deadly spells around that storeroom."

"And if she doesn't?" Torn asked.

"Then you get a gory new story to tell your friends about a foolish faerie princess who got her brains splattered all over the Emporium's rooftop," I said. "Now come on. You too, Padre."

I marched toward the Emporium, teeth clenched. There was no time for elaborate plans. If there were protection wards on that skylight, then I'd be decorating the roof with my brains. I gave myself a mental shrug, and kept moving. There were worse ways to go.

I would have kept stomping forward, but Torn used his feline speed and agility to jump ahead of me, creating an all too effective wall that blocked my path.

"And how do you plan to gain access to the roof, Princess?" Torn asked with a mocking glare. "Are you going to sprout wings and fly?"

A slow grin slid across my face, and Torn frowned. Father Michael blanched, and made a sign of the cross.

"You can't be serious," Torn muttered.

"Oh, I'm serious, all right," I said, stripping out of my leather jacket.

"You do realize you've never tried to fly outside of Faerie," he said, shaking his head.

I shrugged, pulling my long-sleeved shirt over my head. I'd stripped down to my tank top and jeans, eliciting a shiver. But if I was honest with myself, I wasn't cold.

My heart raced, and I reached eagerly for my power. It wasn't as strong here in the human world, but I wasn't without resources. I sent tendrils of magic outward, seeking the wisps who resided here in Harborsmouth.

Even in their weakened state, the recently iron-sick wisps who I'd saved at the Braxton junkyard willingly lent me their power. I sensed others, most in small flocks on the city's outskirts, and tentatively sent a request for their aid.

Back in the wisp court, I'd denounced my right to rule. I'd left my father's court in the capable hands of Skillywidden while a democratic governing body was formed. I'd grown up an outsider, and never fancied myself royalty, but that didn't change the truth of my blood. I was the daughter of the king of the wisps and the queen of Faerie. To the Unseelie fae, I was their liege.

Energy rushed to me, flooding my body with warmth and power. I giggled, magic rising within me to fill every nook and cranny. I had a suspicion that if I gathered any more power, I might burst.

With a sigh, I broke contact and reeled in the tendrils of power that I'd gathered. The entire process took mere seconds, but I still blinked at the sky. The sun hadn't moved any further in its steady decent. We still had time.

"Are y-y-you alright, Miss Granger?" Father Michael asked.

My lips tingled, and my teeth vibrated, as magic hummed through my body. I smiled, and nodded.

"Never better," I said.

"Ready, Princess?" Torn asked.

For the first time since I'd known the cat sidhe, he looked uncertain. I shook my head, unable to keep the wide grin from my lips.

"Not by a long-shot," I said.

I widened my stance, and closed my eyes. I delved deep inside my body, questing for the part of me that I so often rejected.

I'd worried that the insectile wings that were part of my wisp heritage made me less than human. I'd agonized over showing this side of myself to my friends, and I'd wondered if they'd ever be able to accept, and someday come to love, the real me. Oh, the irony that now that very part of myself was what I needed to keep my friends safe.

"Do you need my help, Princess?" Torn asked, lifting a clawed finger.

I knew what he was asking. He'd been there when I'd first transformed in a muddy, gas-filled bog in Faerie. The magic of Faerie, and the proximity of so many of my wisp brethren, had activated a change inside of me, and triggered the first emergence of my wings.

It wasn't an easy transformation.

I'd been wing-bound, and if it hadn't been for Torn and his razor-sharp claws, I'd likely be dead. The outer layer of a cat sidhe's claws grow fresh with each retraction and extension, so there wasn't a strong risk of unwanted psychic visions. But having your back cut open is unpleasant, no matter which way you slice it.

I'd managed to produce my wings, pushing them out through my back and retracting them back within the confines of my skin, during the course of my training with my uncle Kade. Of course, Torn had missed most of that while he languished in my uncle's secret dungeon. He was in for a surprise.

I took a deep breath, and pushed my wings out between the large muscles of my back. The delicate edges were deceptively sharp, and they cut easily through my skin with very little bloodshed. I focused, one wing at a time, carefully unfurling the thin, translucent wings that marked me as my father's daughter.

I rolled my shoulders, making my wings flutter, and pulled a glamour around me—a cloak that shimmered like the air above a bonfire. If I was embracing my wisp heritage, I might as well accept my mother's gifts as well. My glamour gave me the appearance of Mab, the Queen of Air and Darkness. Go big, or go home, as Jinx would say.

Father Michael gasped, and Torn swore an oath. I blinked, opening my eyes, and smiled.

"I'll take the roof," I said. I opened my hand, a tiny ball of flame spinning above my palm. "Unless you have a better idea?"

For the first time since I'd met him, Torn was speechless. I took a running leap and, with a snap of my wings, I was airborne.

"Safe travels, Princess," Torn said, his voice a whisper against the rushing wind and the blood pounding in my ears. I wasn't even sure if he'd said the words, or if it had been my imagination.

I whispered my reply, something I'd heard Jenna utter a dozen times, and aimed for the Emporium, determined to bring our kids home.

"Happy hunting."

CHAPTER 30

I heard shouting at street level, coming from the front of the building where Torn was creating a distraction. Father Michael would be lurking nearby, waiting to get Arachne and Sparky to safety. I also hoped that with Arachne's help, we'd be able to free Humphrey from Kaye's control. Nobody deserved to be enslaved to a revenge-crazed witch, no matter what he may have been forced to do in her service.

I heard a growling rumble, and shuddered, jerking in the air as my wings fought to keep me upright. Humphrey may be a victim, but at the moment he was a potentially deadly threat—just like the glowing sigils below me.

Thank Mab, my second sight revealed the tracery of spells that stood between me and the storeroom skylight. The Emporium's rooftop was covered in an interlocking web of mystical markings. I had no doubt that each glowing mark represented a terrifyingly painful means of death.

Unlike the surrounding buildings, there were no signs of birds, rodents, or insects. No wasp nests beneath the eaves, and no bird's nests, or pigeons on the roof. Even the dust, soot, and grime that you'd expect to see on such an old building were missing.

I tugged at my gloves, sweat trickling down my back. If Arachne didn't do something to take down those spells, I'd never make it through that skylight alive. Another rumbling growl came from the front of the building, and I frowned.

We were running out of time.

"Come on, kid," I whispered.

I held my breath, and waited. My eyes darted from side to side and up and down, scanning the rooftop for a break in the Emporium's magical defenses.

Three interwoven glowing sigils flickered and disappeared. I blinked, and let out a grunt of surprise. Arachne had done it. The spells were down, for now.

I ducked my head, and with a twitch of my wings, I dove straight at the skylight. I kept my eyes focused on that spot, ready to pull myself back at a moment's notice if those glowing sigils began to flicker into existence.

As I grew closer to the rooftop, threatening magic tingled gratingly along my nerves. My body screamed out for me to retreat, but I forced myself further downward. Finally, after seconds that felt like days, I set down lightly on the edge of the skylight. I stepped gingerly, painfully aware of the sun's position.

Not only was it growing late, bringing us closer to Kaye's spell and the Wild Hunt's attack, but I knew that if I allowed a shadow to fall on the storeroom at an inopportune time, it could mean Sparky's life. If Kaye felt threatened, and believed Arachne guilty of betrayal, she wouldn't hesitate to lash out.

Aware of the repercussions, I shifted my position and reached for the window latch with a gloved hand. I bit the inside of my cheek, undid the latch, swung the skylight inward, and froze.

A beetle settled on the wooden sill, its hard legs tapping a staccato rhythm into the stillness of the room. No alarm rang out, and I dared to duck my head into the darkened room. I let my eyes adjust, my faerie enhanced night-vision giving me better sight than a human, and scanned the dark room filled with boxes and crates below.

This was the place from Arachne's vision. I recognized the boxes she'd used as a makeshift table and chairs for her little tea party. There were still crumbs scattered around the room, likely where Sparky had danced around while munching on cookies. The box he'd used as a chair was overturned, its contents spilling out onto the concrete floor.

Had Sparky bumped into it while dancing and playing? Or was there a more sinister explanation for the overturned box? Had there been a struggle? I could make myself crazy speculating over what had knocked the box over. One thing was certain.

They were gone.

CHAPTER 31

My phone vibrated, and I nearly dropped it through the open skylight as I fumbled it from my jacket pocket. I swore, voice barely a whisper, and held my breath as I scanned the room below. When there was no movement except for the beetle flying in lazy circles to the crumb-covered makeshift cardboard table, I checked my phone.

I had two messages.

The first was from Jinx asking how Sparky was, and telling me to hurry my ass up and get back to the industrial park. The second was from Father Michael. He'd finally tracked down Fern Greatoak.

If he wasn't a priest, and I wasn't a touch-phobe who was engaged to a jealous kelpie king, I'd kiss the man. According to his message, Arachne's mother was on her way. She was also sending out the call to the sleeper Circle members to come out of hiding, and a message had finally been received by Circle members in Branford Falls.

Help was coming. I just hoped they'd get here in time. And while I didn't doubt that the witches would help to rescue Arachne, I couldn't place my faith in them to risk their lives for a demon. No, Sparky was my responsibility. He was my kid, and I was going to set him free.

Power poured into me in a rushing torrent, and I had to struggle to maintain control over my magic. Faeries treasure our children, perhaps more so even than humans, because our young are such a rare, precious thing. I don't know how it happened in such a short time, but I'd come to think of Sparky as my own child.

I suppose it had something to do with the way we'd met that fateful day in an alley that smelled of piss and fear. His life had been threatened, and I'd stood up for the little tyke. He'd loved me unconditionally ever since, and, I had to admit, the feeling was mutual. Sparky was my child, my son, and I was Ivy Granger, the daughter of Will-o'-the-Wisp and Mab the

Queen of Air and Darkness. I was a princess of Faerie, and the life of my child was once again threatened.

If Kaye harmed one floppy ear on that kid's head, I'd make a funeral pyre of the Emporium and I'd watch the woman burn.

I shook my head, blinking down at the beetle tapping against the closed door inside the room below. There'd be time for punishment later. For now, I had to make it inside the Emporium alive.

I held my breath, palmed my throwing knives, and flew silently to the floor. With hardly a thought, I folded my wings in close, though I didn't retract them. I'd learned early in my visit to Faerie that wisp wings could act as an antenna, and right now I needed all my senses on high alert.

I moved silently across the room, and turned my head to listen at the door. Even with my enhanced hearing, the shop beyond the storage room was silent. Holding one blade at the ready, I held my breath, counted to three, and turned the knob.

When the plastic skeletons didn't spring to life, and the brooms didn't immediately try to impale me, I let out a shaky breath and risked opening the door wide enough to step out into one of the many maze-like shop aisles. The shelving was stacked high with books, wands, herbs, and other witchy accoutrements.

I was so busy eyeing the magical paraphernalia that teetered precariously above my head that I didn't see the black creature spring toward me until its claws nearly raked my face. I ducked my head, and spun.

That was close, too close. Heart racing, my gaze darted up and down the aisle, but it was just the two of us. Midnight, Kaye's large, black feline familiar, stared at me with unblinking green eyes.

"You scared the crap out of me," I whispered. I smiled, and patted my pockets, searching for something the cat might like. "Want a cracker?"

Midnight hissed, hackles lifting, and I spun to see what had scared the cat. A beetle landed on a shelf, and I frowned. I was sick of this damn hex. The sooner I got Arachne to lift it, the better.

I turned to soothe the cat, but Midnight was gone.

"Damn," I muttered.

Had Kaye been looking out through Midnight's eyes? Was the cat reporting back to Kaye now? If so, there was no time to lose.

I slid forward, rushing as fast as I could without tripping or knocking something over. It was harder than it should have been, a sign that the near-sentient shop was on high alert. The Emporium had been layered in protective magic for so many decades, the building itself often seemed to have a life of its own.

Everywhere I ran, masks leered and normally inanimate objects reached out to ensnare me while others rolled underfoot to trip me or block my path. More than once, an entire section of hardcover spell books and shelving toppled, trying to capture me beneath the heavy remnants of long dead trees. Thank Mab for fae reflexes, or I would have been trapped beneath a mountain of malevolent books and shelving—a tomb of arcane tomes.

I shook off the urge to giggle, and leapt over the final barrier in the ridiculous obstacle course. So much for stealth. It was unlikely that Kaye was unaware of my approach now. Even if Midnight hadn't reported my break-in, I'd made enough noise running the gauntlet of animated shop wares to raise the dead.

Heart in my throat, I slipped through the beaded curtain and into the hallway leading to Kaye's spell kitchen. The kitchen door was on my left, and Kaye's office was further down on the right. The silence of the hallway, after the incessant marching of books and whirlwind of crashing objects in the outer shop, was oppressive.

Blood pounded in my ears, and I took a deep, calming breath. It didn't work. There's no training, no magic ability or power that prepares you for facing a friend's ultimate betrayal. Nothing that can prepare you for seeing harm come to a child you love. So no one can blame me for the pitiful sound that escaped my lips as I crossed the threshold into Kaye's kitchen.

Surprisingly, there was no physical pain upon entry. Apparently, I was still keyed into the kitchen wards as a friend. But that wasn't much comfort. Not with the disturbing tableau, like a scene from a nightmare, frozen before me.

Sparky was laid out on a table beside the center of the spell circle, his tiny form curled onto its side as if he were merely resting. But even I could see that wasn't the case. All the hoping in the world couldn't erase the dark, black-tinged red liquid that oozed from his neck and wrists. He was being bled and, from the volume of blood, it had been going on for some time.

As I lurched further into the room and closer to the table, Kaye's head swung in my direction, but Sparky didn't so much as twitch. Not a good sign. The kid was full of energy and unbridled joy. Even in sleep, he was always moving, always sucking his thumb, rolling in his cocoon of blankets, or giggling. But he was silent now.

A tear rolled down my cheek, and my body lit with fire as my wisp power raged within me, begging for release.

"Where is the piece of Herne?" Kaye asked. "Give it to me, girl. This is no time for sentimentality, especially for hellspawn."

She waved me forward, tattooed hands twitching eagerly. It was then that I noticed Kaye wasn't the one holding the ritual dagger. Arachne held the athame, its blade tainted with blood. My body shook, anger and betrayal and grief raging war beneath my skin.

I could end this now. With a single thought, I could burn us all and erase the pain. I blinked, and shook my head.

"How could you?" I asked, voice ragged.

"Oh, Goddess," Arachne said, choking out a sob. "It's not what you think. It's not what it looks like, Ivy. I swear."

"Funny," I said, lips drawing into a hard line and voice going cold. "It looks like you're bleeding my son."

"N-n-no," she said. "Really. He's fine...he's just...sleeping."

Her wide eyes darted wildly between me and Kaye as she held the dagger out in front of her. Not that the weapon would do much good against a powerful witch or faerie. The only thing that stayed my hand was Arachne's sudden movement to place herself between Sparky and Kaye. Was there a chance, even a shred of hope that she was trying to protect him?

"Sleeping?" Kaye asked, her voice rising into a shriek.

"K-k-kaye said to sacrifice him, to use his blood to fuel the binding spell, but I couldn't do that," Arachne said. "I would never do that. Dark magic is wrong."

I wanted to believe her, but that was a difficult leap of faith considering what my eyes were telling me. I stepped closer, knife in one hand and a tiny ball of flame swirling in the other. Was there really a chance that Sparky might still be alive? If so, throwing fireballs was too damn risky, and that might be exactly why she was telling me that the kid was okay.

"But the blood," I said, waving my hand toward Sparky's bleeding, lifeless body.

"I slipped skullcap, a paralytic, and a sleeping draught into a batch of cookies he ate," she said. "Then I swapped out the real ritual dagger for a fake one we sell in the shop, and filled it with a mixture of fake blood and chocolate syrup."

A prop dagger that squirted fake blood was exactly the kind of thing they sold in the Emporium gift shop. Oberon's eyes, could Sparky really just be sleeping off the effects of a paralytic herb?

For Kaye and Arachne's sake, they sure as Hell better hope so.

CHAPTER 32

I rushed toward Sparky, my every thought focused on checking for a pulse and to see for myself that he was breathing. If Arachne was lying and Sparky had been harmed, I'd burn this place to the ground and spread the ashes in Tech Duinn.

I stumbled as a blast of cold wind knocked me into a nearby countertop. A fiery pain burst from my right hip and wing, but I didn't have time to examine the injuries.

Kaye strode across the kitchen, hair lifting in snake-like tendrils to writhe around her head as her fingers danced to form arcane symbols in the air. The jury was still out on Arachne's involvement, but Kaye was definitely an active threat, and she looked crazier than a pixed bugbear. She'd crossed the line from friend to foe, and an involuntary shudder trembled along my spine. I had a bad feeling that someone was going to die.

I sure as Hell didn't want it to be me.

Panting, I pushed against the wall of wind that continued to assail us, and closed the short distance to where Arachne stood in front of Sparky. Even if Arachne had more magic knowledge than she'd let on, I doubted she could hold Kaye off for long. Too bad her mother and the other Circle members hadn't yet arrived. We could use some backup.

If Kaye decided to do more than toy with us, we were toast.

"You foolish, spoiled, ungrateful girl!" Kaye yelled.

Crap, so much for games. Kaye was escalating, fast.

I bit the inside of my cheek, teeth humming with power, and unfurled my wings to fill the remaining space between me and the table at my back. Ignoring the searing pain in my right wing, I drew more power to me and I began to weave a wall of protective flame around me, Arachne, and the table that held Sparky.

"Oh Goddess," Arachne mumbled.

I flicked my eyes to her, and then to Sparky, before snapping my attention back to Kaye. But in that quick glance, I'd seen what had Arachne worried, and it wasn't just Kaye's tantrum. Not only were we facing down a powerful witch, but the paralytic that Arachne had fed to Sparky had worn off. He'd started to move in his sleep. How soon until he woke up?

Even now his fingers rubbed together, sparks forming between them. He was a demon, and I'd called a wall of flame into the room. The kid hadn't grown into his powers yet, but it was possible that he was responding to his proximity to the fire—like calling to like.

"You got any more of that sleeping draught?" I asked.

I had to shout to be heard over the howling of the unnatural wind that Kaye continued to blast us with. Judging from her scowl, we were giving Kaye more trouble than she expected, but she'd soon think of a way around our defenses, and when she did, we were as good as dead, or worse.

Arachne shook her head, keeping her eyes on Kaye. Damn. As if sunset wasn't already a ticking time bomb, now we had to get this over with before Sparky woke up. He'd be more of a hindrance than a help in this fight, and I had a fierce desire to protect him from ever knowing what Kaye tried to do to him. No child should ever suffer that kind of trauma.

I'd grown up feeling abandoned, and thinking that I was worth less than the other, normal children. I thought that my father leaving and the distance between me and my parents meant that I was unlovable. How would it have felt to learn that a woman who had begun to be like a surrogate grandmother had then tried to kill me? I couldn't imagine the damage that kind of revelation would have, and I wasn't going to find out.

I'd protect Sparky from more than physical blows. I'd end this quick, and keep his innocence intact. It was the least I could do for drawing him into the utter mess of my life.

"Let us go, Kaye," I said. "Last chance."

"How dare you give me orders?" she asked.

A copper bowl lifted from the counter, suspended in the air for a second before plummeting to the stone floor with a loud, metal clang. Kaye ceased waving her hands, and began to massage her temples with tattooed fingers. The skin on her hands had been free of tattoos just a week ago. What the Hell had the witch been up to?

I extinguished the wisp flame I'd held at the ready, and I lifted my left hand, palm out. The right hand I kept pressed to my side as if reaching for my injured hip. Pain flared and I winced, adding to the ruse, my knife at the ready.

No matter how badly I wanted to talk Kaye down from this ledge of my own making, I knew better than to face her unarmed. As it was, she had me at the disadvantage. Even with my newly heightened senses and increased speed, my position was all wrong for an accurate throw of my knife. I'd need to step forward with one foot, and raise my hand above my head if I had any hope of finding my target. At the moment, that target was Kaye's right shoulder, but that could change.

She was faster, stronger, and the madness and compulsion driving her made her actions unpredictable. So focused as she was on revenge, she might take unnecessary risks. The jury was still out on whether that would work in my favor, but it didn't look good. So I kept an eye on the shoulder of her dominant arm, hoping to reduce her ability to cast spells if she pushed her attack.

"Come on, Kaye," I said. "I'm not giving you orders. I'm just trying to help. You've got to see that."

Arachne let out a whimper at my side, but I didn't dare take my eyes off Kaye. My chest tightened, and I struggled to keep my breathing steady. I needed to calm Kaye down, but it was obvious that even now, she hadn't let up on her assault. Arachne was struggling to hold a protective barrier between us and her former mentor, but we continued to be buffeted by an angry wind.

What would happen when Kaye realized I had absolutely zero intent of ever getting her a piece of Herne for her spell? I needed to get through to her before that happened. As it was, she was already recovering from her momentary lapse, shaking her head as she lowered her hands from her temples.

She blinked, and an off-kilter grin spread across her face. Her eyes shone with a feverish gleam, and I had to remind myself that she was sick. Power and age had corrupted her mind, but there still might be a woman worth saving trapped inside. Maybe.

With the flick of her wrist, a row of jars struck Arachne's shield, and I had to renew casting a protective arc of flame around us. The flames shot up just in time, since Kaye's magic had lifted a canister of long-handled wooden spoons, throwing each utensil at us like tiny javelins.

"You're sick, Kaye," I said, lifting an arm against the maelstrom. Racks of spell components were being pulled from the walls to fly toward us. My flames burned most of it to ash or knocked it back, but all it would take is one fork through the eye to lose this fight. I shook my head. "This isn't you."

"You have no idea who I am," she said, spittle forming at her lips. "You call yourself a hero, but I was saving this city when you were in diapers. And I am saving it again."

The objects flying through the air may have been deflected by my flames and Arachne's protective shield magic, but I still felt like I'd been punched in the gut. Kaye might be crazy, but she wasn't wrong. She had been a hero to this city, risking her life to protect its inhabitants from harm. Most of those threats were fae, a fact I was painfully aware of.

I had to force myself to remember that it was her recent actions called into question, not the woman herself. That was a job for a jury of her peers, something that the Circle might already be putting in motion, but we needed to all stay alive long enough to make that happen. Perhaps if I could appeal to Kaye's love of the city, I could get her to back down, and stop trying to impale us with kitchen implements.

"I know what the barghest did to your friends, but there are other ways to defeat Herne's hounds," I said. "We don't need your binding spell to save the city."

I looked around, searching for an opening, some way to end this quick and painless. I was especially keen on that last part. I was all for avoided maiming or worse. We'd all been through enough already, and the true battle facing this city hadn't even begun.

Arachne was shaking, and her skin had taken on a grayish pallor. The kid was running on empty. If only we could get inside the silver-lined spell circle set into the kitchen floor, we'd stand a chance. But there was a crazed witch between us and the circle.

It was then that I noticed the basket of silverware beneath a cloth napkin that was flapping in the artificial wind. The basket was on the floor as if it had been hastily set there to make room for Sparky's body on the table. I hooked the basket with the toe of my boot, not daring to look down at it again and draw Kaye's notice.

I knew from the way that Hob coveted those forks, knives, and spoons that they were made of pure silver. Shiny silver was the brownie's weakness. I drew a breath and flicked my hand, sending a ball of flame to singe Kaye's skirts, and buy us some time.

I inched closer to Arachne, but still had to shout to be heard.

"Can you make a protective circle?" I asked.

She nodded, but her hands shook.

"I can try, but I can't hold it for long," she said. "Not against Kaye."

I pushed the basket between us and kicked it up against her ankle.

"What if your circle is outlined in silver?" I asked. Her eyes widened and she bit her lip, but nodded. That was all the encouragement I needed. "Good. I'll cover you on three."

I widened my stance, and lifted my arm, a throwing knife pinched between gloved fingers. Kaye cackled, but I held my ground.

"You think a mere blade can harm me?" she asked.

Dark tattoos swirled along her arms, but I shrugged, keeping her angry focus on me.

"One...two...THREE!" I shouted.

Kaye frowned, her head tilted to the side, but Arachne dropped to the ground. From the clatter at my feet, she was hastily forming a circle with the silverware. But she'd need a few seconds to build that perimeter and infuse it with magic. It was my job to give her those seconds.

"Kaye!" I shouted.

I stepped forward, and threw my knife. I intended for the butt of the knife to hit her in the shoulder, but Kaye used her magic to swat the weapon aside like it was no more than a mosquito. Sadly, that's all we were to the witch. To someone of Kaye's power, we were no more than a minor nuisance, insects to be swept away—or exterminated.

"Give me the ingredient!" she shouted, sending a large metal cauldron flying toward my head with the flick of her wrist.

By ingredient, I wasn't sure if she meant the piece of Herne she so desperately sought or Sparky. Either way, she wasn't getting what she wanted. I'd tried to reason with her to no avail. I felt Sparky stir on the table behind me, and I lifted my chin and set my jaw.

I was fresh out of patience.

CHAPTER 33

Kaye had done more than threaten my well-being, she'd threatened my family. She'd forced Arachne and Humphrey do things against their wills, things they may never recover fully from, and put Sparky in harm's way. Even now, Arachne and Sparky's lives were at risk.

I'd tried to give Kaye a chance to back down. She was a friend, a mentor, and a former protector of this city. I didn't forget the part I'd played in Kaye's descent into madness, and I wasn't ready to give up all hope for the woman's redemption. But I'd had enough of her threats and demands, and I was done handling the old witch with kid gloves.

My time in Faerie had taught me a valuable lesson, one I focused on now. If those with power become obsessed with greed or revenge, they need to be brought down. Madness and obsession had driven my uncle's actions, and people suffered. I'd made the hard calls then, and I'd do it again now.

That's what heroes do.

I sniffed, and blinked away tears. I knew that what I was about to do was right, but that didn't make it easy. Hurting a friend should never be easy, and if Kaye was of sound mind, she'd be the first to tell me that I was doing the right thing. Innocent children had to be protected, at all costs.

"Arachne, you got that spell circle ready?" I asked.

"One more second," she said.

Her body trembled, but her voice no longer shook. The kid was brave, I'd give her that.

"Let me know just before it closes," I said, keeping my eyes on Kaye.

I threw another knife, but Kaye deflected it easily. She strode toward us, hair writhing in a mass of curls. Spittle foamed at the side of her mouth as she began a new incantation, and I knew instinctively that I needed more than mere blades to keep her at bay.

Arachne held up three fingers, beginning her countdown. It had become too loud for words. The walls shook,

and sections of roof began to tear off the building like cast off
wrapping paper on Christmas morning. But there was no
happy surprise inside the Emporium, only the specter of pain
and death.

That promise was evident in Kaye's wide, unblinking
eyes and in the teeth she now bared as she lurched toward us.
Those teeth swirled with indigo and black arcane symbols, and
Arachne's hand shook as she lowered one finger and then the
other.

Three, two...ONE.

A mere breath away from Arachne closing the protective
circle, I stepped out of the ring of silver utensils and spread my
wings. Pain tore through my right wing, but I forced it open
wide. Without Arachne at my side or Sparky at my back, I had
room to maneuver my wings. More importantly, I'd felt the
influx of magic as Arachne set her circle. My ears popped with
the shift in pressure, and the tension in my shoulders eased.

No matter what happened next, Arachne and Sparky
would be safe inside that circle. I just had to have faith in
Arachne that she could hold her spell in place long enough for
me to take Kaye down. I tried not to think too hard about what
I might have to do to end this threat. It was past the time for
that. I'd do whatever was necessary.

Mind made up, I shot into the air, taking advantage of
the sections of missing ceiling. The kitchen was large, but it
was the gaping holes in the ceiling and roof that really gave me
room to maneuver. I might have gloried in my second time
flying here in the human world if it hadn't been for the witch
trying to squish me like a bug.

Chunks of wood and stone joined the kitchen utensils
shooting through the air and the projectiles had one target, me.
That suited me just fine. The longer I kept Kaye's focus off the
kids, the safer they'd be.

I had the witch's attention. She was on a revenge kick,
but even more worrisome she was hellbent on saving the city
by taking control of the supernaturals here, starting with
Herne's hounds. Demonstrating my otherness with wings and
wisp magic was a surefire way to get on her radar, and I'm
pretty damn sure her lasers weren't set for stun.

A bolt of lightning shot from her fingertips, and I had to
duck and drop like a stone to avoid being barbequed. She'd

guessed my trajectory, and I narrowly missed an entire block of sharp, pointy knives. Oh yeah, I definitely had her attention and from that last attack, it seemed she wanted me dead.

I soared through the room, rolling, dropping, and rising as needed. Taking flight on faerie wings had only enraged Kaye further, but I wasn't done. I was just getting started.

Wings spread wide, I let down my mental barriers and allowed the cacophony of wisp voices to scream inside my head. It didn't terrify me. In fact, knowing that Arachne and Sparky were safe inside a dome of protective magic had eased the band of pressure around my chest and loosened something inside my mind, leaving me in a Zen-like state of calm.

Thankfully, I can move like greased lightning when I'm all Zen. Tattoos crawled over every inch of Kaye's body, but I caught the movement just as she unleashed an orb of endless night. The ball of shadow tore through the room, eating wood, brick, and mortar with a glutton's appetite. It sank into the floor, and I had to wonder if it continued all the way through the center of the earth and out the other side of the planet.

Kaye couldn't be allowed to unleash that kind of magic on the world. She had to be stopped.

Wisp voices buzzing in my head, I began to glow. Light filled the room, and I tilted back my head, basking in the power of my people. Then, I began to sing.

Not all folktales are true. The wail of a banshee doesn't always presage death (though it does often enough to raise the hairs on my neck when I hear their cries), kelpies don't all hunger for human flesh (thank Mab), and pixies aren't cute little cherubic faeries who wear buttercups on their heads (if you believe that, I know a troll with a bridge to sell you). But sometimes, the old stories get it right.

Wisps have long had a reputation for luring their victims into the watery graves of swamps, marshes, and bogs. Some stories say we use our glow to lead travelers astray. Some say we wisps sing a beautiful melody that forces men to dance off the safe path and to their doom. Both stories are true.

We can do both.

I lifted my voice in a humming, haunting tune that vibrated through the kitchen, drowning out the wind and the incessant crash of support beams and roofing tiles. I'd long denied my wisp heritage here in the human world, believing that part of me to be something monstrous. Even after all of my training in the wisp court, and the discovery that I was, in fact, full-blooded fae, I'd doubted my ability to draw on my powers away from Faerie. Those worries were unfounded.

I am wisp, hear me roar.

Have you ever heard the cry of a mother bugbear for her cub, or the shriek of a harpy for her chicks? My body continued to move with a relaxed, fluid grace, easily avoiding the magic thrown at me from Kaye's tantrum, but I was no longer void of emotion.

With the lifting of my voice, and the collective hum of my people, I filled the room with wisp song. The music gathered and built with a crush of power that rode over the kitchen in waves. It pooled in corners, rose in crescendos, crashed upon my enemy, and returned to me to do it all again, the song a constant tide of energy and power.

I was a conduit for a kind of primal magic that required the full commitment of the user. I glanced from tiny Arachne huddled over Sparky's fragile body to Kaye's wrathful scowl and mottled skin, and gave the song my full conviction. I embraced my love for them, and my anger. Kaye had threatened my family, and for that, I would lead her to her doom.

My wings joined the song with a strange chirping vibration of their own, and Kaye's eyes widened. Even in her madness, her judgment clouded by rage and a desire for revenge, she hesitated. She'd miscalculated, only now becoming aware of the true extent of my transformation, the realization that I was my father's daughter and my mother's daughter, no matter the nature of my upbringing.

Kaye had known me as human, and more recently as half wisp, but that had been a lie. I was fully fae. The early deception was a trick of complex magic spells to keep me safe and hide me from Mab and her network of spies. I'd begun to mature into my powers with age, and the spells keeping me human would likely have worn off with time. Cracks had recently begun to form when more faeries had entered my life, but it was my trip to my father's court that had shattered the spells that kept me human.

Faerie had changed me. Kade, with his endless, brutal training sessions and his ultimate betrayal, had molded and shaped me. Sorrow, guilt, and loneliness had hardened me. I was no longer the naïve, young human girl with an unusual psychic gift and a strange aura.

I was the daughter of Will-o'-the-Wisp and Mab the Queen of Air and Darkness. No matter the circumstances of their union, they'd borne a child with extraordinary power. I smiled, baring my teeth. I may not yet know the bounds of that power, but I was willing to test its limits.

Kaye's hands moved in a frenzied dance, hurriedly trying to bring me down, but she was too late. Another wave of wisp song crashed over her, and blood oozed from her ears. I swooped lower, tossing a ball of fire at her feet, and she barely managed to deflect it. The fireball hit the ground mere inches from where she stood, and she had to divide her time between defending against my attacks and using water magic to douse the flames.

All the while, my song lured her closer to the door and farther away from Arachne and Sparky. Getting her away from the kids was good. Trouble was, my wings wouldn't fit through that doorway. To get her out of the room, I'd either have to relinquish control of the wisp song and retract my wings, or grapple Kaye and fly her out through one of the holes in the ceiling. Neither option was without risks.

I was eyeing the door, calculating the force I'd need to try to blast away the adjacent wall, hoping to give myself a third option for taking this battle out of the kitchen, when movement caught my attention. Someone lobbed a cloth bundle at Kaye, and she froze.

The effect lasted only seconds, but it gave Fern Greatoak and the other Circle members the time they needed to make their move. A web of blue and green lines lit the room, quickly spinning to ensnare Kaye.

Kaye fought the magical shackles, but I added my own magic to the attack. Veins burning, body trembling, and chest aching, I gathered more power and pummeled Kaye with wisp song. She sagged, slowing her struggles against the Circle's entanglement spell, but my elation was short-lived.

I listed to the side ungracefully, fatigue and my injured wing making it increasingly difficult to stay aloft. I'd channeled too much wisp power, and my body was reaching its limits. Adrenaline was wearing off, making me aware of dozens of painful bruises, cuts, and a possible tear in my right wing.

I'd sustained a multitude of minor injuries that I'd managed to ignore until now, but now that I was aware of them, pain and fatigue smothered me like a wet blanket. I wouldn't be able to remain aloft much longer.

I frowned, eyeing the web of magic that filled the lower half of the room with a grid of intersecting, glowing blue and green lines. How would the Circle magic react to a faerie?

I had a sudden image of being trapped in a spider's web, my wings buzzing in earnest to break free. The fear wasn't completely unfounded. I'd had more than one run-in with spider fae. Nasty creatures.

Of course, the figures moving below weren't spider fae. They were witches who'd come to our aid to capture a rogue magic user, and help free Arachne. I didn't kid myself that they were here to save the supernaturals in the room. That was the problem.

I shot a worried look at the young witch, trying to gauge her reaction to her mother's appearance. She'd know better than anyone if the Circle members were a potential threat to me and Sparky.

Arachne's gaze was fixed on Kaye, but when she finally looked away, I caught her attention with a small wave of my hand. I didn't dare fly lower or make any sudden movements, but Arachne took in my injuries and her face softened. She answered my questioning look by giving me the universal thumbs up, and waved me to her, patting the table at her side.

That's all the encouragement I needed. If the Circle's magic was going to zap me, let it. I was tired and sore, but most of all I needed to be reassured that Arachne and Sparky were safe.

I was going down there to see to my kids. To hell with the Circle's magic. There are some things worth taking risks for.

CHAPTER 34

The web of magic didn't ensnare me, and although each line hummed with power that made my scalp itch, it didn't hurt. I still inched away from the nearest line, uneasy with the Circle and their magic.

Fern Greatoak and her comrades seemed content to ignore me, but I wondered how long that would last. I was partially responsible for Kaye going rogue, and supernaturals were even now threatening the safety of the city's human and witch population. With Kaye no longer a viable go-between, it was only a matter of time before the witches became directly involved. I wasn't looking forward to that.

Flashing sparks from torn electric lines caused shadows to dance ominously along the demolished kitchen walls. Without the glow from my skin, the entire modern half of the room was plunged into darkness. I looked down at where my scuffed boots stood on the flagstone marking the old section of the room, and took a deep breath.

The ring of silverware at my feet was a mockery of the pleasant meals I'd shared in this kitchen with Kaye, Arachne, Marvin, and Hob. Oh Oberon's eyes, poor Hob. I'd have to break the news to him that his home was in ruins, the kitchen not much more than a scorched pile of rubble.

There wasn't much beyond Arachne's circle, which had only encompassed where she stood and the table where Sparky had been laid out to be bled, that was still in one piece. Even the solid stone of the hearth hadn't escaped the melee unscathed.

A sob climbed its way through my body, stifled only by a fast moving demon and an excited squeak.

"Ivyyyy!" Sparky squealed.

He jumped up, and leapt into my arms. He was alive. He was whole. Tears streamed down my face, and I turned to see Fern and a man I hadn't met wrap Kaye in a straightjacket shot through with glowing, pulsating threads. I winced. To my second sight, it looked like the jacket was woven with the same entanglement spell as the one used to fill the room.

"She can't hurt us anymore," Arachne said. "It's over."

I blinked away the tears, and shook my head.

"You did good," I said. "But it's not over yet. Not by a long shot."

She frowned as Father Michael and Torn burst into the room, Humphrey hot on their tail. I tensed until it was clear that Humphrey was there as an ally rather than an enemy. He was free of Kaye's enslavement, and for that I was grateful, but there was no time to congratulate him. Like I said, it wasn't over yet. We'd won this fight, but the bigger battle was yet to come.

Torn frowned, probably disappointed that he'd missed the fight, but he'd done the job I'd given him. Actually, the fact that a cat sidhe lord had followed my orders was a bit unsettling, but I didn't have time for puzzles or psychoanalysis. He'd kept Humphrey busy, and he'd been our lookout for any Circle members who might show up to lend a hand.

He surveyed my disheveled appearance, and I shrugged. He scanned the room and raised an eyebrow, letting out a low whistle. He'd want the full story, but he'd have to wait.

"Ivy," Father Michael gasped, stumbling in his haste. The floor was an obstacle course of overturned cabinets, furniture, and broken ceiling tiles. "You're alright."

"Yes," I said, turning so he could see Sparky wiggling in my arms. "And so is this little guy."

"Thank the Lord," he said.

Sparky let out a cookie burp, and I had to wonder if that was due to being fed a concoction to make him sleep, or if it was the demon's reaction to the priest's pronouncement. Thankfully, Father Michael didn't seem to take offense.

"Little man, I do believe we have a play date," he said.

He raised his eyebrows questioningly, and I grudgingly nodded. All I wanted to do was snuggle Sparky and savor this moment, but I had to go.

"Yep," I said, giving Sparky one last squeeze before handing him over to Father Michael. "I see pizza and a cartoon marathon in your future."

"Pizzzaaa!" he said, grinning from ear to floppy ear.

"You too, Humphrey," I said. "You're welcome to stay on our building from now on."

His ears perked up when I mentioned his name, but when I told him he could live on our building, his dog-like face split in a grin. I guess that was a yes.

I nodded, but Humphrey reached out a stone arm to block my path. I blinked, and he lost his grin.

"I'll prrrotect them," he said, tilting his head to indicate Sparky and Arachne.

"I don't doubt it, big guy," I said.

He held my gaze and the pain in his eyes spoke volumes. He needed me to know that what he'd done while under Kaye's control wasn't his fault, and that he'd do whatever it took to redeem himself, even if that meant risking his life for those kids. I knew the look well. It was the same one I saw every time I passed a mirror.

"No morrre misterrr nice guy," he said.

He flicked his eyes at Kaye, and dragged a clawed fingertip across a granite countertop, sending up sparks. I might have shivered, but the effect was ruined by the tongue lolling out the side of Humphrey's canine mouth.

"I know, you're a *stone* cold killer," I said. "Take care of them, big guy."

He nodded, and let out a rumbling laugh. Gargoyle humor at its best.

With a smile, I turned away from Humphrey, noticing that he wasn't the only one in the room whose life had changed with this battle. Arachne chewed the tips of her purple hair, shoulders hunched. Her mother was busy with Circle business, and I think it was just dawning on the kid that she no longer had a job. She looked horribly lost.

"Arachne, you want to go with them?" I asked.

I gestured to where Father Michael stood holding Sparky in his arms, Humphrey a vigilant shadow at their side.

"R-r-really?" she asked.

"Really," I said, holding her gaze. "I trust you. I know that Kaye made you do things you didn't want to, but that you always tried to do the right thing. What you held in your heart, that's what counts."

Arachne started to cry, and I took a step away. I couldn't comfort her. I couldn't risk touching her skin and triggering a vision, not now. I had to leave the kids in Father Michael's hands, and pray that we all survived the night.

Somehow I suspected that if anyone was listening, that was a prayer that might get granted.

Torn also backed away from Arachne, grimacing at the display of tears. In fact, he nearly ran all the way to the door, slowing only once to whisper something to Midnight, Kaye's cat familiar. Within seconds, we were out on the sidewalk, gulping in the exhaust-filled city air.

I tried to spread my wings, but the wing on the right protested in pain. I'd have to let it heal before I attempted to fly again. I guess that meant we'd be running back to the industrial park.

"What did you say to Midnight?" I asked.

"I granted him permission to live in my city," he said. "He is no longer Kaye's familiar. The Circle broke their connection when they wrapped Kaye in that magic dampening garment. Midnight is a free cat which means he needs my permission to live in Harborsmouth."

I didn't know much about cat sidhe politics. Torn rarely shared his people's secrets.

"What would have happened if you didn't give your permission?" I asked.

Torn extended a razor-sharp claw, and drew it across his throat.

"Then he would have been executed," he said.

He held my gaze with slit-pupil eyes, and never smiled. A cold sensation hit heavy in my stomach. Torn was deadly serious, and it was a reminder that I was now part of a harsh world that played by a different set of rules—rules that could mean my death if I wasn't careful.

I swallowed hard, and set off toward the industrial park.

CHAPTER 35

I texted Jinx with a status update. I should have called, but I knew that she would start crying at the news that Sparky was unharmed. I tried to convince myself that texting was the better option because we didn't have time for tears, but really, I was just a coward.

I also had a nagging suspicion that Jinx's tears would be contagious, and that if I started crying now, I'd never stop. But I did call Ceff.

According to Jinx's text messages, Ceff had returned to the harbor. He'd gone to rally the water fae to our cause, which would not be an easy task. The water fae would be hesitant to lend the humans of Harborsmouth aid, especially after suffering so many losses here so recently. Kelpies, selkies, and merrow had participated in the battle against the *each uisge* last year, and many of them were ripped apart, their bodies shredded and eaten.

It was a wonder that the harbor waters didn't still run red with their blood.

Now we faced another terrifying enemy, one so powerful its leader was once thought a god. The Wild Hunt may be limited by the restriction to only hunt at night, but that only added to the terror it instilled in the hearts of men and fae alike. At sunset, Herne would sound his horn and the hunt would begin.

The hounds, each a twisted mutation of a barghest, would vent their anger on the free people of this city with tooth and claw. I'd heard of what just one rogue barghest could do. What fresh Hell would an entire pack unleash on Harborsmouth?

Even worse, the twisted hounds weren't the only enemy we faced tonight. The only thing that made a rogue barghest vulnerable was that it always fought alone. The Wild Hunt was something else entirely, a horrific amalgam of order and chaos. The hounds of the Wild Hunt stalked and attacked their prey in unison. They were a unit of monstrous supernatural soldiers whose every movement was controlled by a brilliant tactician.

Before becoming Mab's creature, Herne had been a man. That man was Gwyn ap Nudd, a legendary general of vast armies with decades of battle experience. Mab took that great man and jammed a powerful spirit of the forest inside of him. I'm not sure if the horrific experiment was a punishment or for her amusement, but the Queen of Air and Darkness was never one to pass up an opportunity.

In addition to his physical transformation, Mab gave Herne a horse, a hound, and a curse. It was then that the Wild Hunt was born. And the curse allowed Herne's pack of hounds to grow, so that no matter how many times he lost a hound, there was always some poor soul to take its place.

From what I understood, the curse caused anyone injured by a hound during the hunt to become part of the Wild Hunt. Now we were asking the water fae not only to risk their lives, but also to risk that terrible fate. Anyone injured in this battle could become one of Herne's slaves, a hound forced to eat the flesh of its former comrades. It was a lot to ask.

Ceff would remind the water fae of how the land fae, witches, and human members of the Hunters' Guild had helped to break the enchantment that enslaved him to the *each uisge*. We'd played a role in saving the kelpie king, but not until he'd already suffered captivity and extreme torture. The water fae had died horrible, bloody deaths, and they had long memories.

It would take all of Ceff's charisma and royal negotiating skills to enlist the water fae's help against Herne and his hounds.

The man could use some good news.

I dialed, and Ceff answered on the third ring. I took that as a lucky sign. If he'd been deep in negotiations, it was unlikely he'd have answered the phone. Maybe the talks with the water fae had gone well. Either that or the talks had ended before they'd even begun. At least I had some good news for him.

"Hey," I said. "This a good time?"

"It is always a good time to hear your voice," he said. "Are you well?"

I heard warbling, burbling voices and hurried to give him the news.

"Yes, sorry," I said. "I know you're busy, I just wanted to let you know we're all okay. Sparky too. He's back at the loft with Father Michael and Arachne."

"Thank the tides," he whispered.

He sounded exhausted, his voice ragged with emotion. I wasn't the only one who'd grown attached to Sparky.

"Humphrey is also there to keep an eye on them tonight," I said. "I told him he could stay on my building from now on."

"Then the young ones are in good hands," he said. "The priest is a man of great knowledge, and the gargoyle has the potential to become a great warrior."

"You have no idea," I said, thinking back to Humphrey's fierce declaration that he would protect our hodgepodge family and home.

The gargoyle was keen to redeem himself for the things that Kaye had made him do.

"Am I to understand that Humphrey being without a home means that you have turned the Emporium to rubble?" he asked.

"Of course, she did, Fish Breath," Torn said, interrupting.

I sniffed, spine straightening. Faerie hearing had its disadvantages, namely that my private conversation could be interrupted by the troublesome cat sidhe.

"You make it sound like I destroyed the place on purpose," I said, scowling at Torn.

"I believe what the cat is saying is that you cannot help yourself," Ceff said.

"Not helping," I said, gripping the phone tight.

The plastic case made an ominous cracking noise, and Torn pointed at it.

"Case in point, Princess," he said. "You break things. You stab things. You burn them to the ground. It's what you do."

"You make me sound like a menace," I said, frowning at Torn.

"That's because you are a menace, Princess," Torn said, licking his lips. "That's what makes you so irresistibly delicious."

"She is MY menace, cat," Ceff said, the phone's speaker squeaking in its effort to convey the supersonic power of his wrath. "You would do well to remember that fact."

My chest tightened with pride until I realized he too had called me a menace. I shook my head, and wiggled a gloved finger in my ear.

"While I'd love to debate my being a delicious menace, we don't have time," I said. I eyed the sun's low position in the sky, and a cold, oily sensation churned my stomach. "We're heading to the industrial park. Any luck with the water fae?"

The voices that had been a constant background murmur went silent. A second later, I heard one last intake of Ceff's breath, and the line went dead.

CHAPTER 36

"You tell me," Ceff said, a rare grin making his face painfully beautiful.

I'd nearly barreled headlong into his chest as I rounded the corner, the silent phone still held in a death-grip in my gloved hand. Torn had been a speeding shadow at my side, but upon Ceff's appearance, he leaned against a nearby building and feigned bored indifference. I, on the other hand, thought my heart might pound itself free of my chest.

"What?" I asked, barely able to form words.

It wasn't just Ceff's beauty that had me befuddled. The entire street was filled with water fae.

"On the phone, Princess," Torn said, rolling his eyes. "You asked if fish breath here had had any luck with the water fae. Apparently, he did. Either that or I missed the memo about a water fae street parade."

I blinked at Torn, and back at Ceff whose tanned skin had regained its healthy hue. The trip to his ocean kingdom had restored his vigor, and his smile was contagious. I returned the smile, breath catching in my throat.

"The water fae?" I asked.

"I wanted to surprise you, my love," he said. "An early wedding gift for you."

He knew my abhorrence of gifts, and yet right now I might turn into a sniveling mess at what he'd given me. This was no paper-wrapped vision-inducing bauble. This was a chance to save the city I loved.

A tear ran down my cheek, and I blinked at the kelpies, selkies, and merfolk who'd ventured onto land as a favor to the kelpie king and his bride-to-be. Ceff had given me the best gift anyone could ever bestow. He gave me hope.

"Not very romantic, even for you two," Torn said, squinting at the assembled crowd.

His eyes widened, and he let out an appreciative purr when he noticed one of the drop dead gorgeous, and very naked, mermaids. She too noticed Torn, and I shook my head.

"You think we should warn him?" I asked, tilting my head at Ceff.

"Let him learn his own lessons," he said, lip twitching.

The mermaid ran a hand down her buxom chest, drawing Torn's attention. I'm almost certain he missed the flash of razor-sharp teeth, and the shadows around her brow and cheekbones that hinted at a woman on a starvation diet. She arched her back, posing for Torn, and eyed the cat sidhe hungrily. I'd seen that same look on supermodels in restaurant ads.

"Kind of hard to learn a lesson when you're dead," I muttered.

"The cat is foolish, but perhaps you are right," Ceff said. "We do need him to survive the night. We need the help of every ally in the coming battle."

"You do realize I can hear you, don't you, fish for brains?" Torn asked.

But he was still mesmerized by the mermaid's body. He had no idea how perilously close her shark-like jaws were to his jugular. He froze only when fishy smelling saliva slid onto his skin.

"Cellestrania, my dear," Ceff said, his tone the same one might use when reprimanding a naughty child. "Do not eat our allies."

Vibrant green eyes locked on Ceff's face, but her mouth remained inches away from Torn's neck. Burbling voices whispered up and down the street, and I had the curious notion that the other water fae were placing bets.

My money was on the mermaid.

Saliva continued to pour from her too-wide mouth, but that wasn't all it did. The mermaid was water fae, therefore having power over all liquids. I barely repressed a shudder as a strand of saliva slid along Torn's neck and traveled down his chest and beneath the leather vest he wore. He closed his eyes, and groaned.

I wasn't sure if that groan was due to horror or desire, and I was pretty sure I didn't want to know.

"A little help here?" he asked.

I wrinkled my nose, and nodded to Ceff. I'd seen enough.

"Come on, call her off," I said. "We need to get back to the industrial park and give Master Janus a status update."

"Come, Cellestrania," Ceff said. "Do not make me ask thrice."

Something shifted behind the mermaid's eyes, something that made my bowels turn to icy liquid, but whatever evil lurked inside her soul, it was now under control. Cellestrania giggled, immediately transforming into an image of harmless beauty.

Torn moved so fast, he was a blur that even my eyes couldn't track. One moment he was inches from the mermaid's ample bosom, and the next he was at my side. He shrugged, and I sighed.

"Come on," I said. "I have a feeling we're in for a long night."

I loped forward, Ceff and Torn keeping stride, an entire army of water fae at our back. They remained quiet, each lost in thought. Torn was probably dreaming up a way to turn his run-in with the mermaid into a sexy story, but I knew that Ceff, like me, was strategizing about how best to allocate our new troops. Neither one of us was keen on tossing lives away.

A howl broke the silence, setting my teeth on edge.

"You know, Princess," Torn said with a wink, an eager gleam in his eye. "I do hope you're right."

I wasn't sure if he was eager for a bloody battle, or a rematch with the deadly mermaid. Once again, I really didn't want to know. What I did know was that we had very little time left to convince Master Janus of our plans for facing the Wild Hunt.

The sun slid lower in the sky, and I swallowed hard. I'd lost too much time rescuing the kids from Kaye. Their welfare had kept my mind busy, but now there were no more distractions. I had to face the fact that Harborsmouth was about to face its most dangerous threat, and I had no idea if we could win.

Ignoring the pain in my hip, I broke into a run.

CHAPTER 37

Eyes wide, I scanned the area once again. I almost didn't recognize the industrial park. Master Janus had been busy.

He'd assembled his troops into two squads of a dozen men and women that fanned out to the north and south of the warehouse he'd allocated as a base of operations, and an additional patrol of two dozen Hunters roamed the perimeter. Some were new recruits, but most were seasoned by combat with rogue fae and vamps. All were well trained.

Janus strode forward, and nodded at me before coming nose to nose with Ceff. Hunters tensed, weapons bristling, but Janus smiled and gripped Ceff's forearm in both hands.

"Well met, Ceffyl Dwr," he said. The man was practically vibrating with nervous energy, his excitement evident as his words thickened with the brogue of his native Scotland. "I don't ken how ye've done it, but we got every water fae for leagues pouring into the city offering their aid." He turned to me, eyes twinkling. "This plan of yours might just work after all."

"Thanks for the vote of confidence," I said with a snort. "I didn't hear you complaining when I brought it up before."

"I ken your plan had a yeti's chance in Hell of succeeding, but it was the best option we had. Thanks to this man, we might make it out of this with our hides intact," he said, releasing Ceff's arm, and slapping him on the back.

I might have giggled at the sheer look of bewilderment on Ceff's face, if the topic wasn't such a serious one. Herne wasn't willing to negotiate, and now we knew that not only was the Wild Hunt's presence here intentional, it was the first act in a violent war that could decimate the human population, and turn supernatural friends and family against one another.

Even worse, Mab was pulling at least some of the strings leading us all to war. That didn't bode well, not at all. The Queen of Air and Darkness wasn't known for her sanity, or her mercy.

"You took my advice regarding the merfolk, then?" Ceff asked. "I would hate to waste what good will I've earned."

Janus and Ceff exchanged a look, but the guild master chuckled and slapped Ceff's back one more time.

"Don't you worry yer head now," he said. "Those brazen lasses won't be eatin' any of my men this day, though I appreciate your warnings."

I swallowed hard, trying not to think about the lack of restraint of my boyfriend's mer cousins. I'd seen what a mermaid could do to a healthy man, and it wasn't pretty. In fact, the mer were just the kind of supernaturals who might side with Mab and the rogue vampires who wished to declare open season on human flesh. Thankfully, most mermaids were easily distracted by shiny things, and Ceff had centuries of treasure to dangle before his allies.

"Is everything in place?" I asked.

"Aye," Janus said. "Is it true we'll be losing your demon ally this fight?"

"Yes," I said. "We can't let Yue Fei's rogue vampire faction take over the city. Forneus is the most powerful fire mage we have, and flame is a vampire's greatest weakness."

"I can't say I'll miss his company—don't think I'll ever be comfortable with a demon in my ranks—but I wish him well," he said. "I can't think of a worthier mission. Let us know if Forneus and Benmore need assistance. We're already spread thin, but with the water fae's assistance, we're in better shape than I'd hoped. I'll risk a few of my best if it keeps the bloodsuckers from our necks."

"Thanks, I'll pass that along," I said. I figured my friends had gone over the details of our failed attempt to negotiate with Herne, but it didn't hurt to make sure. Not that I had any good news on that front. "Also, you should know that Herne said Mab is behind the Wild Hunt's escape from Faerie. I don't know her connection to Yue Fei, but with Mab, it sounds like she'll use anyone who will further her goal of inflicting chaos and terror, and gaining power."

He grimaced, but nodded sharply.

"Not welcome information, but good intel all the same," he said. "You did good out there, lass."

I bit my lip, and smoothed a hand down the front of my jacket.

"You might not think so highly of me, or my efforts, if you knew the full truth, Janus," I said.

I'd taken a risk telling him that I was full-blooded fae, but I hadn't gone so far as to tell him who my faerie mother was. It hadn't felt necessary at the time, but circumstances had changed.

"Ivy..." Ceff said.

"No, he deserves to know," I said.

"Whatever you wish to unburden yourself of, I suggest ye be quick about it," Janus said, eyeing the sky. "We're running low on daylight."

I took a deep breath. It was time to rip off the band-aid. I'd vowed not to live a life of dishonesty and secrets. Now was the time to live up to that promise.

"I recently learned something more than just the truth of my fae blood," I said. I stared at my boots for a second before meeting Janus' eyes, and I tried not to flinch at the intensity of his gaze. "I learned who my biological mother was. It's not something I'm proud of, but it's also not something I chose."

"Your mother is the Unseelie queen," he said.

I gaped at him.

"You knew?" I asked.

I had my suspicions, but I didn't ken for sure until my men heard some of what Herne was shouting. That's when it all made sense, as much as faerie politics ever rightly do."

"You do not hold it against Ivy?" Ceff asked, hand going to his side where I knew a weapon could be drawn if needed.

"If we were held for the crimes of our parents, most of my men would be in prison or worse," he said, shaking his head. "We all have skeletons in our closets. You immortals just tend to accumulate ones with sharper claws, and longer memories."

"You have no bloody idea how right you are," Torn said, stepping from the shadows.

I don't know how long Torn had been lurking there, but I figured he'd heard most of what we'd discussed.

"Ready to chase some hounds?" I asked.

Torn's cat-slit eyes widened, and razor-sharp claws slid from his fingertips.

"I'm always ready to show a bunch of pups who's boss," he asked.

I could imagine the cat sidhe lord chasing a barghest up a tree. He'd do it on principle, if not for the sheer challenge of it. At least someone would be enjoying this fight.

"Then let's go wish Forneus luck, and hope this doesn't blow up in our faces," I said.

"It wouldn't be a proper fight without bloodshed, Princess," he said.

"That's what I'm afraid of," I said.

If Forneus and Benmore failed to destroy Yue Fei and his rogue vampires, and my plan to rout the Wild Hunt from the city's population dense downtown failed, there'd be more bloodshed to come. Perhaps more bloodshed than the world had seen in hundreds of years. The only consolation was that we wouldn't be around long enough to see the bloodsuckers, and my mother, take over the world.

Small comfort that.

CHAPTER 38

I'd worried that the night might end with us all on our knees before Herne and his hounds. What I hadn't prepared myself for was finding Forneus in that position before my best friend.

"Good, you're finally here," he said. "You do know how to keep a man waiting."

"And you know how to create a dramatic moment," I muttered, but a smile tugged at my lips.

I may never understand what Jinx sees in Forneus, but I couldn't deny the fact that they were crazy about each other. With all of our lives on the line, emotions were high and the important things were brought into focus. If Forneus wanted to make a declaration of love and commitment on the eve of our potential demise, who was I to argue?

Jinx looked dumbstruck as Forneus reached for her hand.

"You're...you...you didn't drop something, did you?" she stuttered.

"No, my dear," he said. "But I did lose something the day we met. The moment I first saw you, you stole my heart. Though it is already yours, I wish now to give it willingly."

Forneus reached inside his jacket, and pulled out a small, crystalline box that seemed to glow from within. If that was a ring, it sure didn't come from Tiffany's.

He opened the box to reveal a ring set with a ruby the size of a robin's egg.

"Will you restore the piece of my soul that I lost when I fell?" he asked. "Will you become my wings so I may be lifted up once more?"

I'd always assumed that Forneus was a mere demon—a self-aggrandizing demon with delusions of grandeur, and enough titles to choke an ogre—but a demon nonetheless. But if his words were more than mere ceremony, then perhaps Forneus had once been more than a demon. It might explain his capacity for love.

Who would understand love and its loss more keenly than one of The Fallen?

Jinx sucked in a ragged breath, and started shaking her head. Forneus paled, but clung to Jinx's hand, waiting for her reply. I held my breath. Was she going to refuse?

"I didn't steal your heart, you stole mine," she said. Her lip quivered, but she pushed on, keeping her eyes locked with Forneus. "I was so afraid you'd try to steal my soul, I didn't even notice you stealing my heart until I was completely in love with you."

"You do love me?" he asked. "A wretched demon? A creature of Hell?"

"I don't care what you are, or where you're from," she said. "We don't choose our families, or how we come into this world."

I swallowed hard, a lump forming in my throat. Her words were for Forneus, but it was still a relief to hear them from my best friend's lips.

"You are not afraid of me stealing your soul?" he asked.

Forneus slowly stood, and cupped her face with one hand, the fingers of his other hand still entwined with hers. Jinx pressed into his touch, and sighed.

"If the threat is to set me aflame for all eternity, what's there to be afraid of?" she asked.

She moved closer, but he held her from him.

"Is that a yes?" he asked. "Will you marry me, and grant me this one happiness?"

"I'll grant you more than one," she said with a wink.

He groaned, but held her in place.

"Jinx...I must know," he said. "Please do not make me beg."

"I like begging," she said.

"You will be the death of me," he said.

"Yes," she said.

"Yes?" he asked.

"Yes, I will marry you," she said. "But I want..."

He drowned her words in a kiss, swallowing her murmured protest. Her hand fisted on his chest briefly, but quickly spread out and made its way to his waist. I blushed, suddenly wishing a barghest would attack and save me from watching my friends hump each other in the street.

Torn coughed, and I cleared my throat.

"Um, congratulations, you guys," I said.

"May you both find solace in one another to weather all storms," Ceff said.

Forneus and Jinx broke apart, and she smiled as he slipped the ruby ring on her finger.

"Wow," she said breathlessly. "That's some ring."

She slowly moved away from Forneus, and ran a hand over her dress, though I noticed her eyes didn't stray far from his.

"I wish we could throw you two a party, but celebrations will have to wait," I said.

"We'll celebrate with bloodshed," Torn said, his claws extending and retracting.

"And flame," Forneus said, fire flickering along his fingertips.

"Show offs," I said, shaking my head. "Come on. Let's get ready."

With one last heated kiss, Forneus strode away, leaving Jinx licking her lips with a sigh. I sent up a silent prayer, though I'm not sure the sense of praying for a demon. Who would hear that prayer? Lucifer? God? I wasn't sure, but I wished him success against the rogue vampires.

Yue Fei was no green initiate. He had centuries of battle experience, and the loyalty of well-trained warriors. Warrior samurai vampires—Oberon save us all.

"Looks like we might have a double wedding, if we survive the night," Torn said, pulling me from my dark thoughts.

He sauntered off as if he hadn't a care in the world, but I had to wonder if it was apathy or artifice. Torn had lived a long time. Even with his many conquests, it must be lonely to always be a man apart. He'd ruled the cat sidhe for decades, and wandered the world for centuries, but the closest he'd come to love was a tumultuous relationship with a kitsune queen that had ended so badly he refused to speak of it.

How difficult was it for Torn to see us pairing off, and making plans for our futures?

"What did he mean by double wedding?" Jinx asked.

I cleared my throat, mouth going dry. I'd faced down monsters. I could give my friend the good news about my engagement to Ceff, right?

Oberon's eyes, I'd rather battle Herne with a nail file.

"Um, about that…" I said, running a hand through my hair.

"Oh my god," she said, eyes wide. "Ceff proposed, didn't he?"

"Yes," I said.

"And you didn't tell me?" she asked.

She was trying to sound hurt, but the effect was somewhat diminished by the fact she was bouncing up and down, just like Sparky when he'd snuck into the kitchen and ate an entire bag of coffee beans.

"I haven't had a chance," I said with a one-armed shrug.

"Well?" she asked. "What did you say?"

"I said yes," I said.

I sighed, but couldn't control the idiotic grin that took over my face.

"You said yes?" she asked. "Oh my god, Ivy! You said yes. I said yes. We. Are. Getting. Married."

"Yes, well, don't go planning any big parties just yet," I said.

"Double wedding," she mouthed, and I groaned.

Damn Torn and his meddlesome mouth. If I lived through the night, I'd be subjected to an even more terrifying battle—the battle over wedding plans. Death was beginning to sound better by the minute.

CHAPTER 39

Jinx kept up a never-ending banter with mind-numbing wedding plan details, stopping only when we rounded the corner that ended the row of rusting warehouses.

"Wow," she gasped, hand going to her mouth.

Wow, indeed.

Master Janus and Ceff's most trusted kelpie lieutenants had been busy putting my plan in place. Hunters were heavily armed, and assembled in small strike units. Alongside them, water fae flowed through the crowd. Their movements were fluid and graceful, but no doubt deadly.

It was no great surprise that the kelpies, some in humanoid form and others in their horse forms, were there. Ceff was a fair and honorable king who inspired loyalty amongst his people, but the kelpies were not the only water fae to have come. There were selkies with their large, dark eyes, and mermaids splashed tauntingly at the river's edge.

We were at the edge of the industrial part of the city where warehouses sprouted from the harbor and mills grew up from the banks of the brackish river. But we were not that far away from the Old Port Quarter where humans would be getting off work and stopping to grab groceries, or a pint at their favorite dive bar or pub. Just a few more blocks away, tourists dined in fancy restaurants and shopped in stylish boutiques as office workers poured like ants from gleaming towers of steel and glass.

My plan was a simple one. As soon as I learned about the Wild Hunt's aversion to water, I began scheming ways to form a dragnet of allies to harry our enemy, forcing Herne and his barghest hounds away from the population dense areas of downtown Harborsmouth.

I couldn't guarantee that there wouldn't be innocent civilian casualties, but I vowed that we would do everything possible to keep their number to a minimum. In this, we were in perfect agreement with the Hunters' Guild. They would take every step necessary to protect the humans of Harborsmouth.

The water fae's magic was integral to our plan, but I was also counting on their presence to ensure the protection of the other innocents of this city. Just as not all fae were monsters, we were not all-powerful or trained for battle either. Yes, many fae had the capacity for magic and cunning, but some focused on healing, nurturing plants, and raising families.

I'd met some of these fae while rescuing their children from an abductor who planned to use their souls for his own selfish ends. Furred, feathered, spiny, or scaled—fae families had wept and pleaded for their children's safety, and they'd all rejoiced when they'd been reunited. It was for those families that I now fought, just as much as for the humans who remained blissfully unaware of the threat that once more lurked at their doorstep.

My chest tightened as I looked out over our assembled allies, humans and fae come together for a common cause.

"Ceff, you did it," I said, voice hardly a whisper.

"No, Ivy," he said, a satisfied smile on his lips. "We did this."

"And it's not the first time, is it, lass?" Janus asked, stepping forward.

I tilted my head to the side, and frowned.

"I'm pretty sure I've never fought the Wild Hunt before, not even in my nightmares," I said. "Of which I've got quite the collection."

I muttered the last, narrowing my eyes at the assembled crowd. For all their determined faces, this could still go terribly wrong in so many ways it made my head spin. I tried to etch their whole bodies and hopeful faces into my mind. Those images would be preferable to what I might see this night. Our large numbers meant that much more potential nightmare fodder.

I shook myself as Torn slipped out of the shadow cast by the nearest warehouse.

"Janus is right, Princess," he said, waving a lofty hand at the well-armed men. "This isn't the first time you've brought this city together. You have an uncanny ability to bring enemies together as allies. Sometimes you even manage to create lasting bonds between us."

I thought over the events of the past year, the months that passed here in the human world, and nodded. Torn and Janus had a point. When the *each uisge* attacked last fall, I somehow begged, pleaded, and bargained my way into gathering an army of Seelie, Unseelie, and witches. Hell, even the undead had lent a hand in stemming the panic that the monstrous attack could have caused. It had also been the first time I'd worked with any of the Hunters' Guild, and began to build trust between us.

Since then, I'd continued to work with opposing factions of humans and supernaturals throughout the city on various cases. Many individuals—humans, demons, kelpies, trolls, hobgoblins, witches, and Hunters—I'd come to consider my friends. Through blood, sweat, and tears, we'd become a family. That family was often at each other's throats, and dysfunctional as hell, but I couldn't deny that we'd forged something special.

We had a bond that couldn't be broken. In fact, each new threat only made us stronger. I wiped a hand over my face, and sniffed hard. Pesky allergies.

"I didn't do it on my own," I said, nodding at my friends. "I couldn't have saved the city from the *each uisge*, or rescued those kids from the Danse Macabre, or brought an army together today without all of your help."

"See," Torn said, raising an eyebrow. "There she goes, doing it again."

"She really is kind of awesome," Jinx said with a wink.

"You are a natural leader, Ivy," Ceff said. "You care about this city, and all of its inhabitants. That is why people trust you, and rally to our cause. Your love knows no bounds. It is your greatest strength."

And my greatest weakness. But I kept that last thought to myself. No point being a downer. We'd need every bit of hope and good will we could manage.

I wasn't kidding myself. We had a solid plan, but the Wild Hunt was no easy foe. This wasn't the first time this city had faced a barghest. Last time, it had taken every magic user in the city to bring down one beast. Now there were dozens of hounds, and they were led by a powerful faerie who was possessed by a great spirit and driven by a vicious, spiteful queen.

I looked out over the Hunters and the water fae. I'd spent my life on the periphery, never truly belonging. Today, I realized that I was part of something greater, something larger than myself. With that came the heavy weight of responsibility.

For each man or woman who died today, blood would be on my hands. I didn't relish killing, even if it would mean freeing members of the Wild Hunt from decades of enslavement. But my friends were right. I'd become good at fighting our enemies, even when those fights ended with taking a life.

I swallowed hard, and looked to the sky. Giant owls circled ominously overhead, relaying our every move to our enemy. We needed to act soon, before Herne and his hounds began their hunt, but, with a bit of luck, I had one more ace up my sleeve.

I'd sent Marvin and Hob to the suburbs on a mission. That mission served the dual purpose of keeping them out of the action, and to rally the pooka to our cause. Originally, I'd hoped to entice the pooka to use their thief skills to steal a piece of Herne. That plan had changed.

When I learned of Kaye's intention of binding the Wild Hunt to her own will to use as a weapon in the coming war, I began questioning the pooka's mission. Later, when it became apparent that Herne was using giant owls as spies, a new plan began to take form.

I had a new primary mission for the pooka, and I'd managed to contact Marvin with this new plan. Trouble was, there was no guarantee that the pooka would accept the bargain. I watched the sky attentively, releasing a breath only when I saw a swarm of bright, glowing caps flit through the air.

That was my signal. I pulled my gaze from the sky, and looked out over the crowd of Hunters and water fae. I had to trust that the pooka would do their job keeping Herne's spies busy.

I drew my blades, and held them above my head. The steady buzz of a multitude of conversations quieted instantly.

Blood roared in my ears, old fears making my mouth go dry. But I swallowed hard, and met the eyes of the assembled.

"Thank you all for coming," I said. "The Wild Hunt threatens this city. At sunset, Herne will ride, and his hounds will hunt us, both human and fae alike."

"Let 'em try!" someone shouted.

I waited for the chuckles and back slapping to subside.

"Together, we can stop the Hunt, and put an end to the senseless suffering and enslavement of men and women whose only crime was to be in the Wild Hunt's path," I said. "But first, we must nip at their heels before they taste our blades."

I turned to Ceff, and nodded.

"Water fae," he said, raising his trident. "It is time to change the tides of this battle. Tonight, we will coax every river, stream, and wave to our cause. Safe tides and blissful currents!"

"Safe tides!" they shouted.

Water fae lifted their hands, and closed their eyes. Mermaids began to sing. Hunters knocked arrows, or drew their swords.

As the last rays of sun shone on Harborsmouth, we marched.

CHAPTER 40

The pooka took to their mission with enthusiasm. The tiny faeries carried a creative collection of weapons, including an assortment of sharpened tools, but the most effective were the aerosol sprays. More than one owl plummeted from the sky, harried by pooka, after being blinded by bug repellant, pepper spray, deodorant—even silly string.

With Herne's spies temporarily out of the picture, Hunters marched toward the Wild Hunt's position. Our plan was to rout the Hunt further into the industrial district, away from the business and residential areas where there would be a much higher rate of civilian casualties.

Chaos filled the darkening skies as pookas harassed Herne's giant owls, and all around us squads of Hunters fanned out between the warehouses to form a wall of human flesh. But as the sun slipped behind the silhouette of city buildings, a horn rang out—once, twice, three times. A shiver ran up my spine, and I sent up a silent prayer to any gods who might be listening.

Kaye had warned us that Herne would sound his horn thrice, and the Wild Hunt would ride at sunset. She'd ordered us to retrieve a piece of Herne so that she could bind the Wild Hunt to her will. I'd defied that order, and, for once, ignored her wisdom. Hopefully, I wouldn't regret that choice.

I stumbled as a howl split through the night. Ceff hesitated, but I shook my head.

"I'm fine," I said, gripping my blades tight.

True blooded fae can't lie, but we can find ways to bend the truth. When I said that I was fine, I meant that I hadn't injured myself in my fall. But I wasn't fine. After leading the Wild Hunt to Harborsmouth, I wasn't sure if I'd ever be fine again.

But now was the time for false assurances. We couldn't afford any additional distractions. Ceff's attention was already split between issuing orders, summoning the water from the nearby river, and keeping an eye on my safety. Not that I needed a protector, but he ignored my protests, no matter how many times I insisted the last was unnecessary.

So we ran together, Ceff a calming presence at my side. I focused on that sense of calm, and the sound of Ceff's melodic voice issuing orders, as I located and identified targets. Not that the Wild Hunt's hounds were hard to miss.

It has been speculated that barghests originated as the unfortunate offspring of a mauthe doog, a type of fae black dog, and a hellhound. With their bristling, spiny, black fur, needle-like claws, and glowing, red eyes that wasn't hard to believe. They were each larger than a mastiff, with jaws that could snap a grown man's bones, or tear off an arm or leg for a chew toy.

Not only did we rush headlong toward those gaping, slavering, teeth-filled jaws, but we did so with smiles on our faces. In fact, Torn was singing something about dogs and bones with such glee that the nearest Hunters shot him nervous glances, and gave him a wide berth.

Hunters pounded swords against shields as we ran, and dark shadows arced over our heads as bowmen launched a volley of arrows at the hounds. The barghests slowed, for the first time questioning the strength of their prey.

As we closed the distance, Jinx lent her crossbow to the fray, and I set an iron and silver spike flying with the snap of my wrist. It wasn't one of my blades, I'd save those for later, but the spike—a particularly long and heavy nail I'd filled my pockets with from the Hunters' Guild armory—would be a nasty surprise, one that was likely to slow the barghest whose hide I'd pierced.

The air filled with startled whines followed by angry growls. The ground rumbled with the barghest's fierce anger and desire for revenge. We had the hound's attention. Now to give the Hunt what they wanted.

Herne and his hounds wanted a hunt, and we planned to give them a merry chase. We ran, but rather than backtrack toward downtown, we veered hard to the west. With barghests and Herne riding close at our backs, we ran across crumbling pavement and between rusting storage buildings.

Earlier in the day, with the help of Master Janus, I'd pored over maps of the city. The largest area that lay outside the heavily populated areas of the city was split in two by the

Opechobee River. Old mills and docks had sprouted along the banks of the river over a hundred years ago. Now that area was an industrial area housing most of the city's warehouses, factories, storage buildings, and more than a few vacant lots.

It was also, thankfully, not far from Eben Braxton's junkyard. I shuddered to think of the carnage if the portal from Faerie had opened in the center of the city. Thank Oberon, that hadn't been the case.

The Wild Hunt's instincts, and Mab's directive to gather more souls to the Hunt, would drive Herne and his hounds deeper into the city. That's where our revised plan came into play.

I'd been toying with the idea of using the Wild Hunt's aversion to water against them. When I voiced my concern over the location of the river, Ceff had suggested we incorporate that problem into our plan. It relied on a huge outpouring of support from the kelpies and their allies to succeed, but Ceff had somehow enlisted the aid of water fae in large numbers.

Those fae were now hard at work. Kelpies, mermaids, selkies, and other exotic water fae I couldn't name, sang, danced, and lifted webbed hands to the air, and the night filled with the sound of rushing water.

The river to our left kept us from pushing the Wild Hunt farther south, so we did the unexpected.

We moved the river.

CHAPTER 41

The scent of mud, fish, and river water was strong as the water fae lifted the entire river incrementally into the air. It was slow going at first. I caught glimpses of the rising river from between buildings as we ran. It moved inch by inch at the start, and I wondered if we'd misjudged.

Even with my enhanced fae strength, speed, and agility, I was beginning to tire. My calf muscles burned, and the damp air seemed to scrape inside my throat and lungs with each ragged breath. Ceff, Torn, and I were no strangers to hard exercise, but we hadn't had a moment of rest since returning through the portal, and our final day in Faerie hadn't been a peaceful one. I'd risked our deaths passing through the Forest of Torment, entered Mab's winter palace, pushed through my uncle's incarceration, and faced down the entire Unseelie court with the knowledge that once we returned home to Harborsmouth, I could finally sleep in my own bed.

So far, that hadn't happened. They didn't complain, but I guessed that Ceff and Torn couldn't be faring much better. My uncle had imprisoned them in iron chains, and it wasn't the first time that Ceff had been poisoned with iron sickness. Each exposure left him weaker and more vulnerable.

Not that anyone would think Ceff or Torn were weak by looking at them. They both raced along at my side, two wing men who promised death to any barghest that dared take a swipe at me. But I had to wonder just how long we could keep this up. Eventually, we'd tire, and one of us would die.

At least I'd been able to convince Jinx to join the archers on the rooftops. From there she could harass the barghests without the threat of stumbling and ending up as a chew toy. I just had to trust that Janus' men would keep one eye to the sky. Herne and the barghests weren't the only threats. The sky was still filled with the battle cries of pookas as they attacked Herne's giant owls, but the tiny faeries were also tiring.

Fatigue wasn't our only problem. We were running out of road.

Torn wrinkled his nose, and hissed as droplets of river water pelted us from above. The water was cold, murky, and stank of dead fish and a river polluted by factories and city sewage, but I flashed my teeth in a smile, and the men around me threw back their heads and cheered. The water fae had moved the entire Opechobee River.

We'd done it. We managed to lure the Wild Hunt onto a battlefield of our own choosing. The more population dense parts of the city were safely behind us.

"What now, Princess?" Torn asked, as we broke free of the warren of alleys that ran between the warehouses and storage buildings.

I leapt over a dying fish, hoping it wasn't an ill omen. We'd contained the Wild Hunt away from the areas of densest civilian population, but that didn't mean people wouldn't die this night. The first part of my plan was complete, but it was too early to celebrate. We still had a pack of bloodthirsty monsters to battle and an undead uprising to quell.

As the silhouette of Master Janus and his elite unit of Hunters came into sight, I nodded and signaled to our squad to turn and stand our ground. We stopped running, and faced the dark rider with his glowing red eyes and the oncoming pack of angry barghests.

"Now we fight," I said.

CHAPTER 42

Warm blood hit my face, sucking me down into a vision that was blessedly brief. This time I'd had the fortune of being splattered by the blood of a dying pooka, filling my head with a cascade of moments of extreme joy and pleasure, except for the painful moment of his death. Most pookas manage to skate through immortality without the burden of tragedy and mental instability that plagued so many of the larger fae, which meant for shorter visions when my psychometry was triggered by the dying pooka's blood. But even the short visions associated with the pooka's memories were enough of a distraction that I nearly lost a leg.

I sucked in a ragged breath, and struggled out from under Torn who was straddling me with a leering grin.

"Careful, Princess," he said.

"By the tides!" Ceff exclaimed, face blanching as he kicked at the barghest that was snapping its teeth mere inches from my booted foot.

If it hadn't been for Torn's body slam, albeit unpleasant, I'd be barghest food. Even worse, a bite from one of the Hunt would take over my self-control and add me to our enemy's ranks. I'd been fortunate that my friends fought at my side, and that the vision hadn't sucked me deeper into the pooka's memories.

Next time, I may not be so lucky.

Our plan was to try to face Herne and his barghests here, head on, while our archers and our small cavalry of kelpie riders picked off the barghests, drawing them away from Herne, and taking them out one by one. Most of the water fae who weren't needed to hold the river water were set as guards to keep those magic users safe, but some joined in the fight.

It was a good plan, in theory. The terrifying reality was all around us.

For every barghest we cut down, another took its place. It was that horror—the transformation of our friends and brothers in arms—that was the most unsettling of anything I'd ever seen in all my years of observing monsters.

An archer cried out, flailing her arms, as one of Herne's giant owls hooked her shoulder in its talons and tossed her off the warehouse roof where she'd been taking shots at the barghests from behind. I held my breath, watching the body fall, tracing its outline in the failing light. The figure was wearing cargo pants, and I pressed a gloved hand to my mouth in guilty relief that the archer wasn't Jinx.

A large figure rallied a small unit to where the female archer had fallen, and I was surprised to see that not only had the archer survived, but that Hendricks was the man who'd rallied troops to her aid. The large Hunter was a chauvinistic bigot who despised me and everything I stood for, but in that moment I admired his bravery.

It was too bad that the man's courage and loyalty to his fallen guild sister would spell out his doom.

Hendricks and the Hunters he led formed a protective perimeter around the archer as one of them got a shoulder under her armpit, and pulled the injured Hunter to her feet.

A roar to my left tore my eyes from the archer, but when Ceff and I put down our barghest with the help of Torn, a female Hunter with a foul mouth, and a merman who fought with a barnacle-covered sword in one hand and rusty boat hook in the other, my curiosity got the better of me. With a brief moment of respite, I lifted my chin in time to see that the barghest that had targeted the fallen archer was now attacking Hendricks and his men as they tried to make their way back to their position.

Hendricks is a huge man, so large and well muscled that I'd often speculated that he had orc blood somewhere in his family tree. To see a man that size fight was impressive. He swung a two-handed battle axe, and took off the barghest's front legs at the knees. The hound went down head first, eating dirt.

At least, that's what the barghest wanted his enemies to think. Hendricks and his men wouldn't be able to see from where they continued their advance across the body-strewn pavement, but at the last second, the enormous hound ducked its head, taking the worst of the fall on its shoulders. It should have snapped its neck, been knocked out, or been suffocated by a face full of mud launched into its nose and mouth at high speed.

The Hunters turned their attention away from the cut-down barghest, and it was a deadly error.

The barghest didn't stop when it hit the ground, instead, it rolled. Still in motion, it used the incredible strength of its rear legs, and sprung into the air. Red eyes fixed on Hendricks, it launched an attack.

I screamed out a warning, but my cries were drowned out by the clamor of battle, the clash of lightning, and the screech of owls overhead. I couldn't leave my unit, and the barghest was too far out of range for my throwing knives to do any good.

Hendricks tried to hold the creature back with the shaft of his axe, but the weapon's handle was slick with blood that still poured from the stumps of the barghest's amputated front legs. The hound shook its head, wrenching the axe handle from Hendricks, and tossed his weapon out of reach.

The barghest's head snaked in, jaws snapping, and bit Hendricks on the shoulder as he tried to buck and roll. Against another monster, the maneuver might have saved his life. The arm on his injured side hung limp and useless, but he managed to pull himself away as the barghest continued to bleed out from its wounds. Adrenaline and the compulsion of his master had pushed the barghest this far, but it was rapidly weakening.

Hendricks pushed the barghest away, and, this time, the beast didn't get up. Its legs kicked uselessly as it bled out, the fire in its eyes extinguished.

A Hunter reached out a hand to help Hendricks to his feet, but he was hardly upright before he fell to his knees. A hound reached my position, and the next time I checked on Hendricks, the Hunter who'd offered him help was face down in the mud, his neck at an impossible angle.

Hendricks roared, his body bending and contorting as he transformed into a hound of the Wild Hunt. Black hair erupted from his flesh, and when he lifted his head his eyes glowed red. Hendricks howled, and Herne's laughter made my stomach churn.

Hendricks had lost his own will, and became one of Herne's hounds.

I stood dumbstruck, only launching back into battle when Ceff cried out my name. Then there was no time to grieve for Hendricks, or worry about the injured archer. There was only blood, and fangs, and screams that would give me an eternity of nightmares—if we survived the night.

CHAPTER 43

It's amazing how slowly time passes when you are surrounded by absolute horror. Now was one of those moments in my life when seconds stretched into eons as I watched the life bleed out from our friends' eyes, and an emptiness worse than death enter the eyes of more friends still. The battle seemed endless.

As we faced our turned brethren, while choking down snot and tears, we were surrounded by Herne's booming laughter as he goaded us into more and more foolish and desperate acts.

"YOU THINK YOU STAND A CHANCE AGAINST THE WILD HUNT?" he asked with exaggerated disdain. "THEN FACE ME AND FIGHT FOR YOUR FALLEN."

He was taunting us, keeping us distracted and emotionally off balance. The Hunters were trained for that kind of mental attack. I'd witnessed the Guild's instructors berating Jenna during practice, and I knew from our conversations that what I'd seen was just the tip of the drill instructor iceberg. It didn't mean that the guild members who fought with us didn't feel emotion. They were just well trained in either burying their sorrow, fear, and rage, or channeling those emotions in a productive way.

No matter how many losses they took, or how badly Herne taunted them, the fighters from the Hunters' Guild kept their heads and wits about them. Some of the water fae were much less experienced in that department.

Micro storms broke out above the uneven pavement and muddy riverbed that had become our primary battlefield. Herne's owls and hounds shied away from spots of rain, but spell clouds did nothing to even the fight. These were manifestations of the water fae's fears and frustrations, and as such the balls of storm were out of control. Lightning and poor footing brought down friend and foe alike.

A sizzling cloud the size of a pillow opened up a deluge of rain and hail over Torn's head, and he hissed.

"Whose bloody side are your men on, fish breath?" he asked.

A hailstone hit my shoulder, and Ceff frowned.

"For once, cat, you may have a point," he said.

Ceff raised his trident, drawing on his power. The unnatural storm clouds whizzing over our heads began to shift and gather in a dark, flickering funnel above his trident. He took control of the chaotic water magic, his eyes shimmering green as he fought to master all that raw power.

With the possible exception of the ocean god Mannan Mac Lir, I doubted any other man could manage to turn that much water magic to his will. But Ceff wasn't just a man. He was Ceffyl Dwr, king of the kelpies.

Muscles flexing and jaw tightening with the strain of his movements, he swept his trident through the air. Wind and water buffeted him, but he held on. I wasn't sure if it was the tilt of his head or the shift of his stance, but I could tell the moment the storm was his to command.

A funnel cloud formed out of the chaos, and a smile drew my lips from my teeth.

Thunder crashed as the funnel cloud smacked into Herne, sending him from his mount. The smile froze on my lips as a young kelpie, barely more than a colt, spooked away from the herd he fought alongside.

The kelpies had been focused on trying to separate one of the barghests, leading it away from its pack and Herne's protection. When the young kelpie ran, the barghest gave chase.

I knew Ceff would go to him before I even felt the shift in magic, or heard his anguished cry. Ceffyl Dwr had lost his sons, had watched helplessly as they were murdered at the hands of a madwoman. He was incapable of standing idly by and watching another young kelpie die.

I loved him for it, even as I cursed him for his empathy. We were losing our momentary advantage over Herne, who had been struck from his saddle. Torn was rushing in, but with Ceff's magic directed elsewhere, barghests were already coming to their master's aid.

I was torn between going to Ceff, or helping to take down Herne. In the end, it wasn't much of a choice. I would always choose to help Ceff save the life of a child.

I ran to Ceff, glancing back only once to see Torn hamstring Herne's mount. It was a wise strategy, keeping Herne from being able to ride and from gaining the saddle where he had a vantage point for watching over the battle and issuing orders. I gave Torn a crisp nod, and turned back to Ceff.

The young kelpie was in his horse form, and he was fleet of hoof. That speed and agility had served him well so far, but it was obvious the kid was tiring. The barghest was gaining on him, clods of mud and chunks of broken pavement flying behind him as his huge paws struck the ground. Oberon's eyes, it was a huge beast.

Was it Hendricks? A lump formed in my throat, and I swallowed hard, shaking off the thought. It didn't matter who or what the barghest used to be. Now it was an enemy, and one that threatened my mate.

I gripped my blades, and closed the distance between us. I was fast, but Ceff and the barghest were faster.

The barghest let out a terrifying howl as it barreled down on its prey, and the young kelpie froze.

"Run!" I screamed, but it was no use.

Skinny legs shaking, it stood as if rooted to the spot. The barghest howled again, and the kelpie let go of its bladder. Its comrades were running now, but they were too far away, and I was too far out of range to risk using one of my throwing knives. At this angle, I might hit Ceff or the young kelpie.

As if in slow motion, the black fur-covered haunches of the hound's flank bunched, and I knew what would happen next. I poured every ounce of strength into my legs, but I was still too far away. The barghest lunged, going in for the kill.

Ceff pushed the young kelpie out of the barghest's reach, and fell beneath a ton of nightmare muscle, claws, and fangs.

CHAPTER 44

Ceff and the barghest went down in a mass of fur and mud. I paced, heart racing, circling the tangle of bodies, but there was no opening. If I threw one of my blades, or jumped into the fray, I'd just as likely skewer Ceff as the barghest.

I gripped my knives, ignoring how damp my hands were inside my gloves, and waited for my shot. My eyes tracked their every movement, with no regard for the rest of the battle. It was as if everything else fell away. It was just me, Ceff, the barghest, and my blades.

I watched, standing on the balls of my feet with every muscle ready to spring into action. Ceff bucked, creating a few inches of space between him and the barghest. I could work with that.

I leapt forward, blades flashing. A throwing knife went into the barghest's eye socket, extinguishing its red glow. A silver and iron spike went into the base of its neck, piercing the spinal column. The barghest froze, and I dove onto its back, grabbed its head, and dragged a blade across its throat.

I turned my head away as blood sprayed over my gloves and jacket, narrowly missing the bare skin of my face. With a shuddering breath, I heaved with all my strength and pushed the barghest to the ground, freeing Ceff who'd been pinned beneath.

"It's dead," I said, wiping the sleeve of my jacket across my face.

I didn't manage much more than smearing the mud, or possibly blood, spattered across my cheeks and forehead, but I didn't fall into a crippling vision. Thank Mab. The barghest was dead, but the fight was far from over.

"Come on," I said, offering Ceff a gloved hand. "Let's go teach this one's friends a lesson."

He shook his head, coming only to his hands and knees. I looked past him to the battle surrounding us, and bit my lip.

"I c-c-cannot," he said. "You must go."

The battle once again forgotten, I dropped into a crouch. Ceff was clawed and bitten, but the injuries were mostly superficial. I frowned, eyes roving over his body. My brain just couldn't connect what I was seeing with what he was saying. His rib cage wasn't caved in, and his limbs weren't hanging from a thread or bent at unnatural angels.

"By the tides, ahhh..." he moaned.

His tanned face turned ashen, and his entire body shuddered violently, wracked with spasms.

What was wrong with him? A tiny voice inside my head whispered that whatever the injury was, it had to be bad. Most fae can take a beating, but Ceff had demonstrated an amazing ability to withstand injury. He'd remained stoic even during extreme pain and torture.

"I'm not leaving you here," I said. "Tell me what's hurt, and I'll get you back to the nearest medic."

The Hunters' Guild had skilled medical teams who were highly trained in battle triage. Whatever injuries Ceff had sustained, one of Janus' medics could patch him up. They had to.

A figure slid behind me, and I spun, knives drawn. I was prepared to protect Ceff from the entire Wild Hunt if necessary, but it wasn't one of Herne's hounds. It wasn't even one of our Guild or fae allies. It was Torn.

"What's wrong with fish breath?" Torn asked, ignoring the blades held at more than one major artery.

"I don't know," I said. "Ceff?"

Ceff didn't answer, only dug his fingers into the muddy ground and moaned.

"Um, Princess," Torn said, leaning in and stroking his scarred chin. "Is that a barghest bite?"

"Huh?" I asked, staring at my mud-caked boots. When had I gotten so filthy? "Yeah, I guess?"

Torn took a step back, and swore.

"Go...now," Ceff ground out between shaking fits.

I blinked dumbly at the pink-tinged spittle at the corner of his mouth.

"I told you, I'm not leaving your side," I said, frowning. "We'll get you to a medic. Torn, a little help here?"

I reached for Ceff, but Torn lunged to stand between us. What the Hell was wrong with him? The man could be a pain in the ass, but this was no time for games.

Ceff was hurt, and he needed our help before one of Herne's hounds decided we'd make an easy target. The back of my neck itched with the awareness of nearby enemy threats. We had a man down and the battle continued to rage along the mud-slick riverbed.

We were sitting ducks.

"Look at him, Princess," Torn said, voice abnormally soft. "Open your eyes and truly see what is happening to him."

It was the lack of mocking tone that finally cut through the haze of shock and denial. I blinked, a ragged breath forcing its way out of my lungs and leaving me feeling unusually empty inside.

"Ceff?" I asked.

But I no longer expected a coherent reply. I'd not only opened my eyes and looked at Ceff, I'd gazed sidelong at him with my second sight. A fine tracery of magic tore its way through his veins, linking his body to the entire Wild Hunt. Even now, he fought against the onslaught, but the magic was too strong.

Ceff was a powerful faerie, a king, but the battle raged on. And when he lost, he'd become one of Herne's slaves.

He'd be one of the Wild Hunt.

"There must be something we can do," I said. "He's strong, much stronger than Hendricks. He can fight this."

But my words lacked conviction. I bit my lip, drawing blood. I would not cry, not now.

"Princess, we have to go," Torn said. "He's lasted longer than any other man here, human or faerie, but you've seen what a bite from one of Herne's hounds can do. I don't know how he's held on this long."

But I knew. Ceff and I had a bond, a love that we intended to share for centuries, and he was not going to give up on the future we'd promised each other. He wouldn't let go of our dream that easily.

"You can fight this, Ceff, I know you can," I said, ignoring Torn.

"NO ONE IS THAT STRONG," Ceff said, eyes flashing red.

I flinched, staggering back. The face was Ceff's, but the voice and the evil in his eyes was all Herne.

I hadn't known that Herne could speak through his men. It was a nasty trick. My hands began to shake, and I had to bite the inside of my cheek to keep from screaming.

"Ceff?" I asked. "Ceff!"

The red glow faded, and sweat beaded on his brow.

"Too strong," he said, panting. "P-p-please, make it stop."

That one word "please" made my stomach clench and my blood run cold. Ceff was a kelpie king. Faerie kings don't beg.

"You know what you need to do, Princess," Torn said.

I whirled on Torn, nearly taking off his head with one of my blades.

"I won't kill Ceff," I said. "Not while there's a chance of saving him."

"Easy," he said, lifting his hands.

I turned back to Ceff, shaking my head.

"I...I can't," I said. "I won't give up on you."

"Then...RUN," Ceff said.

His voice boomed, full of power, but it wasn't Herne's voice. It was Ceff pouring every ounce of royal command into the word. He wanted me to run. He wanted me to be safe, from him.

"By the tides, I will find a way to save you," I said.

"Save...yourself," he said. "No...more...time..."

Ceff's head snapped back, and an unearthly howl ripped from his throat.

"We have to move, Princess," Torn said. "We'll come back for him, I promise. But we can't help him if he eats us."

Torn had a point. Ceff's transformation was slower than Hendricks' had been, but it was clear that he couldn't hold it off much longer. Even a kelpie king has limits. By the tides...

Tides, that was it.

"Water!" I yelled. "We need water!"

"What are you going on about?" Torn asked. "I think you've finally lost it, Princess."

"Like calls to like," I said, eyes wide, waving to the nearest group of water fae. "He's a creature of water. The barghests hate water. If we surround him with water, maybe...just maybe..."

"Do it," Torn said.

CHAPTER 45

I often forget that Torn is a faerie lord. He wore his air of aloof indifference like a mask, but there is more to him than a pretty face.

The man may act like a carefree, skirt chasing, somewhat deranged buffoon, but he is lord of the cat sidhe. And unlike some of the supernatural factions, the position of cat sidhe leader wasn't decided by birth. Torn had become the lord of the cat sidhe, the king of the Harborsmouth cats, by fighting his way to the top. That took balls, and power.

Torn pulled himself up to his full height, spine straight and shoulders back. The lack of slouching made him remarkably tall and imposing. The random bits of bone and fur tied into his hair and dangling from his tattered ears no longer made him look like an extra from a Mad Max movie. Instead, those trophies seemed to form a crown.

And when he spoke, even in the midst of a chaotic battle, people listened.

I wondered fleetingly if it was indeed that very chaos that gave Torn power. Maybe I'd ask him later, if we lived.

"Water fae," he said, voice echoing through the night as if carried on shadows. "To your king!"

The fighting continued, many having to hold their ground, but those water fae who could break away made their way to where Ceff moaned in agony, still on his hands and knees. As they approached, Torn gestured to me with a wink, his mask once again in place.

"He's been bitten," I said. "He needs to be in water, for water to be brought here. He's in no condition to be moved. And...try not to get too close."

I had to hope they'd honor that last request. It would kill Ceff if he harmed any of his people. He cared too much about the water fae to let such a thing go.

The water fae moved closer, coming to stand in a ring around their fallen king. I stood, fingers clenching around my knives, wishing there was more that I could do. But this was in the hands of the water fae. It was my job to watch their backs, and keep them safe while they worked.

But even as a barghest approached, I kept an eye on Ceff and the water fae. I needed to know that he was safe.

Kelpies and a man with green hair began singing and swaying back and forth. I'd expected to see a mist form around Ceff, moisture being pulled from the air to surround him. Instead, a huge chunk of river water detached from the wall of water that blocked the Wild Hunt from entering the city. The water rushed toward us, and I flinched. But rather than crash over us, it swallowed Ceff whole.

He thrashed inside the murky water, but the transformation seemed to slow. Spiny fur had begun to sprout along his back in a fast moving cascade, but now each hair pushed through his flesh with agonizing slowness. The red glow hadn't returned to his eyes.

I took that as a positive sign.

A howl rose up amongst the other hounds. Ceff's head snapped back, but he didn't return their call. Instead, he shook, writhing in the liquid box that had become his prison and his hope of salvation. He fought Herne's control, and when he next met my gaze, his lips formed familiar words.

"I love you," he mouthed.

"I love you too," I said.

More than the moon.

More than the tides.

More than the stars.

CHAPTER 46

I looked numbly out over the muddy, corpse-strewn patch of pavement. Somehow, Master Janus had rallied his men and managed to help us fall back. Herne continued to taunt us, but for the moment the Wild Hunt's leader seemed content to let us lick our wounds.

I suspected he was taking the time to reassess his prey, and look for vulnerabilities. Heck, he might just be toying with us like a cat with a mouse. I didn't care.

I was numb.

I had nothing left to lose. Nothing left to fear. My greatest nightmare was playing out, and unless we thought of something soon, I'd have to kill the one person I loved more than anything in all the worlds.

The water fae worked non-stop to keep Ceff wrapped inside the ball of water, but that only helped to slow his transformation. There was no known cure. No man had ever been bitten by the Wild Hunt and been returned to himself, I'd checked. Not even Kaye's or Father Michael's books had any helpful information.

Fern Greatoak had promised to ask the network of Circle members and said she would continue searching through the rubble of Kaye's arcane library, and Father Michael had babbled on about immature demons. In the end, I'd tuned them out, and hung up.

Ceff was continuing to change, albeit slowly. He lifted pleading eyes to me, and my lip trembled.

"You need anything?" Jinx asked. "Food? Water?"

She'd remained out of the fray during the fight, but my friend hadn't wasted a second coming to my side when we fell back to our position near the warehouses.

I sniffed, and shook my head.

"No, I'm not hungry," I said.

She put her hands on her hips, and might have chewed me out if tears hadn't started to flow down my cheeks. So much for the gift of numbness. If I was feeling grief, the shock must be wearing off.

"Oh, hun," she said. "I'm so sorry."

"It's okay," I said, even though nothing would ever be okay again, not unless we found a cure for Ceff. "But do you mind giving us a moment?"

"Sure," she said, eyes flicking worriedly between me and Ceff. "I'll go grab some grub. For a bunch of people obsessive about their muscles, the Hunters are surprisingly well stocked with sugary sweets. I'll find us something good.

"Thanks," I mumbled.

She cast one more worried glance, and stumbled off toward a group of Hunters handing out packaged snacks and bottled water. Jinx would give us the space I'd asked for, though I did notice that Torn lingered nearby. I ignored him, and turned my full attention to Ceff suspended in the ball of water.

"Ceff, you fight this and I will love you forever," I whispered. "If you survive this, I will marry you, and fight beside you, and someday we will have a child together."

I couldn't be sure, but a tear seemed to fall down his face. It could have been the water, but I didn't think so. I knew that nothing could ever replace the sons that Ceff had lost, but he loved children. He longed for a child of his own, of our own.

It was the one promise that might help him hold on.

A heavy weight settled on my shoulders, and Torn came to stand at my side.

"Careful with those promises, Princess," he said.

"It's not a hard one to make," I said. "Not anymore."

"No," he said with a sigh. "I suppose not. You've changed since we first met."

"Didn't think I was mother material?" I asked.

"You weren't fit to keep a house plant," he said.

I snorted.

"Thanks a lot," I said.

But it was true. I'd changed. I'd grown up, and I'd met someone I wanted to spend eternity with. I just hoped we were given that chance.

"You think the water will call to him?" he asked. "Keep him from becoming one of them?"

"I hope so," I said. "But I'm not relying on the water alone. I've put in calls to anyone who might have information about a cure. Fern Greatoak is putting feelers out to the Circle, and Father Michael said he'd ask some his contacts in Rome. Even Master Janus said he'd get the Guild scholars searching their libraries."

Torn let out a low whistle.

"The Circle, the Vatican, the Hunters' Guild," he said, eyebrows lifting. "Those are some powerful groups to owe a favor to."

I shrugged. I didn't care who I owed or what kind of insane bargain I had to make. We had to find a cure. There was too much at stake.

"If this doesn't work, I have to kill him," I said, meeting Ceff's eyes through the water barrier between us.

Ceff nodded, a sad smile on his lips. Torn walked away, and the tears I'd been holding back began to fall.

CHAPTER 47

I was arguing with Master Janus about our next line of attack when the Scotsman went rigid. I looked over my shoulder to see Forneus and Gaius striding toward us.

Jinx ran up to Forneus, arms going around his neck, and I looked away. I was happy for them, I really was, but their reunion was a harsh reminder of what had happened on the battlefield and what I stood to lose. The barghest that bit Ceff might as well have torn my heart from my chest, and handed it over to Herne.

"Things are looking up, Lass," Janus said. "Though it's an odd day when the appearance of those two is a happy sight."

It was true. If Forneus and Gaius were here, then Forneus and Benmore must have succeeded in stopping the rogue vampire uprising.

"I can do with some good news," I said as Forneus and Gaius approached. "We're attacking again in one hour, if I have anything to say about it, but if you took down the rogue vampires, you can use the next fifteen minutes to tell us about it."

Janus nodded grudgingly, allowing the delay. He'd wanted to move out now, but I had a possible ace up my sleeve that hadn't arrived yet. We couldn't wait much longer, but he'd give me my hour.

"Always in such a hurry, Corpse Candle," Gaius said.

"Actually, that's the longest I can get the Guild to wait," I said. "If Janus had his way, we'd strike now."

"If we wait too long, Herne might try to bring his hunt to the city," Janus said. "We cannot risk that."

Janus and I had been arguing over our timetable and our best method of attack, but we did agree that we couldn't wait much longer.

"Plus, the water fae can't keep that wall of river water aloft indefinitely," Torn said. "They've been working in shifts, but it can't hold forever."

"I know," I muttered.

I knew they were right, but I needed more time. And if I was honest, I wasn't ready to say goodbye to Ceff. Not in his current state.

"Yes, your water wall gave us some trouble in reaching you," Gaius said. "I would very much like to hear how you came up with such a strategy, but I fear now is not the time."

Yeah, I'm sure the vampire master would love to hear all about how we moved an entire river. Vampires aren't fond of running water, since crossing over it saps them of most of their power. If they knew how to move rivers, it would be a real game changer.

I made a mental note to ask the water fae not to spill their secrets to the vamps. Since the two supernatural groups rarely intermingled, it was a small risk. But it was better to be safe than sorry.

"We do have some good news for you," Forneus said, a smug smile on his lips. "Gaius?"

"Yes, of course," Gaius said. He paused dramatically, and I tapped my foot. I had no patience for vampire theatrics. "I will lend my vampires to the fight."

I blinked at Gaius, and looked behind him at the handful of vampires standing as still as statues at his back. It was then I realized how few had come with him. Gaius rarely left the underground protection of vampire headquarters, but Forneus had set the underground warren ablaze.

Vampires are the dried out husks of long-dead humans, their magically animated bodies a horrific mockery of the living. Unless newly raised, their dry skin is pulled taught over bones. Everything that required moisture in life—eyes, organs, and fleshy tissue—were the first to go. Old vampires weren't much more than bags of kindling.

Gaius was very, very old. He wouldn't be able to return to vampire headquarters until the fires there were fully extinguished. He was more vulnerable than he'd been in centuries, which made the small number of guards at his back so surprising.

"Is this all that's left of your vampires?" I asked. "Are you the only member of the vampire council to survive?"

A shred of worry crept inside the walls I'd erected, gnawing at the numbness that swallowed my head and my heart.

"Already trying to size us up, Little Corpse Candle?" he asked.

"We've earned your trust, Gaius," Forneus said. "Or have you so quickly forgotten that I just saved you from true death?"

"I do not forget our debt, demon," he said, turning the glowing empty pits of his gaze on Forneus. The eye sockets were one of the many things I hated about dealing with vampires. I almost wished I could turn off my second sight and be fooled by their glamour. Almost. "Your assistance in the matter of Yue Fei and his rogues is the only reason we are here. But I do not trust easily, and there is still the matter of our enemy's escape."

"I had nothing to do with Yue Fei's escape, and you know it," Forneus said, narrowing his eyes.

"Wait," I said. My mind was sluggish with fatigue and grief, but I wasn't completely comatose. "Yue Fei escaped?"

"Yesss," Gaius said, the word dragging out in a dry, rattling hiss that raised the hair on my neck. "And he wants your blood, Corpse Candle."

"And why would he want that?" I asked. "Was that part of Mab's deal for helping with this distraction of hers?"

I waved a hand toward Herne and his hounds.

"That and the fact that I made sure to tell him of your involvement in the burning of his men, as he made his escape," he said. "Consider it motivation to take out our shared enemy."

Gaius tipped back his head, and let out a long, wheezy, movie villain laugh. His vampires, who had until now stood stock still, did the same.

For this battle, Gaius and his men were our allies, but it didn't change their nature. Vampires were now, and always would be, the creepiest damn creatures on the planet.

CHAPTER 48

Master Janus and I were finally in agreement. We would attack within the hour. I walked to the writhing mass of water that encapsulated Ceff, stopping to check in with one of the kelpies who stood guard beside his king.

"How is he?" I asked. "Any change in his condition?"

"A bit more of the black fur, M'lady," he said, averting his eyes. "And there is the paw."

"Paw?" I asked, blanching.

"His right foot," he said.

"Thank you," I said.

I swallowed hard, a hand going to my stomach. I took a deep breath, and forced a smile on my face. It wouldn't help to go over there crying and wringing my hands. I'd shed enough tears.

I walked up to Ceff's watery prison, and waved. He lifted his head, and I had to fight not to show my fear. The fur had spread to cover his ears in spiny tufts. The thought of that fur soon sprouting from his handsome face broke my heart.

"I had an idea," I said, knowing he could hear me. He tilted his head, but didn't look hopeful. I suppose, at this point, I couldn't blame him. "What if you change into your horse form?"

He raised an eyebrow, but nodded.

"Just...if it feels like you're losing control, change back," I said. I didn't voice the words, but "if you can" seemed to hang in the air between us. There was no guarantee that he would have control over his change. He may not even be able to shift into his horse form. The only form that might be in his future was that of a hound of the Wild Hunt. I shook off that maudlin line of thinking, and forced hope into my voice. "I have a plan, but we need to buy you as much time as possible."

He nodded again, and lowered himself onto all fours. The water writhed and shifted to accommodate his new posture.

"Do you think this will work?" Torn asked, his voice in my ear.

This time, I didn't even jump.

"You need to stop doing that," I said. "It isn't smart sneaking up on me. One of these days, I'm going to stab you."

"You're avoiding the question," he said.

"That's because I don't have an answer," I said. "I don't know if this will work, but it has to. I can't live without him."

"There are other suitors," he said, staring at his fingernails, smooth crescents that I knew could become sharp claws within seconds if needed. "Some of us have grown to tolerate your royal grumpiness. You do keep life interesting."

"Are you hitting on me, Torn?" I asked, frowning.

I didn't think the night could get any more awful, but Torn hitting on me while I stood over Ceff's failing body was low, even for the flirtatious cat sidhe.

"It worked," he said, waving a hand at the column of water.

At first, I thought he meant that he'd succeeded in distracting me. Had that been his intention all along? If so, I owed him my thanks and an apology. I could be grumpy at the best of times, and tonight was the worst.

I was about to thank him, which would have been an epic error in judgment and was an example of my current mental state, when movement caught my eye from within the water.

A sleek, gray stallion stomped its hoofed feet, and shook its head. Water rippled, swirling around Ceff, but I could see him clearly. I gasped, a gloved hand flying to my mouth.

The paw, and all but one patch of black fur, was gone.

CHAPTER 49

Ceff wasn't out of the woods, I knew that. The black, spiny fur was once again beginning to sprout along his spine. We hadn't cured him, but we had bought him more time. With this battle, I hoped to do more than that.

With a wall of water at our backs, we stood facing Herne and his hounds. Owls flew ominously overhead, occasionally swooping down to pick off our men. Despite their size, the predator birds moved with unnatural speed. More than one man had been maimed by beak and talon. That's why I'd wanted to delay our attack.

I'd last seen our pooka allies harassing Herne's owls hours ago. I'd been scanning the sky, but there'd been no sign of the diminutive fae. Master Janus assumed that the pooka had either fled in fear, or been eaten. Judging from his exasperation each time I asked if any pooka had been seen by his lookouts, the man didn't hold much stock in their abilities to tip the battle against the Wild Hunt in our favor.

He obviously didn't know the pooka like I did. The pooka were resilient and clever. They were low on the supernatural food chain and yet they managed to live in style and reproduce like bunnies. Okay, that last might be due to their love of orgies, but the point was that pooka are survivors.

So I was the only one unsurprised when the air filled with the happy hum of tiny wings, and the colorful glow of pooka caps.

"Oberon's eyes, I'm glad to see you, Red," I said, smiling at the pooka's leader.

I'm not sure what the little man's real name was. Like most fae, he was loathe to reveal his true name, but I'd taken to naming him after the color of the glow-in-the-dark condom he wore on his head. Whether it was coincidence or a sign of respect, none of the other pooka ever wore a cap that color.

He squinted at me, and I could tell he was trying to figure out if I was being sincere. Since most people treated pooka like vermin, I couldn't blame the guy. Heck, I'd met him and his clan while trying to roust him out of an old woman's attic.

"It's true," Forneus said with a sigh. "She made us delay in the hope you would come to our aid."

Not that the demon had minded the delay. It had given him and Jinx some serious smooching time.

Jinx was back in our small camp, watching over Ceff. It was the best excuse I could think of to keep her off the front lines. If she'd come with us, neither me or Forneus would be able to concentrate on the battle. No matter how skilled with a crossbow, the battlefield was no place for Jinx.

The pooka nodded, hands on his hips.

"We have returned, My Lady," Red said.

"Good," I said, lips tilting in a grin. "I have a special task for you."

"Kill the feathered evil?" he asked.

The pooka at his back nodded, and picked up the chant, a murmur of "feathered evil, death to the feathered evil" filling my ears.

"Yes," I said. "Do what you can against Herne's owls. But I have one more task for your bravest soul. But I must warn you, it's a dangerous mission and requires the best thieving skills."

The pooka went quiet, leaning forward with wide eyes to hang on every word.

"And what would you have us steal?" Red asked.

"Herne's horn," I said.

CHAPTER 50

The pooka were more than willing to accept a mission to steal Herne's shiny, magic horn. Their enthusiasm caused more than one raised brow, but there was no time to explain my actions to every faerie and Hunter ally who stood with me. Let them talk.

Those leading the fight, my closest friends and allies, knew my plan. It was, admittedly, a long shot. I wasn't sending the pooka to retrieve Herne's horn for Kaye, who even now was being led to a Circle prison. The horn wouldn't be a component in a binding spell, and I wasn't trying to gain control of the Hunt. I'd been looking at this all wrong.

The Wild Hunt existed because Mab gave Herne his powers. She'd crammed a forest spirit inside his body, made him nearly invincible in battle, and gave him a pack of hounds that created more of their kind with a bite. That was major magic, even for a faerie queen.

That kind of magic usually needed a focus object, like a pendant, ring, or sword. I couldn't see beneath Herne's cloak. Maybe the focus item was hanging around his neck. Or maybe Mab really was powerful enough to create the Wild Hunt with the snap of her fingers. But I'd latched onto the hope that I'd found our enemy's Achilles heel.

It was possible that Herne's horn, the one that called his hounds to battle, was the item that held his power. If that were true, then it gave me a target. If the horn was destroyed, the members of the Wild Hunt might return to normal. Herne might once again become a mortal man. The barghests might return to their former selves.

Ceff might become free.

His absence at my side was like an amputation, and more than once I turned to share a pre-battle confidence only to be reminded that he wasn't there. Ceff was locked back in his watery prison with his most loyal guards and Jinx watching over him, but I wasn't alone.

Torn and Forneus flanked my position. Master Janus and his Hunters were fanned out to my left and the water fae stood along the embankment to my right. Gaius and his vampires lingered in the warehouse shadows at our backs, a silent and deadly secret force waiting to be unleashed.

I stood at the edge of the embankment looking out over the muddy riverbed below and Herne and his hounds beyond. The hounds howled and paced, sometimes snarling and nipping at each other in their eagerness for a hunt.

Herne held his horn, but didn't call for the attack. My guess was that he already had our undivided attention, which fulfilled his mission for Mab to keep the defenders of the city busy while Yue Fei's vampires attacked an unprotected human population. He was probably just waiting for those same vampires to tear their way through to our position, where they could attack our flank while the Wild Hunt decimated our front lines. It was the logical course of action from a brilliant military mind, even one so deranged by dark magic.

What Herne didn't know was that the dwarf leader Benmore had led the vampire master of the city to safety while Forneus had burnt out the nest of rogue vampires. Gaius and the Vampire Council had sustained heavy losses, but the attempt to take them out had been thwarted.

We had our pooka friends to thank for keeping all knowledge of the rogue vampire faction's defeat from Herne. The pookas had taken their job seriously before the battle, and had held an aerial perimeter against Herne's feathered spies. According to Red, not one owl made it outside the industrial park.

It was that tenacious streak and flawless track record that led me to bark out an order of my own mere seconds after Master Janus signaled us all to attack.

"Defeat the feathered evil!" I shouted, as I ran down to the muddy riverbed. "Bring me the horn!"

Squeals of delight and a chant of "defeat the feathered evil!" filled my ears as a gaggle of pookas took to the air. I winced at the high pitch of the pooka war cry, but a smile drew my lips from my teeth. Herne's owls were in for one Hell of a fight.

They weren't the only ones.

The Hunters, water fae, and vampires had all lost friends and comrades to the Wild Hunt. It was time for payback. Swords swung and arrows flew. Rain lashed out and lightening struck. We fought on with a ferocity that would have terrified the old me.

Blood and mud mixed to form a Hellish quagmire that even the barghests couldn't easily navigate, and my friends fell on them like a plague of hungry locusts on a field of juicy corn.

I'd fought alongside a blood-crazed Torn dozens of times and I'd seen Forneus turn all cloven-hoofed and fiery in defense of Jinx's life, but nothing prepared me for the fury those two unleashed on the Wild Hunt. Torn took the cat sidhe art of playing with his food to the next level, and Forneus earned his accolades as the Grand Marquis of Hell.

My friends sought revenge, and they weren't the only ones. Water fae of every color, shape, and size entered the fray, hungry for retribution. The Wild Hunt had sought to entrap Ceffyl Dwr with its foul corruption, and that was a big mistake. The *each uisge* had tried something similar last year, and those wounds were still raw in the minds of the long-lived fae.

The Wild Hunt had signed its own death warrant.

Selkie javelins stopped barghests in their tracks, while their kelpie mounts kicked with bone crushing hooves. More than one mermaid sat atop a barghest's vulnerable underbelly, her shark-like teeth tearing and feasting on the hound's flesh.

Through it all, I remained focused on my target. I threw, slashed, and stabbed with my blades and plunged more than one iron nail into a barghest's tough hide. Unlike my friends, I didn't relish the beast's pain. I couldn't look into the glowing red eyes of those hounds without being reminded of how they never asked for this fate. The barghests were unwilling participants in this fight. I would bring them down, but theirs was not the death I stalked with unholy focus.

I wanted Herne's antler-bedecked head on an iron platter.

Herne was no fool. Despite his godlike strength and virtual invulnerability to injury, he issued orders from behind his barghest army. The cloaked figure rode back and forth, commanding his forces from the back of a limping but speedily healing horse with little risk of harm. Not even the Hunters' Guild's skilled archers could touch him.

It was a good thing then that I had a few aces up my mud-spattered sleeves.

CHAPTER 51

When I reached halfway across the mud and cracked pavement of our battlefield, shadows broke free from the warehouses at our backs. Whether to conserve energy or to put fear into the hearts of their enemies, the vampires didn't bother with their typical glamour. I could tell by the way the Hunters and faeries avoided the silent, creeping bloodsuckers that it wasn't just my second sight cutting through the vampire's glamour. For once, the people around me saw Gaius and his men for what they really were—butt ugly, shriveled corpses that brought death and exsanguination wherever they tread.

Our fanged allies hardly made a dry whisper as they glided over fallen men to their barghest targets, their alien movements a deceptively graceful dance that belied their ferocity. The empty eye sockets and beef jerky bodies weren't the only things that vampires hid with their glamour. They might tempt and tease teen fangirls with tiny, sparkling white, pointy teeth, but the fangs of these ancient vamps were yellowed weapons nearly as long as my forearm.

In the blink of an eye, Gaius and his men were across the field and sinking those fangs into barghest groins and jugulars. I ignored the vampires, especially the way their raisin bodies began to flesh out, bloating like overgrown ticks. I clenched my jaw, and ran.

I was nearing Herne, but that meant the density of barghests was increasing. The damn things were so thick they formed a bristling fur wall around their leader. Being this close to that many teeth and claws was suicide, but I tamped down the cold pit of fear in my belly and soldiered on.

The nearest barghest lunged at me, and I spun. A claw caught the edge of my leather jacket, and I had to dive onto the ground and roll to avoid its snapping jaws. That was too close for comfort. One bite and I'd be barking mad, literally. I'm not sure what would destroy me first, a vision splintering my mind or the magic transforming me into one of the Wild Hunt's hounds. Better not to find out.

I drew my machete as I came to my feet, thankful for its long blade. I nearly missed the glowing red object as it buzzed by my ear, but the pooka's cry of "steal the horn!" was unmistakable. Red and his men had made it past the owls, and were moving in to steal the horn from Herne.

I barely had time to pray he succeeded before the barghest and one of its pals were on me. If it hadn't been for a mermaid and vampire tag team, I probably would have died then and there. Thankfully, the two had an effective routine of suck and maul. With their help, I got my machete between me and the smaller of the barghests, and slit its throat.

I was once again rolling away when Herne's angry roar echoed across the field of battle and vibrated in my skull.

"REND THE INSECT'S SPINE THROUGH ITS MOUTH AND BRING ME BACK THE HORN!" Herne yelled.

Herne's booming voice had one favorable effect. Every barghest turned their full attention to their leader. It was an opportunity we didn't pass up.

We took down more barghests than I could count. I was smiling, enjoying a momentary lull in the battle, when I caught sight of Red flying to me, the horn clutched in his tiny hands.

Except for the glowing red cap on his head, the pooka leader was bedecked in black, ninja garb and wore a look of sheer delight on his face. The pooka prized thievery, the shinier the prize and the more dangerous the mission the better. The little man was in his glory.

He never saw the winged predator hunting him.

The owl swooped in, talons aimed at the pooka's head. Talons slid into Red's eye and through his skull, his small body hanging bloody and lifeless.

"Nooooo!" I screamed.

A second pooka, tears streaming down his face, flew past his leader. I held my breath, too far away to be of any help. The owl shrieked in frustration, but it couldn't shake Red's body from its grip. In striking and killing the pooka, the owl's talons had pierced through the colorful condom that the man had come to wearing as a hat. Now that fashion statement was tangled in the creature's claws, giving the young pooka the additional seconds needed to conduct the heist of a lifetime.

Even in death the pooka leader had managed to save one of his people, and aided in the theft of Herne's most valuable possession. The pooka would sing about his exploits, perhaps even have an orgy in his name. For the pooka, that would be one of the greatest honors of all.

I nodded, and pulled my gaze from the small, lifeless body that hung from the desperate owl's talons. There was nothing I could do for the pooka leader, but I would not waste his sacrifice.

The young pooka grabbed the horn, and flew toward me, eyes big as saucers in his tiny face. I ran toward him, my blades in hand.

The owl finally dislodged Red's skull from its talons and lunged toward us, but I was ready. I'd swapped my machete for my throwing knives, and now released one with a flick of my wrist. The iron and silver blade sunk deep into my target.

Pooka voices cheered as the owl fell from the sky, and seconds later the young pooka dropped Herne's horn into my gloved hands. Magic hummed, its warmth seeping through leather and cloth, sending greed and doubt to wash over me.

Should I try to take control of the Hunt?

I shook my head, trying to fight off the horn's magic. Would that be any better than Ceff being controlled by Herne? It was a temptation, one so great that I had to struggle not to raise the foul object to my lips and blow. My beloved wouldn't be saved. If I became his master and the leader of the Wild Hunt, Ceff would be lost to me forever.

My choice was clear. I needed to destroy the horn, and Herne. It was a risk. There was every possibility that destroying Herne and the horn would kill every member of the Wild Hunt. But it was a risk I had to take.

It was the only hope of stopping the Wild Hunt permanently, and of setting Ceff, and the others, free. Even death would be freedom of a sort.

I grit my teeth and slid the horn into an iron-lined bag, quieting the siren song of its power. I wrapped the drawstring around my fist, cradled the bag against my chest, and ran.

Every second I ran away from Herne was like a dagger in the heart, but I'd get my revenge against the man soon enough. Right now, I needed to get the horn as far from our enemy as possible. It would do us no good if it fell back into their hands. Red's sacrifice would be for nothing.

So I pushed myself faster, legs and lungs burning with the exertion. I had a moment to rue the injury to my wing that prevented me from flying, although there were still enough owls above our heads to make that a risk, and then a familiar horned and hooved figure stood before me.

"Forneus," I gasped, thrusting the bag at him. "Take this. Get it behind our lines, and do whatever it takes to destroy it."

His eyes widened, but only for a second. I hadn't placed much trust in the demon in the past, and my prejudice had burned me in the butt. He knew it, and I knew it. Now I was trusting him with all our lives.

He nodded, and tucked the bag somewhere inside his suit jacket.

"And Herne?" he asked.

My lip curled, baring my teeth.

"Leave that bastard to me."

CHAPTER 52

It didn't take me as long to reach Herne as it had taken to retreat. In fact, the pounding of his horse's hooves were on me almost as soon as I handed the horn over to Forneus. I'd taken something dear from Herne, and he was out for blood.

The leader of the Wild Hunt was pissed.

My heart raced, and I palmed the last of my throwing knives as he came barreling toward me. His eyes and the eyes of his midnight black mount glowed red, and the barghests ran howling at their heels.

Adding the glowing red eyes of the barghests rushing toward me was like something out of a nightmare. Plus, an orange spectral light was on the horizon, and it wasn't the sun. I had a bad feeling that whatever was behind that orange glow was just as scary as Herne. Its power was sizzling over me like supercharged air before a storm.

I was afraid, sure, but I was also mad as Hell. Herne wasn't the only one who was pissed off. Luckily, I could work with that.

I focused on my fear and anger, and drew my power. Forneus was busy carrying Herne's horn away from the front lines, but he wasn't the only one amongst us with the ability to burn our enemies. My wisp powers might not rival the demon's skill with hellfire, but my uncle Kade had taught me well.

I had a fireball with Herne's name on it.

The Wild Hunt had an aversion to water, but Herne was the twisted amalgam of a man and a nature spirit. It was a hunch, but nature had a fear of fire that I hoped Herne shared.

I just hoped my powers recharged as quickly here in the human world as they did in Faerie. While in the wisp court, in the heart of Nithsdale, I'd been in the seat of my father's power. I hadn't had a chance to test the limits of my new powers since returning to Harborsmouth. Battling Kaye at the Emporium had exhausted my power reserves. I wasn't sure what effect the human world, and the prevalence of iron, would have on my powers and on my newly awakened fae blood, but I was about to find out.

The power was sluggish at first, and I frowned. In Faerie, the very air burned with magic. Power flowed through every plant, rock, and tree. Here in Harborsmouth, I had to fight for every ounce of magic, so fight I did.

It was in that tug of war for power that a source of magic showed itself with crystal clarity. Harborsmouth sits on a nexus of ley lines, and those lines now glowed brighter than Herne's creepy eyes.

More howls rose up in a chorus that should have made me sick with terror. But as my head filled with the cries of howling barghests, and the pounding of the hooves of Herne's mount, I drew upon the ley lines that ran through the city I called home.

I'd never tapped into ley line power. I wasn't even sure if it was something that faeries could actively do. That didn't stop me. It was dangerous, perhaps even foolish, but it was our greatest chance of defeating the Wild Hunt.

Especially since with a quick two shot snap, I released my last two throwing knives. If the ley line magic didn't work, I was screwed. I was out of ammo, and I had no delusions of winning this fight with a dagger from my boot and my machete.

"You weren't planning on having all the fun were you, Princess?" Torn said, sauntering from the shadows.

In fact, the more ley line power I absorbed, the greater the night encroached on my sight. I'd lost my peripheral vision, allowing Torn to get the jump on me. Stifling the urge to spin around and check my flank, I nodded at Torn.

"Never doubted you'd have my back," I said.

"Good answer," he said.

Then we struggled to survive amidst a sea of teeth, claws, and bristling fur. It was only when the water fae joined us, repelling the nearest barghests, that I finally faced Herne.

So much had brought us to this moment, including my biological mother's meddling. I couldn't help but think it was such a waste. So many had fallen. So many had died. I'd only made it this far due to the support of my friends and allies, and the power that ran through the city's ley lines.

If it hadn't been for that power source, I'd be a shredded pile of hamburger squishing beneath barghest paws. I continued to draw on the nearest ley line, my teeth vibrating so hard, I worried I might be drinking my meals through a straw if I survived the night.

"IVY GRANGER," Herne's voice boomed. "NOW YOU WILL DIE."

His war horse was a goliath of an animal, and its tons of rippling muscle raced toward me, bringing with it Herne and his wrath. The barghests too continued to fight, hemming us in. They'd sustained heavy losses, but so had we.

Their continued allegiance to Herne meant that Forneus still hadn't found a way to destroy the horn. Or if he had, the object didn't have the significance that I'd hoped. I held my machete in two hands before me, feet planted in a wide stance. The ground was slick, and I knew that I was about to die.

But I wouldn't go down without a fight.

Herne was within meters of my position when I sent a line of flame arcing out along my blade to shoot into his mount. Torn raked the horse's other side with his claws, and the beast stumbled.

Herne just leapt to the ground as if he'd planned to do so from the start. Show off. He swung his sword in a series of impressive moves, and my hands shook. I'd like to think the shaking was from holding in so much ley line power, but I was afraid.

I'd failed Ceff, and now he may never be free of the Wild Hunt. I sent up a silent prayer for forgiveness, and dove forward. I may not be able to save Ceff, but I'd do as much damage as I could before Herne tore me to pieces.

I lunged, running into a slender figure enshrouded in a cloak of living shadow. I blinked, sucking in a ragged breath to replace the one that had been knocked out of me, and the newcomer swung a glowing lantern at Herne's head.

One of the shadowy antlers that flickered in and out of my second sight tore from Herne's head with a terrible, wet ripping sound and hit the ground. Torn's eyes went wide, but there was no time to fear this stranger. No matter the reason, he'd lent his aid and slowed Herne's assault.

In fact, Herne looked rattled. That lantern swung at Herne, and once again rang his bell. Whoever this dark stranger was, his right hook with that lantern was impressive.

I drew my machete across one of Herne's legs, just below the calf, in a spinning move that severed his Achilles tendon. Before he could grab me, I spun away just out of reach.

Torn lunged in for a swipe with his claws, and the stranger grabbed Herne's remaining antler. They harried Herne in a deadly, graceful dance as if they had fought together for centuries. It was almost as if they could read each other's minds, always moving into the exact position the other needed for maximum effectiveness.

Then the stranger began to glow. Upon closer examination, his cloak was not made up of shadows but of tormented souls. I swallowed hard, but some instinct told me to trust this man. We all carried around our demons, some just more literally than others.

Fireballs shot from the fingertips of his empty hand, their light nearly as bright as the lantern he held in the other. The fireballs were tiny, but flew with amazing speed and accuracy. Each ball of flame found its target, burning a scorching path through Herne's mouth and out the back of his head.

I gaped at the lifeless husk that fell to the ground, the once great man now nothing more than a smoking corpse. Herne had deflected all of my magic, always managing to anticipate my move or cause the flame to bounce away from the more vital parts of his body.

"You okay, Princess," Torn asked, moving to my side.

"He's really dead," I said, staring at Herne's body, my eyes unblinking.

"I don't think he's the one you should be focusing on," he said. When I didn't lift my head, he sighed. But I was tired, so tired. The barghests were no longer attacking, but neither had they become allies upon Herne's death. I just needed a moment to catch my breath. "May I introduce to you my friend, Willem."

Willem?

"Hello, baby girl," Willem said.

He pulled the cloak of tormented souls from his head with gloved hands, revealing shocking red hair and a familiar face.

"Daddy?" I asked, eyes going wide.

My father, Will-o'-the-Wisp, had come home.

CHAPTER 53

My father had come home. He'd traveled halfway around the world to heed my distress call, one I hadn't even known I'd sent when I sang the wisp song in my battle against Kaye. I wanted nothing more than to sit with him and ask for answers to the multitude of questions I had. But getting answers to my questions and spending time with my father would have to wait.

Ceff's transformation was slowed, not cured, and the remaining barghests might be without a leader, but they still tried to eat our faces off when we approached. The best bet for saving them was destroying Herne's horn.

Forneus had attempted a variety of ways to destroy the horn, some maniacally creative, but none had damaged the thing, not even a dent. It was my turn.

No one argued when I declared that I wanted the horn. That might have something to do with the scary faeries, Torn and Willem, who strode along beside me. They hadn't left my side, and once again I was left with the impression that these two had fought countless battles together.

But that was a story for another time.

I reached out to the ley lines, power rushing in to flood my veins. Heat pulsed through my body, and I sent wave after wave of flame into the horn. It spun and bounced, but when the fire ceased, the damned horn was just as shiny and new looking as when I started.

Stomping on it also didn't work. I just ended up with a bruised foot, and red cheeks. I tried again with my magic, hitting it in unison with my machete, but to no avail.

Even drawing upon the ley lines until my teeth shook, I didn't have enough power to destroy the horn. My mouth filled with the taste of salt, and I spit blood, swaying on my feet.

"Mind if I lend a hand, Princess?" Torn asked.

He winked and lifted his hands, sending a stream of flickering shadows into the horn. Darkness combined with my fire, dancing along the surface of the horn, and I could feel

Mab's magic begin to fray, her hold on the Wild Hunt weakening.

I kept the fire coming, and nodded.

"More," I gasped.

A kelpie I recognized from Ceff's personal guard lifted his hands, and began to sing in burbling tones. Water magic joined our fire and shadow.

My body shook, racked by spasms, but I widened my stance, and held on to the ley line, sending wisp fire into the horn.

"Air," I gasped. "We need air magic."

A siren tilted her head back, joining her voice to the kelpie's song. My ears popped, air pressure shifting, but it wasn't enough.

"More," I said, though I'm not sure anyone could hear me now.

I caught a flash of purple to my left, so quickly that I couldn't be sure if Arachne was truly there in the crowd, but a breeze began to flow in the direction of the horn.

The horn shook harder, and started to spin in rapid circles, so fast its movement was a blur.

"Fire, shadow, water, air," I said, frowning. "What are we missing?"

"Blood," Gaius said, making me jump as his voice whispered in my ear.

The vampire strode past me, Forneus at his side. They were an odd pair, the short, Roman vampire with his wispy, blond hair and dry, husk of a body wearing leather armor and sandals, beside the tall, dark-haired demon in his expensive suit. I might have laughed if I wasn't on the verge of passing out.

Gaius held his arm over Herne's horn and, with a quick slash of his hand, tore open his wrist. Blood dripped onto the horn and began to sizzle. Oily, black smoke writhed like tentacles around the horn, joining with my wisp fire, Torn's shadows, the kelpie's water, and the siren's air. The wound on Gaius' wrist was already closing, slowing the blood's flow, but I could sense the horn weakening, the blood magic doing its part.

Forneus tugged at his gloves, and lifted a hand toward the horn, but I tilted my head.

"Already got fire," I said.

Not that I could keep my fire burning much longer. Forneus sent flame arcing into the horn, and smiled.

"You will find that hellfire is a different magic entirely," he said.

"I agree," Willem said, reaching to open his lantern and directing its heat at the horn.

They were right. The horn spun faster, wobbling and spinning until it shot into the sky. My head snapped around as a bowstring twanged to my left, but Jinx just shrugged.

"Everyone else was joining in," she said. "It just felt right."

I nodded, and turned back to the horn spinning in the sky. Her wooden arrow moved as if through molasses as it neared the horn, shooting through the waves of magic, but it continued to fly true. I channeled the power of the ley line, sending more wisp fire at the horn with my left hand. I shifted my stance, reached for the iron and silver dagger I kept in my boot, and threw it at the horn.

I held my breath, the salty taste of blood on my lips, as my blade and Jinx's holy water-dipped arrow moved toward their common target. A second later, the horn imploded with a flash of blinding light.

An opening, a tear in the fabric of this world, sucked the light and our waves of magic into its maw, and snapped shut. It was as if I'd been bungee jumping, and when I was at the furthest point of stretch, someone had cut the cord.

I fell back, tumbling head over heels, and everything went black.

CHAPTER 54

I blinked rapidly, lifting my head from the mud-spattered pavement. Warm liquid ran down my face, and I winced. I wiped an arm across my nose to keep from sneezing, and it came away slick with blood. I forced myself to breathe through my mouth, and pulled myself to my knees.

"Give her a moment," Torn whispered, holding my father back.

Willem glanced at my gloved hands, and nodded. I blinked, trying to make sense of everything around me. Even my dreams weren't this weird. They were scary, yes, but not weird.

Forneus shook his head, catching my attention, and groaned. His gloves had burned away, and Jinx was bandaging his blistered hands. I hadn't known that demons could even get burns, not until now. Father Michael would probably want a look at those injuries when we went to pick up Sparky.

These thoughts and more raced through my head as I dragged myself to my feet, turning slowly, my eyes searching through the crowd for one familiar face. There would be time to check on my friends later. Right now, I needed to know if destroying the horn had finally freed the members of the Wild Hunt from Mab's twisted magic.

My chest tightened, and my limbs grew heavy, stopping me dead in my tracks.

Herne and the horn were gone, but Ceff and the others weren't free. They stood stock still, gazing blankly into space.

"Ceff?" I asked. "Can you hear me?"

I stumbled toward Ceff.

He gazed ahead, eyes unfocused, and I let out a choking sob.

"Ceff," I gasped.

It couldn't be. It had to have worked. The spell should have been broken. But here he was unresponsive, his eyes glazed over.

I reached out, tearing off my gloves. I had to find my way to him, even if it meant losing my own freedom. I wasn't willing to leave him trapped in this hell of my mother's making. I would not leave him to suffer this alone. We'd vowed to be together forever.

"Ivy, no!" Willem screamed.

But his voice was already tumbling and fading away, becoming less real as I cupped Ceff's face with my bare hands. I fell into the visions of Ceff's past, rushing at first through the familiar visions leading up to before the summer solstice. The time of Ceff's captivity at the hands of my uncle was tortuously slow, but every second he was enslaved by the Wild Hunt was sheer, endless agony.

But that agony ended with an explosion of light and a tearing of reality that sucked away the painful, icy tendrils of Mab's spell. Icy talons slowly retracted from my skull, but I couldn't move, not until I felt the touch of my beloved.

I'd feared that I might have harmed her in the battle, but she felt whole as she cupped my face with bare hands. Wait, what? Oberon's eyes, I was seeing me through Ceff's eyes, now after the spell had been broken.

The spell had been broken.

"Ivy," Ceff said.

I blinked, and moved to pull away, but Ceff arms enfolded me, holding me close. Was this real? Or was this some new kind of trickery, a magical booby-trap set by Mab to ensnare my mind with wishful thinking made to seem real?

"Ceff?" I asked, my hands shaking as I traced the line of his jaw.

"You saved me," he said. "You brought me back."

CHAPTER 55

It took over an hour before we made it home. Some of the faeries were celebrating our victory, while the Hunters cleaned up and tended their dead.

Surprisingly, some of the lost had returned, though the haunted look in their eyes gave me chills. Hendricks had been one of those to return, his body shifting from beast to man sometime after the horn was destroyed. Dark circles ringed his eyes, and he flinched at every loud noise, but he'd had it easy compared to some of the former members of the Wild Hunt. Some had been in hound form for so long, they could no longer speak. They howled with human and faerie throats, and more than one took his own life.

After what some of those men had seen and done under Herne's command, it wasn't surprising. The Guild's medics did their best for them, but time would tell if the rest made it.

I thought of Kaye and the hurdles she would face in the coming months. I had a feeling I'd be visiting a lot of patients and praying for their progress.

Master Janus had barked out a series of cuss words when I told him about Kaye's situation, but in the end, he'd grudgingly admitted that he'd have done the same. We can't let someone with that kind of power threaten the city, not even if they're our friends.

It was a point worth remembering, and one that Janus had repeated in earshot of my father. I guess demon lanterns and creepy cloaks of tortured souls don't make a good first impression.

Not that it kept the vampires from staring at both longingly. It fit with their flair for the overly dramatic.

Gaius promised to scour the area before sunrise, making sure that any human who'd ventured into the industrial district had their memories wiped.

That left a bad taste in my mouth, but it was a necessary evil. And I had to admit that the vampire master's willingness to help was refreshing. I still didn't trust the man, but he'd kept his word and backed us up tonight.

It was a start.

Ceff finally said his goodbyes to the water fae, but only after promising that tomorrow he'd attend a welcome home feast in his honor. He'd be returning to the ocean soon, but we had today and what was left of the night.

We walked hand in hand, a fact that Torn pointed out mercilessly.

"Willem, have they asked your permission yet?" he asked, lips twitching.

"Torn," I growled.

The damn cat was enjoying this. My father had only just arrived, and during an epic battle at that. Of course, we hadn't asked his permission to marry. We hadn't even had a chance to tell him about our engagement.

"Permission for what?" Willem asked. "Ivy?"

"Um, well, Ceff and I are engaged," I said.

Willem's eyes narrowed.

"Sir, I know this is not the best timing," Ceff said. We were still holding hands and I gave his hand a reassuring grip. "But would you allow me your daughter's hand in marriage."

My father's pale, freckled cheeks turned red, and Torn slapped him on the back.

"Go on, Willem," he said.

"I will think on it," he said.

I bit my lip. In all my fantasies of my father's homecoming, this conversation had never happened. I tried to think of something to say, but Jinx broke the uncomfortable silence.

"At least now I'm not the last to know," Jinx said.

"Come on, dear," Forneus said, tightening his arm around her. "They were busy traveling to Faerie and back."

"Now that is a story I would like to hear," Willem said.

I swallowed hard, as Torn launched into a tale of his marvelous exploits, and my bumbling. I groaned, but I had to admit that Torn was one Hell of a storyteller.

He'd reached the point in the story where we were entering Donn's castle. It was time to bring that tale to a close, or part ways. I didn't want Jinx anywhere near when he mentioned Donn's hearth. There was certain knowledge that wasn't meant for human ears. The backdoor we'd used to enter to Faerie was a well-guarded secret, and one that could get my human friend killed.

"Dad, are you staying with us?" I asked.

We were close to the building where Jinx and I shared a loft apartment. I didn't usually invite people up, especially those who wore a cloak of tortured souls that might taint everything I owned with nightmare visions, but I'd searched for my father for months. I didn't want to let him out of my sight.

He started to nod until he caught sight of the glowing lantern clutched in his hand. A dark look crossed his face, and he shook his head.

"No, sweetheart," he said. "Get some rest. I will come by tomorrow."

"You can stay at my court, Willem," Torn said, nearly bouncing with excitement. "It will be like old times, and I can finish my story."

Willem sighed, a weary smile on his lips.

"Good night, baby girl," he said.

"Good night, dad," I said.

An involuntary tear slid down my cheek as they turned the corner, my father disappearing from sight.

"He will return tomorrow," Ceff said.

"I know," I said, shrugging with one arm. "It's just been a long night. Sparky being kidnapped, fighting Kaye, my dad showing up, almost losing you...my heart hasn't quite caught up with my brain."

He pulled me close, and whispered in my ear.

"I can think of ways to convince you that I am alive and well," he said.

A shiver ran up my spine, and I licked my lips.

"Promise?" I asked.

"I promise," he said.

As far as bargains go, it was a good one.

CHAPTER 56

Humphrey announced that all was well when we arrived at our building, and Father Michael and Sparky were asleep on the couch. I looked around for Arachne, careful not to wake the priest, and found a note in her handwriting on the kitchen counter.

I have something important I need to do. When I'm finished, I'll go home.

She'd signed her name and drew a doodle of a beetle with a smiley face.

P.S. I got rid of Ivy's curse. Sorry about the beetles.

I was dialing Arachne's number before I realized I had a missed message from her cell phone. I'd seen a flash of purple hair just before someone had sent a second wave of air magic to help us destroy Herne's horn. But that was over an hour ago. Was she okay? A lot could happen in an hour, especially in Harborsmouth.

I fumbled with the phone, and selected my voicemail.

Hey, Ivy. Don't be mad, but I was down by the warehouses earlier. It's hard to explain, but I had to help. I'm home now, and my mom is back from that place they took Kaye. She said Kaye's sedated, but she can have visitors soon. Want to go with me? Okay, I gotta go. Hope you're not mad.

The call ended, and I stared at my phone, shaking my head.

"Everything okay?" Jinx asked, her voice a whisper.

"Yes, everything is good," I said. "I'm going to grab a shower."

"Good, because I want some time with my man before those two wake up," she said.

She grabbed Forneus, and dragged him into her bedroom, not that he wasn't willing.

"Don't use all the hot water, Miss Granger," he said with a wink.

I looked into Ceff's heavy-lidded gaze, stomach tightening with need.

"I make no promises," I said.

I pulled Ceff into the bathroom, and closed the door on Forneus' laughter. I turned on the shower, and Ceff pulled me close and slid a hand down my chest.

"But I keep mine," he said.

Oh yes, he was very good at keeping his promises.

CHAPTER 57

"Ivy, get up," Jinx said.

"What?" I asked, brain fuzzy. "Is my dad here?"

I blinked around the room, eyes lingering on Ceff's tanned chest, trying to remember where we'd left our clothes.

"No, he's not here," she said.

"Then go away," I said.

"I second that decision," Ceff said, mumbling into his pillow.

"I hate to be a buzzkill, but there's something you've got to see," Jinx said.

"Can't it wait?" I asked.

I groaned, and threw an arm over my face. What time was it, anyway? Sun streamed into the room. From the angle, it must be before noon.

"Something happened at sunrise, out in the industrial park," she said. "Come on. You really have to see this."

She threw a bundle of clothes at me, and I sighed.

"Fine," I said, reaching for the clothes. "Give me a second. I'll be right out."

She tapped her foot, a slow smile tugging her lips.

"You too, lover boy," she said.

Ceff sighed, and rolled over. He stretched, making his naked muscles flex, and I blushed.

"A little privacy here?" I asked.

"You sure?" she asked, with a wink. "Ceff's been through a lot. I could help him get dressed."

A muttered curse and footsteps coming from the kitchen meant that Forneus hadn't missed that comment. Knowing Jinx, that had been the point.

I rolled my eyes, and Ceff shook his head.

"That will not be necessary," he said. "But I believe Ivy requires coffee."

"Make that a barrel of the stuff," I said.

"You got it," she said with a wink.

Jinx shrieked, and was pulled from the doorway. I tensed, reaching for my blades before my sleep addled brain registered the playful laughter coming from the other room. Forneus had finally had enough of Jinx's flirting with Ceff, and had dragged her off into the kitchen. If her delighted squeals were any indication, he was obliterating thoughts of any other man from her mind. So long as she remembered to make a pot of coffee, and they didn't leave any sex visions on the kitchen counter, I was cool with that.

The last few days had been Hell, for all of us. And if reports were to be believed, the nightmare wasn't over. Mab was still out there, a black widow manipulating the threads of our future. As if that wasn't bad enough, my psychotic birth mother had friends. We hadn't seen the last of the rogue vampire and fae factions. Jinx and Forneus deserved what moments of happiness they could steal.

Ceff stood and crossed the room, shutting the door with a sigh.

"Wishing I lived alone?" I asked.

I pulled myself out of bed with one last longing look at my comfy mattress, and shrugged into the jeans and long-sleeved t-shirt Jinx had tossed at me. Ceff was still staring at me, the silence stretching between us when I sat on the edge of the bed and started pulling on my boots.

"What?" I asked, tilting my head. "You okay? You can stay here if you're not up to it. Who knows what Jinx has up her sleeve."

Ceff strode toward me, and knelt at my feet. Clothes materialized to swirl and wrap around his body as he moved, a display of his kelpie shapeshifter magic and a sign that he really was okay.

"I am fine," he said. "I will accompany you."

"Then what is it?" I asked, reaching toward him, but stopping before we touched.

We didn't have time for a vision.

"When we marry," he said, lips so close now I could feel his breath on my face. "Will you live with me?"

I frowned, trying to puzzle out what he was asking. Ceff was a kelpie king. His domain was beneath the waves. I couldn't travel there, let alone live with him.

"That's not really possible, is it?" I asked. "And...I...I have duties here. I can't leave the city unprotected."

That realization, and the weight of it, settled heavy on my shoulders. I slumped, and stared at the boot laces in my gloved hands. What were we doing getting married? How would any of this even work?

"I would never ask you to shirk your duties, or to abandon those you love," he said, voice gentle but firm. "What I am asking is to build a new life together, one that includes both of our worlds. I cannot reside on land at all times, but when I do, I wish for us to do so together."

"Oh," I said, voice catching in my throat. "You mean, give up the loft?"

He wanted me to leave Jinx? Did that also include Sparky too? Ceff narrowed his eyes, and his hands twitched where they gripped the bed on either side of me.

"I would never ask you to abandon a child," he said.

"But...you said..." I stuttered.

"Keep the loft," he said. "All I ask is to consider living with me part of the time. To find a place that we can call home. That you and me and Sparky can call home."

My vision blurred, and tears trailed down my cheek.

"Really?" I asked.

"I want a family, Ivy," he said. "And I want you."

"But he's a demon," I said, wiping a hand across my face.

"And I will adopt him as my own son," he said.

Ceff's face was deadly serious, and I gasped.

"But your people, what will they think?" I asked. "That would put Sparky in line for the kelpie throne, wouldn't it?"

"Yes, it would," he said with a nod, his entire body rigid.

I felt lightheaded, mind spinning at the possibilities and repercussions of what Ceff was suggesting. If we married, and he adopted Sparky, then the kid would become our son. That idea was enough to make my head explode, but it was what the kelpies would gain that had my heart racing without so much as a drip of the heavenly coffee brewing in the kitchen.

We would gain a son, and the kelpies would gain a prince.

A demon prince.

But first thing was first. We still needed my father to approve of our engagement.

CHAPTER 58

I had to blink away happy tears as Ceff and I followed Jinx and Forneus with Father Michael at our backs and Sparky skipping back and forth between us. I was so busy watching the floppy-eared kiddo that I nearly stumbled into Jinx and Forneus when they came to an abrupt halt.

"I told you that you had to see this yourself," Jinx said.

I lifted my head, jaw dropping at the sight before us. At the edge of the city, where we'd fought the Wild Hunt, and where the most rundown section of the industrial park had grown like a rotten sore on the face of Harborsmouth, nature now took hold.

"What...how?" I asked.

"Nature free," Marvin said, lumbering up to us.

"Aye, Lass," Hob said, hand-in-hand with a female gnome. "Ye freed the nature spirit when ye broke the dark queen's spell."

"The nature spirit?" I asked.

"The spirit of the forest that Mab forced inside Gwyn Ap Nudd to create Herne," Torn said.

He walked up to us with my father at his side. I smiled up at Willem, and he smiled back before frowning at Torn.

"I told you never to speak her name," he said. "That name invites nothing but pain and torment."

Torn shrugged.

"I was just explaining her twisted ways, not asking the dark queen to dinner," he said.

"Right, so mom's an evil bitch, got it," I said. "What about this nature spirit? Did we free it when we killed Herne?"

Willem gaped at me, but I ignored his surprise. Evidently, Torn hadn't told him that Kade had spilled the beans about my parentage. I wasn't looking forward to that conversation.

"It appear so, Lass," Hob said. "Though Marvin and I missed that fight."

He kicked at a rock on the ground, and slouched.

"You helped us win, you know," I said. "Even helped bring Ceff back to me. For that, I'll always be in your debt."

A heavy weight settled on my shoulders. I'd acknowledged my debt to Hob and Marvin, but it was one I'd gladly pay a million times over. They were family, and I'd do anything to help them. That included finding Hob a new home.

"We help?" Marvin asked.

I nodded.

"You went and convinced the pookas to join us, and they were the ones who stole Herne's horn," I said. "They also helped to fight Herne's giant owls."

Gretchen shivered, her conical gnome hat twitching, and huddled in close to Hob. He blushed, but patted her arm.

"There, dear," he said. "I'll let no owl near ye garden."

"Speaking of gardens," Jinx said, waving an arm at the vibrant blossoms that burst from plants as far as the eye could see. "Holy wow, right?"

The river was back in its original location, but there was no sign of the abandoned lots that had been on either side. Cracked pavement and tufts of grass had been replaced by flowers, trees, and flowering shrubs.

Greenery had erupted from Herne's corpse, his body feeding the nature spirit we set free. Flowers scented the air, erasing the smell of blood and death, and pookas flit from blossom to blossom. Even the river water appeared cleaner and clearer than before.

"Your handy work?" I asked, pointing at the river and raising a questioning brow at Ceff. "Or was that from the nature spirit as well?"

"Our magic would have aided in this river's recovery, but it would have taken time," he said. "This cleansing is the spirit's handiwork."

"It's a miracle," Father Michael said, eyes blinking owlishly.

"But it didn't come without a cost," I said.

"The important things rarely do," Willem said.

CHAPTER 59

My father stayed in Harborsmouth for a week. I monopolized his time, though he did spend his nights out carousing with Torn. When I asked if he wanted to visit my mom, his human wife, he'd gone sad and quiet. He came with me when I went to help the gnomes and pookas move out of my mother's garden, but he didn't speak to her. He stayed behind a tree at the edge of the woods near her house, an extra shadow beneath its branches.

But he'd helped carry the lumber from the old treehouse when we left. The gnomes and pookas had outgrown my mother's garden, so we were relocating them to the new gardens along the river.

The faeries didn't have much, but the pooka refused to leave the neon painted treehouse behind. We erected it in a tree overlooking a bright red patch of poppies, a shrine to a man who'd given his life in the battle below.

I spent days walking those gardens with my father. We shared stories, laughed and cried, and I learned more about why he'd left, and why he couldn't stay.

The lantern he carried held an ember from Hell, and that cursed thing brought disaster and destruction wherever it went. For that reason, my father would once again travel far away to somewhere remote where he'd do the least harm. I knew he was leaving to protect me, but it still hurt.

I vowed to find a way to free my father from his curse. No more cursed lanterns and cloaks of tormented souls. I thought back to the grief stricken look on my father's face when he watched my mother from the shadows. My family had suffered enough. I would travel to Hell and back if that's what it took to bring him home for good.

But for now, we had to face goodbye.

"You know I must leave, baby girl," he said.

I nodded, blinking rapidly. It took more than one attempt to say the words I needed to say. The old me would have given up and run away, but I'd learned the importance of

sharing my feelings with the people I cared about. The past
year had taught me a hard lesson about regret. My voice
quavered and shook, but I choked out "I love you" through a
cascade of sobs and tears.

My father, Will-o'-the-Wisp, turned and walked away.

I'd lost him for twenty years, and now he was gone
again.

*****

Even after my father left Harborsmouth, I walked the
gardens along the river. In that place, I felt close to him. I also
had a few friends to visit.

Engineers from the Hunters' Guild had helped to build a
footbridge over the river, and it hadn't taken Marvin long to
move under it. He said it was because it was so clean, but I
suspect the bridge troll also wanted to keep an eye on Hob.

The hearth brownie had taken Kaye's madness hard,
but he didn't respond whenever he was asked about his hearth
back at the Emporium. One day he just helped Gretchen move
to the garden, and never left. He was staying at her place, but
I wasn't sure how permanent the arrangement was. They'd
built a hearth that was tiny by human standards, but seemed
to work, for now.

I stopped by their place daily, only missing a day when I
went with Arachne to visit Kaye. I'd worried that our visits
might agitate her, but Kaye seemed to have vented all her
rage. Sadly, there wasn't a lot of the spunky woman left. She
knitted and talked about the weather, only becoming animated
the day I brought in Midnight.

Torn had asked me to bring the cat, and I had to admit
that Midnight seemed content to curl up on Kaye's lap. I'd
offered to take him with me when I left, but he'd hissed and
shown me his teeth. I'd check with Torn next time I saw him,
but I figured that meant the cat wanted to stay.

Unlike Midnight, Humphrey wasn't so forgiving. When
I asked if he wanted to visit Kaye, his hackles rose and his ears
flattened to his head. He was here to stay and that was fine by
me. He was the only one of my friends who got my jokes, and it
was reassuring having a gargoyle guarding the building.

I still hadn't decided on living arrangements with Ceff. I liked the loft apartment that Jinx and I shared above Private Eye. And now that the faerie courts had cleared my name and I was off the Moordenaar assassins' hit list, I could take on cases again.

With my father gone and a growing demon toddler to feed, I was ready to go back to work. Plus, as Jinx repeatedly reminded me, we had a double wedding to pay for.

Oberon save us all.

Ivy Granger World

Don't miss these great books set in the world of Ivy Granger.

Ivy Ganger, Psychic Detective Series

Shadow Sight

Welcome to Harborsmouth, where monsters walk the streets unseen by humans...except those with second sight, like Ivy Granger.

Blood and Mistletoe: An Ivy Granger Novella

Holidays are worse than a full moon for making people crazy. In Harborsmouth, where many of the residents are undead vampires or monstrous fae, the combination may prove deadly.

Ghost Light

Holidays are worse than a full moon for making people crazy. In Harborsmouth, where many of the residents are undead vampires or monstrous fae, the combination may prove deadly.

Club Nexus: An Ivy Granger Novella

A demon, an Unseelie faerie, and a vampire walk into a bar...

Burning Bright

Burning down the house...

Birthright

Being a faerie princess isn't all it's cracked up to be.

Hound's Bite

Ivy Granger thought she left the worst of Mab's creations behind when she escaped Faerie. She thought wrong.

Hunters' Guild Series

Hunting in Bruges

The only thing worse than being a Hunter in the fae-ridden city of Harborsmouth, is hunting vampires in Bruges

Coming Soon

Blood Rite

Ivy Granger psychic detective takes on a simple grave robbing case, but in Harborsmouth nothing is ever simple when dealing with the dead.

Warning: This book features grave robbing, an abandoned amusement park, necromancy, and zombie clowns.

Tales from Harborsmouth

Short stories set in the city of Harborsmouth.

Dressed in White

Something old, something new, something borrowed, something blue...

On the eve of Jinx and Ivy's double wedding, a sinister figure is terrorizing Harborsmouth.

When reports of a homicidal jilted bride threaten their wedding plans, Ivy and Forneus set out to put a stop to the string of heinous acts. What they discover might just send the faerie and demon straight to Hell, and set Ivy on a path to rectify more than one evil deed.

Will Ivy tie the knot with her kelpie king, or will she be saying "I do" to the king of Hell? Her father's curse is on the line, and lives hang in the balance. No pressure.

Praise for the World of Ivy Granger

"Stevens draws you in instantly with well-developed and likeable characters."
-Ted Fauster, author of the World of Faerel series

"Move over Harry Dresden fans, Ivy Granger is here."
-Kelly Abell, author of the Haunted Destiny series

"I haven't met an Ivy Granger story I didn't like. ...I love a good Urban Fantasy and the Ivy Granger series is not just good it's great."
-James A. Moore, Bram Stoker Award nominated author of the Seven Forges series

"If you're a fan of Kim Harrison or Patricia Briggs kind of Urban Fantasy then you will love the Ivy Granger series."
-The Keeper Shelf

"E.J. Stevens did a great job creating a unique Urban Fantasy world."
-Parajunkee

"There is romance, action, mystery, plenty of things that go bump in the night, all told with humor and style."
-Paranormal Romance Guild

"Stevens has done a fantastic job with bringing her world to us."
-Urban Fantasy Investigations

"Want a clever, fun and unique Urban Fantasy? This is the series to check out."
-The Jeep Diva

"The Ivy Granger Series is fantastic!"
-Book Bite Reviews

E.J. Stevens is the author of the HUNTERS' GUILD urban fantasy series, the SPIRIT GUIDE young adult series, and the award-winning IVY GRANGER urban fantasy series. She is known for filling pages with quirky characters, bloodsucking vampires, psychotic faeries, and snarky, kick-butt heroines.

BTS Red Carpet Award winner for Best Novel, SYAE Award finalist for Best Paranormal, Best Horror, and Best Novella, winner of the PRG Reviewer's Choice Award for Best Paranormal Fantasy Novel, Best Young Adult Paranormal Series, Best Urban Fantasy Novel, and finalist for Best Young Adult Paranormal Novel and Best Urban Fantasy Series.

When E.J. isn't at her writing desk, she enjoys dancing along seaside cliffs, singing in graveyards, and sleeping in faerie circles. E.J. currently resides in a magical forest on the coast of Maine where she finds daily inspiration for her writing.

CONNECT WITH E.J. STEVENS

Twitter: @EJStevensAuthor
Website: www.EJStevensAuthor.com
Blog: www.FromtheShadows.info

www.ingramcontent.com/pod-product-compliance
Lightning Source LLC
Chambersburg PA
CBHW071253250626
47159CB00004B/1158